WAGES OF SIN

AN INSPECTOR DEACON NOVEL

SHANE PAYNE

DEACON

For Karin, Jamie & Zoe

CHAPTER ONE

SEEING the result of an extreme murder was not something Harold Timmins was expecting as the engine of the tractor roared, echoing in the barn. The vehicle jolted as he engaged the gears and drove onto the stony, uneven track leading to the south fields. He bounced and rolled from side to side as the giant wheels hauled the tractor along the peaks and troughs of the track, densely packed with clay, pebbles and small sharp stones that crackled under the vehicle's weight. The surface of the trail was now dry, save for the occasional patches where the puddles had yet to disappear.

He momentarily caught sight of something in the rearview mirror. Yet, before he was able to register what it was, it disappeared. It must be a bird, he thought. They often followed the vehicles along the fields as the vibrations brought up the worms, making easy pickings. On second thoughts, it most likely flew from the hedgerow, startled by the noise. Whatever he saw was a brief glance, too quick to make a judgement. He caught sight of it again. Intrigued, he flicked quick glances towards the mirror as he drove, hoping it would return into view. But it didn't reveal itself again.

The engine slowed as he prepared for the sharp right turn leading to the field entrance. Steering the vehicle towards the gate, the source of his puzzlement appeared in the right-hand mirror. He supposed it could be a log being pulled along the ground, but it seemed peculiar in shape and not as rigid. Anyway, there weren't even logs on the farm. No, it was most probably one of the empty feed bags caught on the back somehow.

He climbed from the cab to open the field gate. Its high-pitched squeak seeming much louder in the morning silence than normal. Prior to going back to the cab, he checked the back of the tractor to inspect the dragging object. The muddy coating on the track made it difficult to identify at first. Kneeling down to take a closer look, the sight caused him to jump backwards, heart pounding his chest like a hammer. He placed his hand to his mouth but was unable to stop the vomit spraying through his fingers.

———

'It's good to see you back,' said Chief Superintendent Pau as DCI Alex Deacon sat in the chair strategically placed in front of her desk. There followed a grinding sound behind him and a hum resembling that of a vacuum cleaner. Pau returned and placed two coffees down on her desk that she had made with her new coffee machine.

'Good to be back,' he said. He took a sip of the hot frothy coffee, which was strong, just as he liked it. 'This is good.'

'It is. That machine is the best toy I've bought myself in years.' She sat behind her desk, her face becoming sterner. 'I think under the circumstances, it would be best, from a mental health and well-being perspective, to have you oversee operations from a more *organisational* standpoint, than having you directly involved on the ground, so to speak. I don't want you to throw yourself into the mix until you are fully settled back in with us and ready.'

Deacon felt his heart sink. This was exactly what he didn't want, although, in truth, he was expecting it.

'With all due respect, I'd rather jump back in. I need to be immersed in the job. Sitting at my desk isn't going to help.'

Pau fidgeted in her chair whilst holding his gaze, before composing herself.

'Alex, I have a duty of care. You've been through a lot, with your wife's illness, her passing, *your* recovery. I can't risk it.'

'I understand you want the best for me. But I need to be doing my job, having things back to normal again.'

I can't risk putting you out there with all the demands and pressures. You know the consequences. If you're not ready – emotionally?'

'It won't be a problem. I know what the job involves, I've been doing it long enough. Ok, so I've had some time off to support Claire and sort things out at home. But now I'm back and I'm *ready* to be back.'

Pau closed her eyes and massaged her forehead with her hand.

'Yes, you are, and I'm incredibly pleased, as is most of the station I would imagine. But are you ready? Really? How do you know? How can I be sure? Your life's different now, Alex, whether or not you admit it. Listen to yourself.'

Her voice was increasing in volume. Deacon could see her taking deep breaths to calm herself. Again, she stared at him before continuing.

'Claire was an absolute rock. She was always there, supporting you through thick and thin. Those tough assignments, the cases that consume us, the stress and emotional turmoil, the toll it puts on us. Your wife was there with you. She deserves more credit than, "I know what the job involves, I've been doing it long enough". And that's what's bothering me. The denial. Claire was as much a part of your job as you were. Kind words, the comforting shoulder. Now it's different. You're going to have to deal with it on your own. That's why I'm acting with a degree of caution and want to reintroduce you to your full role slowly.'

Alex looked intently at Pau, slowly nodding in response. She was right. Claire was always there. Prepared to listen to him offload the problems of the job. The frustrations of the cases, helping him unload the sights he's seen for his own sanity. The terrible things he discovered can easily eat away at you. Yes, things have changed, not by choice. He would have gladly given his life to spare hers, if such options existed, but they didn't. Not when it came to cancer, anyway.

'I completely understand your reasons. Sitting all day at a desk won't help me. I need to be involved *operationally*. Pair me with team members if necessary, but I must be involved.'

Deacon could sense she was conflicted. They had known each other for many years, worked on cases together as young police officers and detectives as they rose through the ranks. Surely, she could see how him being back in the field would help him acclimatise into his role. However, he knew the potential risk to her position. The higher you climb, the harder you fall, as they say. This was a case of heart and head. And at this moment in time, he was hoping that her heart was edging in front of the pragmatic, sensible approach of her head. His thoughts were broken by the ring of the telephone.

'Excuse me, Alex,' she picked up the receiver. 'Pau?' She listened to the caller for a short while, staring at Deacon. 'Where are you? No, no, I'll come to you.' She put down the phone and rose from her chair. 'Apologies, if you could just wait here. I'll be back shortly. Make yourself another coffee'.

Pau marched from her office, the clicking of her shoes disappearing along the corridor as the door of the office shut.

In the three months since he had been in the office, Pau had made some nice changes. The walls had been painted a fresh pastel blue colour, complementing the white ceiling and the fitted grey carpet. The large desk was the same, but the rest of the furniture seemed new. There was an oval teak table and six matching chairs with light grey seats and backs, used for small meetings, he presumed. Certainly, an upgrade from the tired looking set that was there before. A wall unit along the side wall replaced the grubby-looking filing cabinets that once presided in the space. On it were a couple of photo frames, with some glass ornaments and a vase full of multi-coloured tulips displayed in the centre, which gave a fresh perfume to the room. In the back corner was a small yet tall table that supported the coffee maker and cups. The colourful prints on the wall seemed to come alive as the light shone through the large window, now fitted with vertical blinds. In fact, it looked better than some of his rooms at home.

Deacon was about to help himself to another coffee when the door flew open, and Pau quickly settled in her chair with her elbows on the desk and chin resting on her clasped hands. She stared at Deacon as if trying to penetrate his thoughts.

'So. You've been away for what? three months? How have you been coping during that time? *Honestly?* We tried to call, but you wouldn't pick up. At the funeral, you seemed to disappear into thin air. As a friend, not your superior, but as your friend, Alex. please tell me the truth.'

Deacon was uncomfortable with the question. He stared down at the carpet. It's not something he'd thought about. That wasn't true. It was something he'd thought about but chose to push into the dark corners of his mind. Pau was right. He had avoided talking to people, ignoring phone calls and emails. Why? Because he didn't want to answer *that* question. But Pau was right. They're good friends; in fact, she's friends with all his family. Well. With the two of them who are left, anyway.

'It was difficult seeing Claire like that in the final week.' He let out a sigh. 'And then we lost her. Susan was in bits. Still is, I suppose. You know how close she was to her mum. The last six weeks have been about us readjusting to life without her. Setting the house up for the two of us without erasing Claire's memory completely. So, that's what the following weeks were for.' He raised his head and looked at Pau. 'Now that's done and I'm back to do the job I love and start the next chapter of my life.'

'But what about you, Alex?' said Pau. 'You said it was hard, you said your daughter is still upset, and you've set up for life without your wife, but not once have you said how you feel? How you're dealing with it?'

'I've accepted it is what it is, and you have to move on.'

'And that's it?' she asked.

'Yes.'

Pau slowly shook her head. 'You, see? Even to a friend, you're not prepared to share your feelings or state of mind during that time. And that worries me, because you may not have fully grieved for the loss of Claire. And that could eat away at you and potentially cause you and, from a selfish point of view, *me* problems in the future.'

'It won't.'

'I don't know that,' snaps Pau.

Again, she seemed deep in thought. Eyes piercing into his. She suddenly sat upright and folded her arms.

'Ok, I'll give you the benefit of the doubt. But if I sense something's not right, you're behind the desk. Do I make myself clear?'

'Crystal.' Deacon felt a weight lift from his shoulders.

'The call I took earlier. There's been an incident at a farm. DI Foster is already at the scene and would like you to join her there. I'm sure she'll fill you in with the details.'

Deacon felt himself smile. 'Thank you, seriously, thank you.'

After arriving at Bakewell Farm, Deacon was swiftly transferred into a waiting Range Rover. The vehicle was driven slowly, but Deacon had to grip the door handle firmly to stay in his seat. Rattling and banging, they crawled up the track. The front wheel dropped into a deep pothole. The Range Rover lurched to one side. Muddy water sprayed across the windscreen. Deacon bounced, banged his head against the padded roof and muttered a curse. If the driver heard, he didn't show it and continued on until they reached the crime scene. The car slewed to a halt. The door was opened by a face he knew well. He stepped out of the car and DI Gill Foster gave him a hug.

'You, Ok? You're looking well,' said Deacon.

DI Gill Foster gave a smile and nodded. 'Yes, I'm fine. It's good to see you back.'

'It's good to be back, Gill. So, I'm intrigued. Where's the body?'

'Come with me.'

She led him towards the back of the tractor. The pathologist was packing up while the photographer continued taking pictures as if working on commission.

Staring at the body, Deacon felt the colour drain from his face and his mouth go dry. Goosebumps rose on his arms, a sensation he had only experienced once before when looking at a dead body, in a case many years before. The body was severely cut and gashed along its length, probably due to the journey from the farmhouse. The open wounds were filled with mud and stones. Material around the body suggested evidence that the person was at least partially clothed. It was impossible to tell if the body was that of a male or female. It was so broken and contorted. Yet, with all the damage the body exhibited, it was the face that drew the attention. Deacon felt the bile rise towards his throat when he first glimpsed the head. He swallowed quickly to hold it at bay, resulting in a bitter tasting, burning sensation in his throat. He stared out at the surrounding fields to absorb as much of the scenery – nice things — before returning his gaze towards the head.

A steel hook had been inserted into the socket of the left eye, exiting through the right. Nylon rope, about three metres in length, he guessed, attached it to the tractor. The remaining space within the eye sockets was packed with mud. A large lump showed damage where the eyebrows met. The skin at the end of the nose was worn away, leaving the bone exposed, the mouth open, full of everything that it had scooped up as the body was dragged along by the tractor. The chin was ground flat.

Deacon turned to the Pathologist, Dr David Freestone.

'What do you make of it, Dave?'

Dr Freestone was in his early fifties but looked much younger. He wasn't stuffy about the use of his title when addressed, especially with those he knew. Though, like Deacon, he would follow the relevant protocols if there were any top brass in earshot. His soft and well-educated voice was in stark contrast to his six-foot-tall frame, that showcased a muscular and toned physique. His cauliflower ears, a result of too many rucks and scrums, were the only feature that spoilt what many would consider a handsome and well-chiselled specimen. He turned to Deacon.

'He's a chap, he's dead and he'll never need glasses.'

Many found Freestone's sense of humour inappropriate, distasteful even, but Deacon didn't mind. It lifted the mood, especially at times like this.

'So, it's definitely a "he"? And time of death?'

'Difficult to say, Al. You can see what I've been left to work with. Rigor mortis has set in and is well established, so, within the last twenty-four to thirty-six hours.'

'Cause of death?'

Freestone smiled. 'Alex. As you can see, all areas of damage are either contaminated or covered in mud. If and where bleeding occurred is impossible to assess here, it's been soaked up or scraped away. So, you'll have to wait until I get him on the table and conduct a full post-mortem.'

It didn't help Deacon, but he could see for himself there was nothing the Doctor could do that would be useful. He stared at the body, once again finding his gaze drawn towards the hook. Surely an afterthought? He tried to imagine the body being pulled along the floor by the tractor, bouncing and rolling. The rough track cutting through the skin as earth and stones forced their way into the wounds, with bones creaking and fracturing under the strain. Thank God he was dead. But there were a couple of questions that sprung to mind.

'Tell me. Would it be easy to do that? You know…. Force a hook through somebody's eyes?'

Freestone turned towards Deacon.

'Eyes are well protected, as are most sensitive areas of the body, in their case by bone. In my view, the hook would have needed considerable force applied to get it in there. But once again, we'll hopefully find that out during the PM.'

'Could he have been alive when that happened?'

Freestone raised his eyebrows. 'Hopefully I discover he wasn't?'

There was an awkward silence. Deacon turned to Gill.

'I take it the driver of the tractor found the body?'

'Yes. A farmer by the name of Harold Timmins. He ran back to the house to raise the alarm. His wife called us. He didn't take the shock too well, began complaining of a mild chest pain. She was a bit worried because he had a heart attack a few years back. The local doctor was called to check him out.'

As uncaring as it seemed, Deacon knew for the accuracy of memory, especially when shock is involved, the first twenty-four hours of an investigation is crucial.

'Is Mr Timmins still at home or hospital?'

'As far as I know, he's at home. Do you want to pay a visit?'

'I think so. My guess is he only noticed the body dragging behind him, in which case I doubt we'll gain much. But, just on the off chance, I'd like a word before his imagination distorts the facts.'

They climbed into the unmarked Range Rover, used to ferry the team up and down the bumpy track. The driver carefully turned the car and took his passengers towards the farmhouse. Along the way, the SOCO's van squeezed past, causing the Deacon's driver to move to the left, dropping into another rain filled pothole, causing the car to rock unsteadily side-wards. Deacon gave them a cursory wave, received by the usual sour faces.

'As happy as ever.'

Gill smiles. 'They probably think we've trampled over their evidence.'

'I'm sure they do, but until we're able to hover over the scene, they'll continue to be disappointed. And one minor point, it's *our evidence* too.'

During the brief journey, Deacon reflected on how one

telephone call changed the whole complexion of the day. Returning to work after a prolonged absence; especially in this job, was always going to feel strange. Being a detective often involves spending time among society's dangerous and dead people. Not your average nine-to-five job. He knew the meeting with Pau this morning would be intense and was expecting to be assigned to desk duties, managing the team at arm's length from the station. Once Pau was fully satisfied with his mental strength, she would then grant him permission to resume full duties as DCI. He completely understood that. He'd refused a phased return that HR was pushing for because, simply, he wanted things to get back to normal, or as close to what he considers being normal at any rate. Yet, it was looking like the desk was going to be his primary place of work for a while until *that* phone call. And credit where credit's due, Pau made a big call. She was prepared to cut him loose.

It wasn't long after leaving Pau's office that Gill had rung him directly from this place, between the villages of King's Norton and Great Glen. She said someone discovered a body tied to a tractor. That was the only actual information she offered, followed by, "You have got to see this for yourself. My God, I've seen nothing like this before in my life". The quiver in her voice didn't go unnoticed, so he decided not to push for more detail.

They've worked together for around seven years. She joined his team as a Detective Sergeant, transferring to Leicester's Headquarters from Manchester. In all that time, he'd never known her to be affected by anything. In fact, that's one of her unnerving characteristics—if she has feelings, she never lets them show. That's one reason she commands so much respect from her male colleagues. Well, that and the fact she stands five-foot-ten inches tall and was a very good kick boxer during her early teens, winning several trophies and medals along the way. Although muscular in build, she's by no means overweight and has an attractive rounded face and nose with large brown eyes. She has her straight brown hair cut just below her shoulders and usually wears it tied back in a ponytail or braid. Deacon liked her inquisitive mind, which is a good attribute for a detective. She takes his sarcasm and occasional stinging outbursts in her stride. He knew others in the force had the opportunity to work with him in the past but had declined; in a couple of cases missing out on promotion. But he didn't care. With Gill, he has someone he trusts who is not afraid to air her views.

Deacon had enjoyed the drive along the narrow winding roads of the Leicestershire countryside towards the farm. He couldn't help noticing the riot of colour in the grass verges, with clumps of daffodils and snowdrops bursting through the ground like illegal aliens. They grew with urgency anywhere they could, as if making up for lost time, absorbing as much sunshine as possible. Technically weeds, he thought, fondly remembering his grandfather who, after years of growing his own vegetables, decided to turf his garden. His frustration over the following years amused the rest of the family as his beautiful lawn was invaded by a number of potato plants that inconsiderately tunnelled up from the soil below. The memory of his grandfather cursing raised a smile.

The milky coffee Mrs Timmins made upon his arrival at the farmhouse was as good as any Deacon had bought in the many bistros that were popping up throughout the city. He took a sip from the China cup, assuming it was reserved for special guests. Closing his eyes momentarily, he inhaled the warm aroma. He sat in a very comfortable armchair in the living room, which was spotless and tidy, although cluttered with lots of porcelain ornaments. Someone had covered the two armchairs and sofa in matching floral-patterned throws, even though they didn't match. In fact, as he scanned the room, the table, sideboard, and drinks cabinet were all different styles, yet worked well together. Gill sat next to him on the sofa, notebook in hand, as he asked the questions.

Harold Timmins recalled the events of the morning. He was still visibly in shock, occasionally shaking his head as he described what had happened. The frown on his face seemed to stress the wrinkles in his leathery skin from many years working out in the elements, day after day. His white hair was short around the sides of his head, his crown bald. Even for his age, which Deacon guessed to be late sixties, early seventies, he still looked to be a powerful man. He wasn't particularly tall, at around five-foot eight, and wore baggy jeans and a mustard-coloured jumper that had various holes. The sleeves, rolled up to the elbows, revealed a heart-shaped tattoo on his left forearm.

'Was there anyone about?' asked Deacon.

'Nah, I would've noticed. You don't see many folks around here. Definitely not in the morning.'

'Did you notice anything out of the ordinary? Odd? You know, noise, lights, this morning or even last night?'

'Nothing. It's a pretty lonely place in the fields, so I'd remember if there was. Anyway, it was just after ten when I got back yesterday, and after a quick bite and a bath, I pretty much fell into bed. This game takes a lot out of you at my age.'

'What time did you go to bed?'

'No later than eleven, I bet. The missus stayed up longer. I'll ask her.' He shouted towards the kitchen. 'Mary, pet? Have you got a minute, love?'

Mrs Timmins came into the room from the kitchen,

wiping her hands on her apron, where she had been busying herself with the odd clatter of pots and pans. The result manifested itself in a rich smell of beef stock and vegetables that wafted through the air. She was smaller than her husband. Probably about five-foot five, Deacon guessed, thin in stature but not in a frail way. Her sandy-red coloured hair was curly and just about reached her shoulders. She had one of those happy, friendly faces, if there was such a thing, and appeared to be a few years younger than her spouse, although that could be because she spends less time outside. Her husband repeated Deacon's question. She shook her head.

'Sorry, I've been asking myself the same thing. After Harold came back and had his food, I washed the dishes and sat here watching the news on television.'

'Until when, Mrs Timmins?' asked Gill, noting the timelines.

'Just before midnight.........yes, I switched off the television about midnight.'

'And went straight to bed?' asked Deacon.

'Yes,' replied Mrs Timmins.

'Is there anything else? Something that springs to mind?'

She thought. 'I don't know. I can't swear to this, it could have been nothing, but as I switched the television off, I thought I heard a vehicle of some sort. The only reason it sticks in my mind is that when I switched the news off, I thought the noise carried on for a second longer and that's what caught me a bit strange. I thought it odd how the sound of the TV didn't switch off straight the way.'

'What do you mean, a vehicle of *some sort*?' asked Deacon. 'Could it have been a car or a tractor? High pitched or low?'

'I don't know, let me think.' She thought a while. 'It definitely wasn't a tractor or any heavy farm vehicle, I'm sure of that. I suppose it reminded me of our old Rover estate that I used to drive when I went shopping or visiting friends. I couldn't use the dirty things he uses around the farm. It was quiet and smooth. I don't know if there was anything else I noticed?' She thought for a few seconds. 'Probably not, but then again, my memory isn't what it used to be,' she smiled and rolled her eyes.

'It'll come to us all,' replied Gill. 'And just to confirm, the time was?'

'It wasn't long before I went to bed, so about midnight, ten to twelve, around then.'

Deacon felt that they were not going to get any more from the couple at this point. Maybe there would be some information that springs to light that will warrant another visit. The sound of a vehicle was interesting, though. It would be worth getting the team to look for any fresh-looking tyre tracks or open gates that could suggest someone driving close to offload the body.

'Do you know of any reason why the body would be left here?' asked Deacon.

The couple shook their heads.

'Have you had any threats or disagreements with anyone recently?'

Once again, they shook their heads.

'Could you do one thing for me, please, Mrs Timmins?' asked Deacon. 'Switch the TV on and off for me, please?'

She gave a rather puzzled look, but switched on the television as he asked. Within a few seconds, it was transmitting a twenty-four-hour news channel. When she switched it off, the picture disappeared, and the sound cut off immediately.

Thank you, said Deacon. He gave Gill a slight raising of the eyebrows, the well-rehearsed sign to end the interview. The detectives thanked the couple for their time and gave them a business card.

'If you think of anything else, no matter how small, please call us.'

'Thank you, we will', said Mr Timmins. 'By the way, when will I be able to get in the field, because if I don't get the seeds in, it'll be a disaster for us?' Harold's voice was desperate. He wore a frown on his leathery face as his watery brown eyes pleaded with Deacon. This was part of a crime that people often never consider. The disruption, losing wages and revenue to those innocent bystanders caught up in such situations that are not of their doing. Deacon had witnessed it too many times for his liking.

'I'm afraid the track to the field and the tractor will most certainly be off limits—indefinitely, while the team gathers evidence.'

Mr Timmin's face seemed to drop. His wife walked over to him and held his arm. 'There's another gate to the field that I can get to from the village,' he said. 'Will that be alright to use if I just use the bottom half of the field? I can borrow a tractor from down the way?'

Deacon knew this was too close to the crime scene for comfort. The couple seemed desperate, broken. He was probably going to regret what he was going to say, but it's not like they'd be trampling on evidence. 'As long as you keep clear of this end of the field, I don't see any problem with that.'

The sigh of relief from the farmer, along with the smiles exchanged between Harold and his wife, warmed Deacon's heart.

Stepping out into the warm, fresh air, Deacon and Gill saw an ambulance carefully driving up the hill to collect the body.

'Sir?'

'I know what you are going to say, and I'm not interested.'

'But you've no right to allow him to go back on the field. It's a potential crime scene. What if there's....'

'Stop!' Deacon turned to Gill, eyes burning into hers, his face taught. 'All I know is there's a couple who are spending the last years of their life working their arses off to make a living. And because some sadistic shitbag offloads a body on their land, we're expected to deny them the right. No, I'm not letting that happen and I don't care who it upsets. Do I make myself clear?'

Gill stared intensely into his eyes. 'Crystal.'

CHAPTER TWO

The rain splattered against the window from which Deacon stared, watching the morning traffic taking its occupants to their destinations. After leaving the farm yesterday, he had been busy ensuring that all the mechanisms were in place. Deacon allocated an incident room at the station and commanded DS Buxton to assume the role of office manager. Buxton was usually Deacon's first choice. Although not the most dynamic in normal duties, at fifty years of age and more interested in retirement than policing, he always excelled in this role. He meticulously logged, audited, and ensured that everything was above board, dotting all the Is and crossing all the Ts. In late afternoon, Deacon advised his team to go home and get a good night's sleep because experience suggested with cases of this kind, it would be of a premium, once things started rolling.

Well rested, he wasn't. Images of bodies hijacked what little sleep he had. One hung from a crane, swaying and spinning in the wind. A train dragged along another, bouncing up from the sleepers as it raced along the track—an arm severed from it, flying into the air. He also remembered another body held down on the riverbed, feet floating vertically towards the water's surface, arms stretched out wide like an inverted crucifixion. Was it St Peter who suffered a martyrdom like that? He couldn't remember. Religion was never Deacon's strong point. There were many more images. Vivid. All with a common theme—the bodies were attached by hook and rope. Some through the neck, a few through the stomach, one was in the ear—anywhere where his mind decided. They were like scenes from horror movies.

He knew that unless the SOCOs came up with something like a miracle, there was going to be little to go on. A gentle tap on the door snapped him from his thoughts. DI Gill Foster stood in the doorway.

'You ready, sir?'

He glanced at his watch. Eight-thirty. He quickly finished his coffee, wincing as he did so. Why he always felt compelled to drink the stuff when it was cold, he never understood. After all, it tasted bad enough when it was warm.

'Best not to keep her majesty waiting,' he said, tossing the paper cup into the bin. He held out his hand toward the stairs. 'After you, Gill.'

'Ah, Chief Inspector, DI Foster, glad you could make it.'

As the pair entered the conference room, they could not miss the sarcasm in Superintendent Pau's voice. It seemed those present had made sure they were especially early, knowing how nauseatingly anal the Superintendent was with lateness.

Deacon tapped his watch. 'Seconds to spare,' he countered with equivocal sarcasm.

The only empty seats were located each side of the Superintendent, so they did their walk of shame past their colleagues who sat quietly, not daring to look up and make eye contact. Just like school, he thought, with all the seats filled from the back of the classroom as far away from the teacher as possible. Superintendent Pau started proceedings before they had even sat down, as if to make a point.

'Good morning, everyone. Obviously, I have some grasp of the incident at Bakewell Farm, but I'd like to use this briefing to get myself and, of course, the team up to date. Chief Inspector Johnstone, I imagine it makes sense to start with you?'

Johnstone, a well-respected officer nervously brushed down his already neatly groomed hair with his hand before clearing his throat.

'Yes, ma'am. Mrs. Timmins called us at zero five fourteen hours and informed us that her husband had found a body tied to an agricultural vehicle.'

'Was it a tractor?' intervened Pau.

'Er, Yes, ma'am.'

'Well say so then,' snapped the Superintendent.

'Yes, ma'am. Tied to a *tractor*. I deployed my officers immediately where we could establish the scene of crime and secure the area. The Divisional Surgeon was called along with our colleagues at CID. DI Foster arrived approximately forty-five minutes later, and I handed the scene over to her and organised door to door at nearby farms and villages.'

'Any luck?'

'Nothing as yet.'

'So, is the farm quite isolated?' asked the Superintendent, writing relevant points into a notebook. Johnstone confirmed this. 'And the Divisional Surgeon was?'

'It was me, Dr Oliver Morton, ma'am.' Pau turned towards him to put a face to the name.

'Ah, Dr Morton. Forgive me. And you could declare life extinct?' He nodded. 'Did a pathologist attend?'

'Yes, ma'am. Dr Freestone,' said Gill.

Superintendent Pau glanced at Gill before looking around the table, eventually returning her gaze.

'Is the pathologist unable to attend?' asked Pau, making no attempt to disguise the annoyance in her voice.

'Dr Freestone is unavailable, ma'am. He's conducting a lecture to medical students at the university this morning, but has agreed to conduct the autopsy sometime this afternoon,' replied Gill, fully aware that this would not go down well with the mood Pau seemed to be in.

'How good of him to fit us in to his busy schedule. I would like to think that our needs are a higher priority than some pubescent wannabe doctors, but I'm obviously mistaken. All the same, for the benefit of the team, can anybody tell us what his initial conclusions were?'

Deacon gave a rundown of the few deductions that Freestone could make. He also pre-empted the obvious next question by telling everyone of the interview with the Timmins's, and his belief that they were not involved. However, he couldn't provide a reason at this stage for why their farm was targeted. It was feasible that it was a random location that was off the beaten track. The Superintendent listened intently as she continued to write, lightly biting at the nail of her nicely manicured thumbnail as she did so. After Deacon had finished speaking, there was a long silence as the Superintendent digested what she had heard. She eventually turned to Deacon.

'So, where are we now?'

'Door to door enquiries are still in progress. There's been a couple of males reported missing over the past two weeks. One of them could be the victim, so we have sent their details to Dr Freestone too, which would give us a start. But until the autopsy is done, and DNA samples analysed, or even better, someone offers some amazing information, we still have nothing.'

Pau gave a slow, purposeful nod of agreement before addressing the team.

'Well, I will not state the obvious, but because of the remote location of the farm and the speedy response from us, the media seems unusually slow off the mark. As you know, we have released a statement to the press stating that we found a male body in a field. However, we have tried not to arouse too much interest by avoiding the phrase "suspicious circumstances", hoping to make the story less sensational. However, at some point, we'll need to come clean. After all, the press can be useful to us too when required, so we don't want to dampen relations with them. I'm sure you'll appreciate that we can only keep them at bay for a day or two. For that reason, I want you to give one hundred percent commitment to this case to get a speedy result. Otherwise, things may escalate and blow up in our faces. Are there questions?' Everyone remained silent. 'No? All right, let's continue with our duties. Alex, a word, please.'

Once the room emptied and the door closed, Superintendent Pau positioned herself on the desk, facing Deacon as he sat cross-legged in his chair.

'Never do that to me again,' she yelled.

'What?' replied Deacon with a smirk.

'You bloody well know what? "Seconds to spare" crap.'

Deacon held up his hands as a half-hearted apology. Pau held a piercing stare before letting out a sigh, which seemed to release at least some of her anger.

'About this case, Alex? What's your gut feeling? Is this a spontaneous murder or could it be something more calculated?'

Deacon shook his head. 'I honestly don't know. The extremity of it worries me. It's so over the top, so unnecessary. It's like someone is trying to make a point, you know, a statement saying, "do that and this is the consequence", like a gang killing. But if that was the case, the perpetrator or perpetrators would aim to make headlines, or they would waste the message. Leaving the body in the middle of nowhere on a couple's farm - who I'm certain have no connection, is pointless.'

'It could be a psychopath?'

'It's possible. Christ, who knows these days? How many cases have occurred in recent years from around the world of so-called normal people from relatively unassuming mundane existences, who are loved by their mum, dad, cat, neighbour, neighbour's dog, that suddenly go on a rampage in schools with guns, or murder their families for no apparent reason. Society has become messed up.'

Pau moved from the table and sat in her chair. 'You know who this reminds me of, don't you?'

'Yes, but he died in jail two years ago.'

'I know. But do you remember how that started? That's still the most heinous crime I ever investigated. *We* investigated. I hope this doesn't take the same trajectory.'

Deacon locked into her stare. 'So do I.'

'Ah, good of you to come. You're a smaller audience than I had this morning, but I'm sure I'll perform just as well. I had twenty-five medical students hanging on my every word. I was rather good, if I say so myself.' Dr Freestone held out his arms and stared at the microphone that hung above him. 'Hello Wembley!'

The image before Deacon was incredibly odd, with a dead, naked body laid out before the doctor like a human sacrifice.

Freestone shrugged. 'Well, it's as near as I'll get to fame and fortune.'

'Their loss,' jokes Deacon with a smile. 'Anyway, back to the day job. What do we have that's new?'

Freestone adjusted the clipboard held by his assistant to read the notes.

'So far, a male as we know, one-point-eight metres tall or five -feet-ten-inches in old money, and seventy-eight kilograms in weight—what's left of him at any rate. I'll need to do a few more tests before I'm able to give an age, but at this moment in time, I can say he's definitely an adult but not a pensioner. As you can see, the patient has cleaned up well so we can get a better idea of damage. And one of the first points of interest is that our friend here shows signs of hypostasis. So, I can say that if someone did not position this chap on his back when he died, someone moved him into that position shortly afterwards.'

Deacon observed the body through the large glass window of the viewing area and the difference in its presentation struck him compared to his first view yesterday at the farm. The greyish pink colour of the skin was clear among the cuts and serrations, along with the minor features such as knuckles and fingernails. However, with the mouth and orbs cleared of soil, the horrific injuries appeared more striking. Freestone must have noticed him staring at the hook because he suddenly seemed to feel the need to explain that earlier he had x-rayed the head to give a better insight of the damage.

The doctor continued. 'Judging by the damage to the orbital bones, someone forced the hook into the left eye and it exited from the right. Although I don't claim to be an engineer, the hook shows signs of flattening on the outside edge that would be consistent with hammering.' Gill passed a glance at Deacon before addressing Freestone.

'Excuse me, Doctor. Could you please clarify that point?

Are you saying that whoever committed this act had to physically hammer the hook into place?'

'Without a doubt. It would take genuine force to push it into position. The resistance of the bone and the muscle would be quite considerable. Before we continue, I believe we should remove it.' A dull clunk showing it being placed into the metal tray.

'When you people have got what you want from that, we'll need it to find the manufacturer and supplier,' said Deacon.

'Of course.' Freestone returned his attention back to his patient. 'Now, this small area between the eyes took the full weight of the body as it was dragged along the ground, which is why there is a lump on the top of the nose. The bones in this area fractured under the load. We can see the integrity of the procerus muscles and the skin because they literally prevented the hook from ripping out from the head. By the way, following both external examinations and this autopsy, no other wounds on the body appear to be fatal.'

'So, the hook caused death?' asked Deacon anxiously.

'Judging by the bruising around the wound, the evidence from the x-ray and the position of the body at death, I'd say so, yes. However, Mr and Mrs Detective, did our friend remain conscious when the hook was applied? I'd like to see the results from toxicology before I say either way.'

'Do you think he was drugged first?' asked Gill.

'I think nothing at this stage. But if he was sedated, at least his last moments would have been more bearable.'

Deacon and Gill sat silently, reflecting on what Dr Freestone had said. Deacon wondered how much pain a person really feels when they were unconscious. After all, if the signs of the trauma surround the wound, surely the intensity of the pain is the same. The same intense, agonising pain as someone hammers out your eyes with a hook, but unable to scream. A terrorising thought. He broke from his unnerving thoughts and spoke to Freestone.

'When will you have the preliminary findings?'

'Hopefully, by this evening. I'll pass them on to you as soon as I have them. It's up to you, but do you want to stay for the main bill?'

'I think we'll give it a miss.' Deacon never enjoyed seeing a body opened and its contents removed, examined, and weighed. That was a tad too much for his stomach. How people like Dr Freestone could do such a job and break off for lunch without losing their appetite was beyond him, but he guessed it took all sorts. Besides, there seemed little help in terms of clues to identify the body, so he needed to kick start the process, although he was buggered if he knew what that was. Going back to the farm may be useful. It would give an opportunity to get a feel for the geography of the place. And he could inspect the barn. One could assume the body was attached to the tractor there.

Sharing thoughts on what little information they had and suggestions to improve the situation, Deacon and Gill crossed the busy Aylestone Road from the hospital towards the car park. Deacon's mobile rang. He pressed the device firmly against his ear and used the finger of his left hand to plug the other from the din of the traffic emanating from the multi lane traffic passing around them. Gill stared at the imposing silver and white structure of the Caterpillar stand at the Leicester Tigers rugby ground as Deacon listened intently to what the caller had to say; only speaking to clarify points. Ending the call, he turned to Gill and gave a smile.

'This could be nothing or a lucky coincidence. There's been a report of a burglary.' He could see the confusion on Gill's face. 'Look, it's too noisy here. I'll tell you on the way.'

The stones crunched evenly as the Audi made its way along the endless driveway leading towards a large, modern, symmetrical looking house. Rounded leaded bayed windows and the three acutely angled gables, which inspired the name of the property, created a blend of contemporary and traditional elements. The large entrance with the double doors achieved the stately look of the place, without being too extravagant.

Inside, access was restricted. Forensic teams collected samples after sealing off a couple of ground-floor rooms. But looking through the doorway of the living room, it was easy to see the disruption, with furniture overturned and a large glass display cabinet lying on the floor. Deacon leaned over the police tape to get a better view but could not see any more from this vantage point. He caught the attention of a police photographer and called him over.

'Is the rest of the room like this?'

'Pretty much, sir, although this may be of interest.' He scrolled through the pictures on his digital camera before showing them a picture of a wall on which the words SCUM was crudely painted, by hand he guessed by the run marks that dropped from the letters.

'Is this here?' Deacon asked.

'Yes, sir. It's here behind the door.'

In which case, it was fair to assume what happened had more purpose than a simple burglary. Deacon didn't want to impede the people scurrying about around him, collecting samples, bagging potential evidence, and powdering for prints in the main room. With the knowledge of the graffiti on the wall, he decided that a causal search through the rooms upstairs may be useful to look for any documentation such as passports, bills and such like relating to the occupants. He and Gill made their way up the staircase to see what they could find.

During the drive to the Three Gables, Deacon told Gill about the phone call. Although sketchy, the station informed him about a burglary. However, what was unusual, and the reason for Deacon's interest in the place, was the disappearance of the occupants. No one had seen John McGregor and his two adult sons for days. Their PA had raised the alarm after trying to contact them. Neither of the men answered their mobiles. According to the PA, John McGregor and his sons, Danny and Terry, ran a very successful business dealing in real estate and high production farms around the United Kingdom. So, they know who lives here. Well, ninety-nine-point-nine percent confirmed, but Deacon never took information on face value. He always liked to triangulate. Point one of a percent ran the risk, admittedly tiny, of providing a surprise, which he didn't like.

They entered the first bedroom, both putting on their silicone gloves to avoid leaving prints and traces of sweat on anything they touched. The walls were the same colour as the rest of the house, from what he'd seen, which was a rich matt cream. It made the rooms feel clean without seeming clinical like you get with white. A maroon shag pile carpet that covered the floor of the upper floor and the stairs contrasted this. Sunlight poured through a south-facing window, bathing an office desk. Gill searched through the drawers as Deacon slowly walked the perimeter of the room, memorising the general layout. She found nothing of interest, just pens, a calculator and business letters that seemed legitimate. Deacon would get the guy from the station to go through them more analytically. After pressing the power button using the end of his pen, the screen of a laptop that sat in the centre of the desk lit up and went straight to the password command. It was no surprise he thought. Even children lock out their PCs from prying eyes.

His initial impression of approaching the large king-sized

bed was of extravagance. Gill whisked the tips of her fingers along the silk quilt as she walked along the carved oak frame towards the matching bedside table. She opened the top drawers of the bedside table carefully, revealing more pens, a packet of cigarettes, two large boxes of condoms, and three used ones that had been pushed back into their opened packets, making her wince. Pornographic magazines filled the lower two drawers.

'These look interesting.'

Deacon joined Gill and flicked through the titles and some of the content. They were not your typical top-shelf publications. These were really hardcore. Imported, some appeared to be German, but most were from more eastern European countries.

'These are as explicit as any I've seen before,' said Gill.

Deacon put the magazines back into the drawer. 'You know, I saw some with similar content a few years back when we did a raid on a shop. And that investigation ended up exposing a sex ring. Early days, but could these gentlemen be involved in such activities? It's certainly an angle to pursue, I think.'

Deacon pointed to the long blue ribbons that were tied to each side of the bedpost.

'Pervert? Casual interest or active participant?' said Gill.

'Well, he seems to practise what he reads.'

In contrast, the main bedroom showcased conservative yet elegant furnishing. The multi-paned window that stretched from the floor to the ceiling lit the room like a floodlight. The double bed that unusually occupied the centre of the room left an ample space around it for sparsely placed furniture and for viewing the many framed photographs that adorned the walls. Deacon spent some time looking at the pictures that all appeared to feature who he assumed to be the missing men. Most of the photographs seemed business related, taken at functions and receptions. There were some from more personal endeavours; trout fishing, riding camels, at a casino playing blackjack. One particular picture seemed rather pretentious, with whom he assumed to be the McGregors' kneeling next to their cars with big smiles. A Bentley, a Jaguar and a Ferrari, all parked in line, grills facing the camera, headlights on. Were the pictures here as a personal reminder of their success and achievement? He couldn't help thinking there was something missing, but could not pin-point what it was. It would come in time, it always did. But first, the brain needed to digest it all.

The next south facing bedroom was bare of any belongings, so they assumed it to be a spare room for guests. Directly opposite was another bedroom with a wall full of shelves that accommodated sets of James Herbert and Stephen King novels, along with a Sherlock Holmes box set. These shared the space with business management, agricultural and property books and magazines.

The room did not have the sun shining through the windows, but it had a partial glass ceiling that adequately compensated, illuminating the room from the top down. A mixture of original oil paintings by artists Deacon had never heard of and several framed prints by Picasso adorned the walls, adding colour to the pale cream interior. A thorough search had revealed little of immediate interest but revealed a passport along with clay shooting trophies, also engraved with the same name.

'So, what do we have, Gill?' asked Deacon, admired the glass ceiling. 'I think the large bedroom is John MacGregor's. He seems to enjoy surrounding himself with photographs of himself and his sons' success. Whether it's preserving wonderful memories or to pet his ego, I don't know. But from what they show, they appear successful and reap the benefits.'

He looked up at the glass ceiling. 'The view at night looking up at the stars must be stunning.'

'It'll give whatever tart he's laying something to admire while he's performing, I suppose,' said Gill. 'Although I'd guess it's better than a mirror. The last thing you'd want to see is his arse.'

Deacon laughed.

'Anyway, this appears to be Terry's,' continued Gill, 'there's a guest room, by the looks of it. Oh, and a pervert's room.'

Deacon raised his eyebrows. 'So, that makes Danny our potential pervert? You know, I wouldn't mind a look in the garage before we ask questions. I'll be interested to see if there is anything stored in there. Talking of which, give Buxton a call and get the contact details of the McGregors' PA.' He looked at his watch. 'See if we can meet her around four-thirty ish.'

CHAPTER THREE

SWILLING the liquid in her mouth for a few seconds before swallowing, Margaret Wilson opened her eyes as the warmth of the Whiskey seeped into her body. Her hands still trembled, not as uncontrollably as earlier thanks to the medication of the Scotch, but enough to hear the ice rattling against the glass. It'd been a hell of a start to the day, and she feared the worst. If it wasn't for the need of an urgent signature, she'd never had gone to their house. She often went there if a customer needed to go away on business. But today, it seemed different, somehow. It was quiet—too quiet. That's what scared her the most. No, that's wrong. It wasn't scary at that point; it was *unusual*. When she looked through the large bay window into the lounge, seeing the furniture strewn all over the place, her heart beat ten to the dozen, and she felt scared. She would have left there and then but felt compelled to check that the boys were not inside, lying on the floor bound and gagged. She forced herself to look through the window once again, hands cupped each side of her eyes, pressing hard against the glass. There was no sign of the McGregors on the floor. But as she raised her head, she caught sight of it. That word painted on the wall. It made her feel nauseous and short of breath. She feared the worst for them - and herself, if she was honest. Running towards the car, she fumbled through her handbag, dropping the car keys. She blindly grabbed at the gravel to retrieve them, tears blurring her sight. Still, at least she scrambled into the car and get away.

She took another swig of whiskey, this time swallowing immediately. Her hand gripping the tumbler with fingers showcasing chipped nails still packed with dirt. Knocking back the remains of her glass, she wondered whether to buy another. It was good of the detective—what was his name? Deacon, Chief Inspector Deacon, to offer to bring her here to the Baker's Arms pub in Oakham for an informal chat after noticing how upset she was. Sitting outside in the beer garden, the blend of fresh air and warm sunshine, along with the trickle of the stream that cut through the garden all helped her to relax and to talk through events. Because it was between the rush of the office lunch hour and the evening crowd, there were very few people in the pub and no one was sitting outside. A female detective had sat next to her as the Chief Inspector asked questions. Some were what she expected, like how long had she worked for the family and what were the McGregors like to work for? But others were weird. Has she ever experienced sexual harassment or bullying? Were they easily annoyed? Were they motivated by money? Did she know their dentist? Who was their doctor? Did they have any enemies, or had they been involved with disputes will clients? What cars did they drive? What was their relationship with their cars? Really, what kind of question was that?

She guessed that the reason for her questioning was because she'd been working for the family for almost twenty-years, *twenty years*. Had it really been that long? Starting originally with Christopher Dudbridge, before he died, and his wife Alison married John McGregor. For that reason, she had a lot of background information that the police officer could tap into. She wasn't sure if it was her imagination, but she could have sworn that as soon as she mentioned the tragic death of Alison, his eyes lit up. He wanted to know about Dudbridge Holdings, and seemed intrigued why her second husband, John McGregor and his sons, ended up taking over the running of the business long before Alison died. His curiosity seemed further aroused after she mentioned Alison's daughter, Libby. He fired a barrage of questions about Libby and her whereabouts. She hadn't seen Libs for years, but that didn't stop him from pressing for information. How many years? Is it three, four or more? Who might know where she could be? Did she have friends, boyfriends, or relatives that she liked to visit when she was young? All questions fired at her at a faster rate, and all questions she couldn't answer. All she could say for sure was that Libby had obviously severed contact with the rest of the family following her mother's funeral.

Throughout the interview, she had expected Chief Inspector Deacon to ask about her relationship with her employers. They always do on the detective programmes on TV. That was something she would rather not discuss. Hopefully, they wouldn't bother to ask now. Although he seemed interested in everyone else's relationships with each other, so why didn't he ask her? He certainly seemed inquisitive enough. Unless, of course, he knew—or had figured it out. A tingle of anxiety seemed to trickle through her body. She stood up, quickly grabbing the back of the chair to steady herself for a few seconds, before carefully walking towards the bar for another whiskey and dry. What did it matter? Her home was only a ten-minute walk away.

'There you go. One Pedigree bitter as requested, and if you don't mind, I've opted for the G and T.' Gill placed the beer onto a sodden mat in front of her superior before sucking the froth of the overspill from her hand.

Deacon looked like he had swallowed a lemon.

'What's wrong?' she asked.

'Your drink is going to taste revolting after doing that.'

'Probably, but it's a double so I'll have plenty of gin to help get the taste back,' she gave a smile and a wink, tipping the change from the twenty-pound note onto the table in front of Deacon as he gulped his beer.

He was enjoying every bit of the hoppy brew. The ringing of the tumbler signalled Gill's assault on her drink. Following a few moments of silence, they settled down to business.

After informally interviewing Margaret Wilson, they needed to compare notes. Margaret politely declined the offer of a lift home, deciding to stay for one more drink to "relax her nerves". Instead of the station, Deacon opted for the more appealing location of the George and Dragon. It was a modern, open plan pub with seating bays along one wall opposite a long bar. Ideal for those who wanted to eat and drink in relative privacy. One bay was a particular favourite with the CID because it was more isolated, in the far corner of the room. Gill shimmied herself along the seat opposite Deacon as he took another long swig of his beer.

'You know what?' he said, wiping froth from his upper lip. 'I'm certain that the body at Bakewell Farm is one of the McGregors'.

Gill opened her mouth to speak, so Deacon quickly continued.

'It's a huge assumption, I know, but from what we've seen, I think there's a very good chance.'

Gill savoured the aftertaste of her gin and tonic. 'There's nothing to suggest a link. But who knows what'll come to light? There's no evidence of conflict within the family as far as we know, although that might change as when we speak to the rest of the employees at Dudbridge. If the body turns out to be one of them, the other two are going to be in the frame for murder, in hiding or victims themselves.'

'My gut feeling is victims.'

Gill shook her head. 'Why? They could just as well be hiding on a Caribbean Island somewhere.'

'They could, but I find it unlikely. Remember what Margaret said when we spoke about the cars? She probably thought I was barking mad, but all I wanted to understand was how important it was to the McGregors to be seen driving their expensive cars—advertising their success, letting people know what big shots they were. And the answer seemed to be - very. Margaret laughed at the suggestion that they may have taken a taxi somewhere. Christ, she'd even arranged for limos on business trips abroad.'

'*Never in a million years* was the actual phrase she used,' said Gill, 'insisting they would always go to the office in their own cars. Would never share, which I found amusing.'

'Which seems bloody pointless to me. They live in the same house. They work in the same place. Yet, where did we find their cars?'

'They are at the house in their garage, but that doesn't mean someone has murdered them.'

'No, it doesn't. But it's out of character. Look at the way the room was turned over. It looks like there's been quite a struggle in there.'

'Or made to look like there was,' countered Gill, feeling his enthusiasm was clouding his judgement.

'What would be the point?'

Gill could only shrug her shoulders. 'To make it seem more dramatic. Like an insurance scam?'

Deacon remained unconvinced. 'Ok, we'll see what's found when the team go through the accounts.'

'However,' said Gill, crunching on an ice cube, 'the writing on the living room wall is interesting.'

The message also intrigued Deacon. 'SCUM? It seems like a person or persons were not impressed by something.'

'Oh, while I remember, I passed on the name of the dentist to the team. Jonesy caught her before she shut up shop and got the McGregors' dental records.'

'Good stuff, Gill. Get them to Dave Freestone first thing in the morning.'

'Already done. He said it shouldn't take long to check for a match with the victim, so he'd include the result along with an overview of the key findings from the autopsy early tomorrow, as promised.'

Deacon held out his arms. 'This is why I have people like you on my team, Gill.'

She emptied the remnants of her gin and tonic into a wide-open mouth, which reminded Deacon of a basking shark, and placed her glass on the table as her teeth broke through the final ice cube.

'Another pint?'

Deacon looked at the small amount of beer left in the bottom of his glass, swilled it around before drinking it—froth moving slowly down the sides of the glass.

'Why not?' he said.

'Your shout,' she replied.

He raised his eyebrows. 'How does that work?'

'Because you're grateful for the work I've done and, I quote, "why I have people like you in my team," and obviously, you still have change from the twenty-pound note handy.'

'Alright.' Deacon shook his head. 'But you can fetch them. I pity the person you marry.'

Gill scooped up the change from the table into her hand with a smile and made her way to the bar.

The place was filling up now, and the volume levels rising. Deacon could see Gill among the crowd at the bar, which looked about four people deep. It was one of those situations where you had to be selfish and fight your way to the front and grab the bar staff's attention. He smiled when he saw a young lad with his mates try to barge past her in the queue. Rather him than me, he thought. Seconds later, Gill whispered something into the young man's ear, after which he made a hasty retreat to the back of the queue. Deacon took the opportunity of solitude to text his daughter.

It was ten minutes before he was once again in possession of a beer. After Gill settled back in her seat, Deacon raised another aspect of the case that puzzled him.

'Those photographs on John McGregor's wall? At first, I assumed they were random snapshots, you know, memories, but the more I think about it, the more I'm convinced it's about what they have — success. They're the trophies, proof of what they've done and achieved.'

'Ah, egos gallery! It's boys and their toys stuff. I'm surprised there are no pictures of them surrounded by gold digging bimbos.'

'That's it!' Deacon felt his face light up, as if radioactive. 'John McGregor had a wife. His sons' a stepmother. According to Margaret Wilson, there was a stepdaughter, a stepsister. Tell me, of all the photos we've seen at Three Gables, did you see any pictures of them at all?'

'Now you come to mention it, no.'

'Don't you find that strange? His wife died in a tragic accident, so why is there no memorial to her anywhere?'

Gill placed her glass on the table before speaking. 'Some people can't deal with things well and don't enjoy being reminded. It happens. I remember when my uncle died, my aunt removed everything of him from view in the house. She couldn't cope with being reminded of the loss of the man she loved and shared her life with for forty-odd years. It was like he never existed.'

'And in some ways, I understand that. But ignoring Alison McGregor for a moment, there is, of course, a daughter who, as far as we're aware, is alive and breathing. So, I would have expected to see something with her, surely?'

Deacon was feeling there was more to the McGregors, whether one of them turns out to be their dead body or not. Even if they returned from some secret fishing trip tomorrow, there is something odd about them. Deacon emptied the last of his drink.

'It seems odd. I'll give the guys back at base a bell to crank things up, as far as she's concerned. We need to trace her, just for peace of mind, that she actually exists. First thing in the morning, can you get in touch with the troops conducting the door to door and Dudbridge staff interviews? Tell them to squeeze the staff for any information on the daughter as well. If they find someone who knows or knew her, get them to focus more on specifics; how they know Libby, the last time they saw her, if they keep in touch, boyfriends. Sorry, I'm teaching you to suck eggs. But literally, anything that will help locate her.'

Gill nodded. 'Tomorrow has the makings of an interesting day.'

Staring trance-like at the television, watching the glowing images moving without registering what they were, Deacon's mind was far, far away in a place of darkness, a place of death. His brain tormenting him with snippets of information he had so far. Yet, trying to put together such a puzzle now was impossible. There were too many missing pieces.

Shortly after arriving home, he switched on the TV, more through habit, to the BBC's 24-hour news, to catch up on what's going on around the world. Although, why he bothered, he never understood. He'd long since concluded that you get the same ingredients every day. More royal gossip. Another government leak to test the waters for a new controversial idea. A potential terrorist attack foiled by our effective secret service, and another celebrity who's had her heart broken after discovering her husband's been screwing around. Obviously, she would be devastated and want everyone to respect her privacy at such a difficult time, but she is accepting exclusive interviews for six-figure sums.

'Would you like another drink?' The voice jolted Deacon from his thoughts. He allowed his eyes to re-focus and turned towards the doorway, where Susan looked in.

'Why not, so kind of you to ask.' He held out his glass.

'So, kind of you to ask,' Susan mocked, snatching the glass from his hand. 'Yeah, right? If I was to rely on you, I'd die from dehydration.'

'Oh, you've cut me like a knife.'

'Don't tempt fate, Dad.'

'Ah, moaning and moody. Good female attributes. You have developed into a real woman.'

'You're such a chauvinistic pig—a typical male. Anyway, do you like the wine because I'm not sure what to look for in a red. It all tastes too much like the remnants of the gherkin jar.'

'It's very nice, thank you. Tell me what I owe you and I'll give you the cash, or would you prefer a new jar of gherkins?'

'Yeah, whatever. Hilarious as always.'

'I do my best,' he said with a smile. Susan dropped onto

the couch next to him, nearly causing both to spill their drinks.

'Whoops! Dad, I appreciate that you're still engaging in conversation, even if it's filled with sarcasm. You're obviously at that stage in an investigation when stuff is happening. You just start sitting, staring at the telly or whatever, completely lost in thought. It's like sharing the house with a stranger. You have no interest in what's going on or what I say, only what's in your head. I suppose stuff you're trying to figure out. It can't be good for your mental health.' She got up and went into the kitchen.

Susan delivered the comment without her usual venom, but it still had the desired effect, like being shot with a bullet wrapped in cotton wool. The aftershock was silence accompanied by the occasional clinking of the cutlery as it was placed on the table. She had obviously prepared a meal after Deacon had texted her from the pub to say he would soon be home. He walked into the kitchen.

'I'm sorry, Susan. Am I always that predictable?'

'Afraid so, but, hey, you've been like that for as long as I can remember, so I wouldn't expect you to change now.' She placed a steaming plate of spaghetti bolognaise on the place mat in front of her father. 'Eat, enjoy, and try not to choke to death after the effort that's gone into making it.'

Deacon smiled and felt the need to force himself to facilitate some small talk, considering what she had made for him.

'So, what have you been up to today, besides surprising me with this wonderful meal?'

'Don't overdo the niceties. First, as for the food, I felt that the occasional rounded meal other than toast would do you good, after finding breadcrumbs scattered all over the worktops for the past couple of days.'

'I'll make a detective of you yet.'

'Whatever. Anyway, Hayley from university came over. We're working on similar psychology projects?'

'Hayley? Is she the one with the long legs, short skirts and big...'

'You know damn well she is! Oh, you're such a sad purvy, old man. Means other than their cup size can identify women, you know.'

'Really? I'll have to change my procedures.'

Susan gave a contemptuous smirk before continued, deliberately not rising to the bait.

'Anyway, she stayed until around four o'clock. After that I ordered some flowers for mums...' She stopped eating and looked down at her food. 'Please find time to go there. Last week...I waited at her grave hoping you'd turn up, but once again...'

The playfulness had gone from her now. The voice was barely audible. Her shoulders shuddered, followed by the clunking of the knife on the plate as she covered her face with her hand. Deacon moved around the table and wrapped his arms around her, placing her head against his shoulder. They both embraced. This should have been a special moment between a father and his daughter. Yet it felt awkward to him, worse—alien. As he held her, he realised why, and it came as a shock. He couldn't remember comforting Susan since she was a child. Had he become that distant? Had he become so absorbed with his work that his own flesh and blood took second place? Tears filled his eyes as he stroked her hair.

'I'll be there. I promise.'

At such an early hour in the morning, the lingering mist made the moment seem eerie, like a scene from a horror flick. But this was real. And what reality does that cinema doesn't quite achieve is to blend the bizarre with the extreme. Immersed within the soundtrack of happily singing birds was the creaking timber, like that of an old wooden boat dancing in the swell. The occasional dripping sound that accompanied it had long since stopped. The only evidence was the crimson stain on the grass; muddy boots swaying lightly in the breeze about a metre from the ground.

The ragged bloody line across the neck showed the cause of death - razor wire that was tied in a loop had sliced through the neck. Its torso seemed like it was only kept attached to the head by the vertebrae. The wire had the other end wrapped around a branch several times to ensure it would not slip. The face, grey in complexion, was a mesh of minor cuts and scratches, possibly done when placing the makeshift noose over the head. Although it could just as likely result from birds' claws trying to get a purchase, enabling them to peck away at the eyes; two black holes in the face, the result of their efforts.

Deacon surveyed the area around the tree. Stepping back a couple of paces to get a better perspective of the scene and assess the height of the branch. Deacon inferred the victim must have been sitting on the branch when the razor wire was put around the neck, as the length of the wire prevented him from standing. With the length of the body and the razor wire, there would be a drop of three metres. Add to that the weight of the victim, he guessed the chance of a quick death was highly probable. This raised the question - did he jump or was he pushed?

There was no sign of an aid to get up to the branch, which was odd. If the dead man had taken his own life, one would expect to find a chair or ladder in situ. So, did this suggest foul play? That they'd find out in good time, but he'd seen enough for now. It was time to make himself scarce before the SOCOs arrived and accused him of trampling over the evidence. From where he stood, he couldn't see any indentations in the ground, but he didn't want to get too close in case he damaged or flattened potential evidence. He looked at the large oak tree from which the victim was hanging. Maybe, if agile enough, a person could climb up the trunk of the tree, but to carry up the razor wire too? He didn't think so. He used something to get up there, or someone used something to get him up there. So, there's the mystery.

He went into the house where Gill was doing a good job of probing Rosemary Hawthorne for information in the living room. Rosemary sat rather uncomfortably on the front edge of the sofa with her knees pressed tightly together. Her red swollen eyes were wet and stared vacantly at the handkerchief clutched in her hands that rested on her lap. Stands of her blonde shoulder length hair stuck to her cheeks. Deacon guessed her age to be around forty-five and couldn't help thinking that in normal circumstances she would be a very attractive woman. She pondered all the questions posed before answering in a whisper. Gill sat next to her, diligently scribing the responses into her notebook.

Gill exchanged a glanced at Deacon, allowing him the opportunity to intervene.

'Mrs Hawthorne?' His voice seemed to startle her. She turned in his direction, her eyes darting from his face and back down to the carpet, avoiding any eye contact. 'My name is Chief Inspector Deacon and I'm in charge of this investigation into the death of your husband. I apologise for the difficulty of the questioning and what may seem the apparent disregard for your feelings, but I must stress that we have to ask these questions, and there's never a good time. I'm sure you can appreciate the need to gain an understanding of the circumstances of the death of your husband and his state of mind.'

Rosemary nodded.

'DI Foster will need to ask a few more questions and then we advise you get some rest because you've had a very traumatic morning. Do you have a friend or relative who we could contact to keep you company or is there somewhere we can take you?'

The tears streamed down her cheeks.

'Rosemary's brother-in-law is on his way.' Gill glanced at her watch. 'He should be here in about thirty minutes. Mrs Hawthorne wishes to remain here.'

'Very well.' He knelt in front of Rosemary. 'You're in excellent hands. DI Foster is a very experienced officer, one of the best. So, if you've anything you want to ask her, don't hesitate.' He signalled Gill towards the door. 'Anything?' He whispered once out of earshot.

She shook her head. 'The victim has a kind of study where he hides himself away. I'll ask the forensics to look around to see if there's anything useful to us. I had a quick look, but it just seems full of books and drawings. To be honest, it's a bit of a mess, so they'll probably need to box them up and take them back to the station to scour through. He may have a diary or such like that offers some kind of explanation.'

'Ok. I'll take one last look around and meet you back at base later.'

The latch of the front door clicked loudly as the front door closed behind Deacon. He turned to the uniformed officer who stood guard on the doorstep.

'Tell whoever is on duty here to keep a log of everyone who arrives and leaves, and the times.'

The officer nodded.

Deacon wanted to take a last look outside. It wasn't that often he could be at an incident for so long before the SOCOs appeared and restricted access. A large, prefabricated outbuilding housing ploughs and farm equipment would need to be searched by officers at some point. Added to the end of the building was a small extension. When he peered inside, he found it was used for storage. It had everything from tools, which were coated in rust, to furniture decorated by dust and cobwebs. Everything was unstacked or disordered, far from it. The stale smell of damp wood and corroding metal was strong. His mind was already starting to formulate questions, consider conspiracies and bond theories. Everything was becoming urgent. Worrying, even. Two deaths and three disappearances within three days, all on farms, all within a ten-mile radius. Coincidence?

It was just after noon. Gill felt tired and hungry as she drove back to the station. After getting home last night and soaking in a nice hot bath with a Catherine Cookson novel and a bottle of South African merlot, she had slept well. Even following the telephone call from the station at four-thirty-five, she felt well rested. Understaffing because of another flu epidemic had placed her as the next available name on the rota. When she arrived at the Hawthornes' place, the sun had not quite risen and there was a mist that restricted the vision, but there was enough light to see the spectacle before her. Although one would question any connection with the McGregors' case, the timing and the cruelty of the situation shared similarities. That's why she called Deacon. It would make sense for him to see the victim for himself to make his own judgements. She gave him a head start before calling the SOCOs.

Make no mistake, she was pissed-off having to attend a suicide whilst investigating a murder *and* a missing person's case. However, to add an element of interest, there seemed to be some rather odd factors surrounding the victim. How did he get into position on the tree's branch? There was nothing about that he could have used. Anyway, if he had used a ladder, for example, it would still be in place. Maybe he climbed up the tree, but judging by its size, she didn't see that could be possible. Was he helped? If he was, why not leave ladders or whatever was used to make it look less suspicious? Questions to be debated with Deacon, for sure. There were now two deaths that demanded considerable thought. The mobile rang. Deacon's name lit up on the screen.

'Ah, Gill, how's it going?'

'I'm hungry, fed up, and would rather have a drink than mull over the information I've gathered. Anyway, what do I owe the pleasure?'

'I thought you'd like to know the results from the pathology report.'

'You bet. Fire away.'

'The good news is we have a name based on the dental records. It's Terry McGregor.'

'Bloody hell! So, the Three Gables turned out a good hunch. Where does that leave us with the others?'

'Hmm, that's the bad news. John and Danny are still missing, so it's serious whichever way we look at it. Obviously, someone felt the need to kill Terry in the way they did. I'll feed you in with the smaller details when you get back.'

'Excellent! I should be with you in around twenty-minutes, but you know what the ring road's like.' She hung up and pondered the news.

This intensified the gravity of the McGregors' case. Although happy in so far as it gave them somewhere to start, she knew that it now posed more questions. The obvious one being, are the other family members involved in the death or are they to be victims themselves? As she drove, her thoughts strayed back to the recent assignment. Does finding a man hanged with no sign of a note or any sort of access to the position he was found in suggest influence from elsewhere, or is it too obvious? The wife seemed genuine enough. Her grief was clear during the interview. In fact, she was absolutely distraught. It was only when James Hawthorne, her husband's brother, arrived and intervened that she seemed to calm down and relax. He was concerned for his sister-in-law, holding her hand and comforting her throughout the rest of the questioning.

In truth, the more she thought about the interview with Rosemary, the more she realised they got very little information. Not through lack of trying. Rosemary was simply beside herself with grief over the loss of her beloved. Maybe it was the shock of finding him as she did? Whatever it was, she was inconsolable. Although when James arrived, she seemed different somehow. Gill tried to pin-point what it was. It was nothing obvious, but she seemed to become... stronger. Gill wasn't sure if she was imagining it, but with James there, she seemed no longer unable to focus on the questions asked—but had the strength to avoid answering them. So why was that?

CHAPTER FOUR

THE INCIDENT ROOM was a hive of activity, with the team scurrying from desk to desk, passing on information and discussing leads. There was a small din because of endless conversations and ringing phones. DS Buxton ensured that all information, no matter how small, was logged. Deacon brought Gill up to date regarding the McGregors' case.

'Terry is thirty-one years old, two years older than his brother Danny. Their dad, John, is fifty-six.'

'And we've no information yet regarding Danny and his father?'

'No. They're officially missing persons. Our people are talking to the staff at Dudbridge Holdings, so hopefully someone there will have heard something, seen something, and come up with a description.'

'Ok. And what did Dr Freestone have to say?' asked Gill.

'That the hook caused death, and he's pretty sure Terry was alive when it was hammered into place. Well, at the start, anyway.'

'Oh, my God! Please confirm if someone drugged him.'

'I could say that, but Freestone says not.'

Gill shook her head.

Deacon continued. 'His initial assessment of time of death was pretty accurate. He puts it at around twenty-four hours before finding the body. Therefore, Freestone determined the victim was murdered sometime on Saturday night, possibly early Sunday morning.'

'He will not sit quietly while that's done to him. The pain. If killed out in the open, you'd expect the scream to carry for miles in the countryside.'

'You'd think so. Hopefully, our enquiries will bring up a witness or two. Anyway, there's more.' He flicked through the report. 'The food in Terry's stomach was nearly digested.'

'So, could someone have held him for some time before they killed him?'

'It would seem so.' Deacon flicked through the remaining pages of the pathology report. 'No fibres or skin found under the fingernails.'

'There's no surprise. The body was caked in so much crap when we got to him.'

'True.' Deacon placed the report on his desk. 'You know what, Gill. I was thinking, if all the McGregors end up as murder victims, it's fair to assume they were they taken together, hence the cars still in the garage. But surely they could over-power the perpetrator? Unless, of course, there was more than one person involved. A gang, perhaps? Rivals of some sort? Disgruntled customers? Who knows, it could be anyone.'

'I agree. Talking of anyone, any luck finding, Libby?' asked Gill.

'Not yet, but the team is working on a few leads. She's moved around a bit. But I think we've about caught up with her.'

'It'll be useful to talk to her and get a better picture of the family dynamics.'

'Judging by what Margaret Wilson implied, I think it'll be more *interesting* than useful. I found Margaret to be very informative.'

'Especially after a few drinks,' said Gill with a smile. Her brow furrowed. 'You know what really surprised me? How much input she has in the organisation and the McGregors' lives. She arranges everything. Stuff beyond the business remit. Meals, dental care, holidays, boiler servicing, you name it, her name's against everything. Christ, she's almost like ...'

'A wife? A mother? I think she, if not *is—was* something more than a personal assistant to one of them. Probably, John McGregor. Either way, I think she'll have more to offer in terms of information. It'll certainly be worth us paying her another visit.'

He looked at the scraps of information they had written on the whiteboard. There were names, places, and some theoretical thoughts—fragments, really.

Deacon sighed. 'So, we have a victim. We're looking for a murderer or murderers, two missing persons, a lost relative, and a motive. Anything else to add?' Gill shook her head. 'No? I think we have enough to be getting on with.' He rubbed his hands together. 'Let's lace ourselves with caffeine before we discuss the recent addition to our workload.'

The vending machine had pride of place below the staircase in the corridor. Deacon muttered his disgust at the extortionate cost of the drinks, as he always did, rummaging in his pockets for change. They carefully carried their hot drinks towards another board, which only had the name "Steven Hawthorne" written on it. Deacon grabbed a black marker pen and offered to write the relevant details. Gill sat on the edge of a desk, opened her notebook, and read.

'Steven Hawthorne, a fifty-year-old farmer, married to Rosemary for twenty-seven years. They have no children. He owns the farm with his brother, James. Their father passed the farm onto them in nineteen-ninety-two. According to Rosemary, her husband had suffered bouts of depression for around five years, for which he had medication. He'd threatened to take his own life on a couple of occasions, normally after arguments, but she never took them seriously.'

'Was there a catalyst for the depression?' asked Deacon, pausing with the pen on the board.

'I tried to probe for more detail but Rosemary said that no-one was really sure what triggered it. Although she believed it was the stress of running the farm. There was a serious difference of opinion about the direction that the farm should go in. Financially, the business hadn't been doing so well for some years and a few years ago, they lost some land in a poor deal of some sort. According to Rosemary, Steven's brother, James, was more business minded and had plans to modernise the farm and their practices to make it more competitive, ideas that she supported, apparently. But Steven was resisting any proposal put forward. He wanted to keep to the traditional practices that their father used.'

'What do they deal with?'

'Livestock, mainly sheep.'

'Were Steven and James equal partners?'

'I'm not completely sure. I'd have to clarify that. But I get the impression that James is more the man in the office than a hands-on farmer covered in shit.'

Deacon wrote the relevant facts onto the board.

'Anyway, to cut to the chase, Rosemary found her husband hanged at around four-fifteen this morning. She had woken in the early hours and realised that he hadn't been to bed. She assumed he was sleeping downstairs on the sofa; he'd sometimes do that if he stayed up late to avoid waking her. She went downstairs to get herself a glass of milk and became concerned when she realised he wasn't there. So, she went outside to look for him. The geese were making a bit of a row.

Apparently, they're better than guard dogs for raising the alarm. She made her way towards them and found Steven hanging from the tree.'

'That's when she called us?'

'Not exactly. She said that she stood staring at the body for ages. It was probably shock.'

'Is that your assumption or hers?'

'Mine, sorry.'

'Just tell me what she said for now, so I can get a picture. We'll add our take later.'

Gill took a deep breath and continued. 'She said that a couple of crows landed on his shoulders, flapping their wings, seeming quite agitated with each other. It was then she saw them pecking at Steven's face. The sight made her feel sick and dizzy, and she thought she was going to faint. She said that she somehow made her way back to the house. At that point she called nine-nine-nine.'

'Had he threatened to kill himself recently?'

'Apparently not. In fact, she said that Steven had seemed to get better. More like his old self, *she said*.'

Deacon noticed the sarcastic emphasis, but he ignored it.

'Maybe he took his own life and had resigned himself to the deed. Like it was a weight off his shoulders?'

'It's possible, but I'm not allowed to make assumptions, apparently,' said Gill.

The response pissed him off, but was deserved. He smiled and held up his hands in a gesture of apology. 'Tell me, you saw the body. What struck you about the scene?'

'I wondered how he got up the tree.'

'Me too. The branch must be three metres?'

Gill nodded. 'If it was a suicide, and for argument's sake, let's assume it was, he would have needed some way of getting up there. A ladder or chair, perhaps? And there is nothing there. So, either he had help, or for some unknown reason, someone removed the ladder or chair. But as things stand, we're not able to offer an explanation. So that raises questions about the whole suicide aspect. I asked Rosemary if she recalled anything lying about when she discovered her husband, but she kept saying that there was nothing but Steven's body. And obviously she was getting more and more distressed recalling the scene.'

'Did she seem genuinely upset?'

'She was definitely upset by the experience, to where it was near impossible to get answers from her. It wasn't until James arrived she seemed to calm down.'

'Was she more responsive to your questioning then?'

'I wouldn't say that I got any more from her. She was ... more thoughtful.'

'Cautious?'

'Possibly. I was thinking about this during the drive back. James seemed to have a calming influence on her. I got the impression, and I could be wrong, here, but I felt she could not help until he arrived and then possibly less willing, and less vulnerable. But you'd expect that, a familiar face and all that.'

'A special relationship? Lovers?'

'Maybe. I wasn't sure at the time but, on reflection, their relationship felt restrained, kind of playing it down. Like there's more to it than they want people to know. But, it may be because you've suggested it. I'm interpreting things that way.'

'Fair point,' replied Deacon, 'screwing the brother of your husband isn't a crime, but it offers a motive? We need to delve deeper into those two. Get some background. Christ, we're pushed for resources at the moment, what with the McGregors' case.'

'Hopefully, the SOCOs will find something useful at the scene,' said Gill.

Deacon didn't hear the comment, instead grabbing DC Karl Goodman as he returned from the photocopier.

'Do us a favour, Karl. Could you fetch us a cappuccino and a black coffee with extra sugar? He opened the Sergeant's hand and tipped a handful of coins into it.' Goodman stared at the money, looking slightly irritated, which didn't go unnoticed.

'Problem?'

'No, guv.' He whispered. He turned and made his way to the drinks machine.

Deacon watched as he stormed away. He returned his attention to Gill.

'The razor wire struck me. Hardly a painless way to kill yourself?'

'Maybe it was all that was available?'

'What, on a farm?'

Gill shrugged. 'But razor wire creates a new question. Did he choke or bleed to death?'

'I'm sure Dave Freestone will give us his rundown in his own inimitable way,' said Deacon with a smirk.

Karl returned with the coffees. They thanked him.

'Service with a smile. I'm sure he wanted to throw them over our heads.' He took a sip. 'Do you think I should send him back for sugar?'

Gill rolled her eyes. 'On a serious note, how are we expected to investigate the two cases effectively with such a depleted team?'

'It's going to be tough, but that's the way it is these days with government cuts and sharing of resources. I'll speak to Pau and see what she can do for us. You follow-up on the Hawthorne incident. You've already made the contact and done the preliminaries. It'll probably be straightforward, anyway. I'll stick with the McGregors. We'll try to meet daily to swap notes and bounce around ideas. Take Cara

Matthews with you. Get her up to speed. I'll take our friend Smiler.'

———

The rainbow that arched across the landscape was absolutely stunning. The young woman stared at its beauty, the full spectrum of colours from red to violet so clear to the eyes. She remembered as a child running across the fields trying to find the rainbow's end. But it was unreachable. A smile softened her face at the memory. It was a time when life was simple and all she wanted to do was play without a care in the world. Her parents would encourage and cheer for her to find the pot of gold, but no matter how hard she tried, it was never in sight. Her childhood was wonderful and fun, surrounded by love.

She felt a lump in her throat. It had been a while since anything had stirred up such emotion. It was long ago. A different time. So much had happened since—bad things. Her resolve had been put to the test multiple times. Yet, standing here today was a testament to her survival. Yes, she was scarred, damaged and alone, and would be the first person to admit that. But did she feel unhappy with her life? She had a small circle of friends whom she could trust. The ever-expanding garden centre, which now boasted one and a half acres of land, had grown from her ambition and vision. It was a small florist shop when she bought it, but now it was a popular and profitable business. It hadn't been easy, but she had invested every penny and hour of her time to achieve it. Now she reaps the rewards from such single-mindedness and determination.

Yet, standing and staring at the colourful phenomenon, she would give it all up to be that little girl again. Laughing out loud as she ran in the fields, chased by her dad and cheered along by her mum. But things changed following the death of her father. And years later when she lost her mother, too. That's when she had to make a new life. She hoped that one day, even with such baggage, she would find true happiness. Maybe someday she would find Mr Right and have a family of her own she could love and cherish, as her parents did with her. She watched as the image in the sky slowly faded and wondered if she would spend the rest of her life chasing rainbows?

'He's an arsehole, and the fact he goes running to you like some schoolboy snitching to teacher shows it.'

'Alex, shut up!' Pau pointed at Deacon. 'You're testing my patience.'

He was about to respond, but she held up her palm to his face.

'Remember what I said the other day? If you make me question something you've done, I'll remove you from ground and have you overseeing the investigations with your arse glued to your desk chair. And do you know what? I'm getting very close to that point. So, I suggest you think a bit more about your actions and show me a little more respect. Trevor Jardine dislikes you as much as you do him, so he could have been much more vindictive earlier and forced my hand to remove you from the case, so think yourself lucky. But you are taking things too far. Now, I don't know if this is a one off or if recent months are clouding your judgement, in which case.... please talk to me because we can get you help and support, there's nothing weak in that. God knows, after what you went through with Claire would destroy many people. But if not that, please think about what you're doing. Do I make myself clear?'

'Completely.' Deacon was feeling numb. He wasn't expecting a full scale bollocking when he came to the office. He just wanted to know the situation regarding extra legs on the ground, as the investigations were expanding at an alarming rate and the team he had were struggling to keep up. It turns out that Pau had taken assertive action to draft in officers to help from nearby Hamilton and seconded a couple of administration staff from Market Harborough to help with calls and collection of data. But as soon as Pau mentioned that Principle SOCO, Trevor Jardine, had complained about him giving Harold Timmins permission to work on an adjacent field, the hairs on the back of his neck rose and it was always going to go downhill from that point. But Pau hadn't got to such a high rank in a predominantly male environment by allowing people like him to argue with her like he had. Old friend and colleague or not. If he was honest with himself, he deserved it. And he'll always have respect for her. They might not always agree, but she wasn't one of these power-hungry ambitious chiefs who seem to run other areas. No. She was fair and knew when to exert her position of power and resume control. Now was such a time.

'Now listen to me because it's the last time I'm going to say it, Alex. What you did was wrong—fact. Now, I don't care how much you think you have the moral high ground, you cannot allow people to trample on or in this case *around* a crime scene, no matter how desperate their plight.'

Deacon was about to respond.

'Shush!' Pau held up her hand. 'I know it stinks and innocent people can suffer financially; especially when murders happen in their backyard, so to speak, but that's the way it is. You know that. I know that. Now stop being so bloody contemptuous towards Trevor Jardine and let him do his job.'

'He cost a girl her life, and what does he get? Promoted to Principle SOCO! So, I would imagine I'll always be a little contemptuous towards the arrogant pile of shit.' Deacon knew she agreed with his sentiments, but she was clearly towing the official line.

'The incident you're referring to happened a long time ago. Whatever you think of him is irrelevant. His team are scientists. You know as well as I do it's a highly skilled profession that doesn't pay anywhere near as much as it should. And let's take that case in question with that young girl. Would we be where we are now if it wasn't for that case? I doubt it. We all made mistakes along the way, me included, and dare I say it, even you. In our job, there are some things we have to live with. But in the face of adversity, we jailed one of the cruellest killers in British history.'

'I don't deny their contribution is important—vital even. But when they're strutting around with their heads stuck up their own arses, it can get a tad irritating, especially when I'm trying to do my job and gather as much information at the start of the investigation. The last thing I need is being shooed away like some kind of naughty schoolboy.'

'So, he's a schoolboy for snitching. And you're a schoolboy being shooed away. I agree. You both act like a pair of immature little boys. And by strutting around, I presume you're referring to Trevor rather than his team? You know where I'm coming from with this, Alex. Yes, they can slow things down. He runs the team very old school, but you're going to have to grin and bear it, I'm afraid. They need to be methodical; *we need them* to be methodical. I've got enough to worry about, *as have you*, judging by your cases, so please.' She tapped her lips. 'Keep it shut, behave and close the door on the way out.'

Deacon felt he had riled his leader enough for one day, so rose from his chair and left the office.

Pau stared at the door for a while after he left. Her heart was pounding. It took a lot to keep an element of composure with him. He's a brilliant detective, one of the best she's ever worked with, that was for sure. But he could be an antagonistic sod towards some factions. The SOCOs were a case in point. An example of what made commanding him so difficult. Not that he disrespected her position or disobeyed orders that often.

Their friendship was special. Throughout many years, they built their friendship by sharing a lot together as uniformed officers, detectives, and during undercover operations before opportunities arose. No, what made him difficult were the complaints and disputes from those he riled. People who had betrayed him at some point or another. One of his great assets is also his downfall—he has a memory like an elephant. And he'll hold a grudge forever. One day, the murmurs will become too loud for her to suppress any longer. That's when she'll have problems. Some had already questioned her judgement why she allowed him to return to full duties with the stresses and responsibilities associated with it —especially following the personal trauma he'd been through. It's the reason she tries to nip every tiny incident in the bud as quickly as possible, before they blossomed into more problematic issues—preventing him from jeopardising his career, and possibly hers. She smiled. Yet, you can't help but admire his cheek and audacity.

Karl Goodman was waiting in the car with the engine running by the time Deacon left the station. He pulled away with a screech as Deacon closed the door.

'Bloody hell, Karl. It's not the Monte Carlo Rally. I'm sure a second here or there won't change anything.'

'Sorry, guv.'

Deacon understood the excitement. This was a big moment in the case. Finally, some movement, and all thanks to Karl's methodical and patient detective work. Just after leaving the dragon's den, Karl had come marching to him wearing a very rare grin and waving a piece of paper. He had located Libby McGregor. So, with a 'what are we waiting for?' they had scrambled themselves into action—the mauling in Pau's office forgotten.

It turns out that the girl's done well for herself. The owner of Petals Garden Centre, off of the main A47 just north of Uppingham. Deacon knew it well, visiting it on a number of occasions when going through his sporadic gardening phases. It seemed to stock about everything a person would need. A small coffee shop housed within it made the experience more pleasant and kept the punters on site long enough to see something else to buy. If he remembered rightly, when he was younger, it was a small flower shop. He assumed that's where the name "Petals" originated.

The road was getting busy with the rush hour traffic, but it didn't affect the speed that people were travelling up and down the hills, around the bends. No wonder the road had such a reputation for accidents. They had passed at least half a dozen bunches of flowers laid at the side of the road, some with pictures attached, reminders of where the lives had been lost. He'd called Libby from his mobile as he and Goodman set off to ensure that she would be available. He didn't give her any details of why they wanted to speak to her, but said that she was in no trouble, but they really needed to talk. A couple of hundred yards beyond the Uppingham-Oakham roundabout, a sign directed them to their destination. The car park was empty except for a silver transit van emblazoned with the centre's livery. Karl parked the car in front of the main entrance.

The centre's aroma was a strange mixture of soil and plants, reminding Deacon of his grandfather and the visits to his allotments as a child. His greenhouse had the same smell, only a warm smell. Can a smell be warm? Who knows, but he always associates the smell with heat? Although this place was not hot, it was very comfortable, leading Deacon to assume that there was an automated temperature-controlled system inside. The place's tasteful presentation gave the impression of a more upmarket business than your average garden centre. Yet, the prices seemed very reasonable, but in all fairness, he hadn't a clue. All around were plants and flowers of different types, sizes and colours which look randomly placed. Yet, it all felt picturesque, suggesting far more thought and creativity than Joe Bloggs would ever give it credit for. Interspersed among the foliage and blooms were statues of Cupid and birds, jumping fish and deer, to name a few. All tastefully done and cleverly placed.

Both sides of the room had windows which, along with the Perspex ceiling, gave the feeling of the outside being inside. Ideal when it was slinging down with rain. There was a constant sound of running water that directed the visitors' attention towards the centrepiece. A large water fountain that took pride of place in the middle of the shop in the shape of a water well. The rocks around the bottom supported two wooden posts, from which there were two buckets. Water poured from the top bucket into one below, and then into the well itself. Very whimsical. People had thrown coins into the surrounding pool, where a sign encouraged them to make a wish. No doubt a bonus for staff, thought Deacon, reading the notice informing the customers of the local charities who were to benefit—right!

The loud thud of a stack of clay plant pots being dropped onto the display area and dragged into position caught the attention of the detectives, who then noticed the tight-fitting denims showcasing two beautifully shaped legs that stretched up to a very sexy bottom. Deacon caught himself staring a little longer at the sight than he should, so diverted his eyes quickly towards Karl, who was still engaged in visual contact with the posterior. He soon diverted his gaze as the owner of the rear stood up and turned towards the detectives, adding an equally pleasant upper half to the body. Deacon guessed she was probably in her early forties, but could be mistaken for someone a few years younger. Her smooth, lightly tanned complexion and high cheekbones were accentuated by her straight, brown hair that was neatly tied back into a ponytail. She was thin but not bony. Sporty looking. And even dressed casually with her skin-tight jeans, military green Che Guevara tee shirt and Doc Martin boots, looked great. She stared at the men with soft brown eyes.

'Libby McGregor?' Deacon asked.

She nodded. 'Chief Inspector Deacon, I presume?' she smiled. 'When the police ask to speak to you, it's accusing you of something or telling you bad news. To my knowledge, I've done nothing wrong, therefore I qualify for the latter. Although, for the life of me, I can't imagine what that could be.'

She was well spoken. Deacon looked around the room for an area of privacy where he could break the news. Whether Libby noticed he wasn't sure, but she suggested they went to the café area. After making all three of them a milky coffee, she joined the detectives, placing the cups on the table with long tapered fingers with neatly shaped nails, spoilt only by the soil trapped at the tips.

'So, Inspector, sorry, *Chief Inspector*, what do you need to tell me that qualifies for a personal visit?'

Deacon hated these moments. They got no easier. During the journey here, he had tried to plan the right words in such a way to soften the news. But as always, he told it as it was—

no frills. As he was about to speak, his mobile phone rang. Annoyed at the timing, he apologised and quickly switched it off.

'I'm afraid your brother Terry has been found dead. Also, Danny and your father are missing, which is of grave concern to us.' He looked at Libby. She stared motionless at the table. Deacon has seen this scene so many times before. The shock, followed by silence, then disbelief, and tears. Libby cradled her face in both hands.

'Was he killed?' was her muffled question.

'Yes. It was a brutal attack, I'm afraid.'

'Brutal?' she said, still talking through her hands. 'So, he suffered?'

'Yes, he would have. I'm sorry,' replied Deacon empathetically.

Libby's body jolted, her shoulders and chest shaking in unison. Hands still covering her face. Here we go, thought Deacon. The realisation. The pouring of grief. And then it exploded into a roar.......... of hysterical laughter. Deacon turned to Karl, who looked puzzled.

It was a while before she composed herself. The outburst was not only unexpected but unnerving. Tears Deacon expected, but the laughter that accompanied them he didn't. He initially thought it to be a reaction to the shock of the news, as some had before. Although that was sad laughter, if there was such a thing. Libby's response was unbridled joy. She wiped her eyes with a tissue and blew her nose. Turning to Deacon, she smiled.

'Sorry, but that's the best news I've had in years.'

'So, it appears,' said Deacon, puzzled by the reaction. 'I take it there's no love lost?'

'None. And to correct what you said earlier, they're technically my *stepbrothers* and *stepfather*. I disowned them a long time ago.' She drank her coffee, seemingly thoroughly enjoying the taste.

'When was the last time you had contact with them?' asked Deacon.

'Don't know. Twelve months ago, maybe.'

'And where was that?'

'I went to the house to collect something of mine, but they wouldn't let me in.'

'Why not?'

'Because it was me and they're scum of the earth. I hope they all rot in hell.'

'Would you like to elaborate on why you have that opinion?'

'Not really.' She leaned back in her chair and casually crossed her legs.

Deacon sensed he would not get too much more from this visit, but tried anyway.

'How long has this family feud been going on?'

'I really don't want to talk about it.'

'Ok, Libby, but we will need to know more about your relationship with the rest of your family at some point, as this is now a murder investigation.'

Libby shrugged.

'Do you know of any reason someone would want to harm Terry? Did they have any enemies that you know of?'

'Are you kidding?' replies Libby. 'He was a shit. All three of them are shits. I would imagine there is a queue a mile long of people they've crapped on and trampled over, ripped off, or double-crossed. I don't envy your job if you intend to speak to them all.'

'And you? Have they done that to you?'

Libby momentarily paused. 'I got out, but they'd done enough damage by then. Now, if you don't mind, I have work to do. Thank you for the news. I'll certainly be opening a bottle of wine tonight to celebrate.' She stood up and stared at the police officers. Her point made.

The detectives thanked her for her time, with Deacon re-emphasising that it was a murder investigation, so they would most likely want to speak to her again. She said nothing as they left for the car.

Driving back towards Leicester, Karl commented on Libby's reaction to the news of her family. But Deacon said nothing. Lost in thought, reliving that very moment, and trying to interpret the response. It was the strangest reaction he'd ever experienced after breaking such news. He couldn't help thinking that there was more to learn from Libby. He also guessed that something very bad and painful must have happened for her to dismiss her own family, albeit, half family. And she used the word 'scum'. Coincidence?

They'd been travelling steadily among the Leicester bound traffic for a while before Deacon remembered to switch on his mobile phone. Within seconds, the device showed that there were text messages to be read. They were all from Susan. He opened the most recent one, which simply read, 'Bastard'. The power of the word shocked him. It was not the language he would expect or ever had directed at him from his daughter. He opened its predecessor, which read, 'Don't let us down again, Dad'. He let out a groan, causing Karl to look his way. If he was going to say something to Deacon, he chose the better of it. The guilt he felt seemed to squeeze around his body, causing his breathing to get heavier. He paused before opening Susan's first message. 'Where are you?'

He felt like shit. Once again, he had allowed the job to take precedent over his daughter's needs and his wife's memory. Not purposefully, he'd never do that. It just seemed that his job occupied his mind more, pushing aside anything else of importance. Was the job that important to him? He realised it probably was. His life revolved around outwitting the bad guys and putting the pieces of the puzzles together. It was the thrill of the chase, the intellectual nous and the potential danger associated with his job that kept him going. And he needs it more since the death of his wife. Susan dealt with it differently. Like him, she missed her mum terribly, but she needed to deal with it on a more spiritualistic level. The weekly visits to the grave, flicking through family photographs and watching home movies of the family at Christmas, were how Susan connected. He had to work. That was the distraction. His daughter did not know how badly her mother's death affected him. She had no idea how close she was to losing both parents.

CHAPTER FIVE

Following the fourth ringing of the doorbell, James Hawthorne finally opened it. He wore a white knee length bath robe that was tied at the waist. His hair looked greasy and ruffled. He checked the time on the gold watch that graced his left wrist, as if to make a point. Gill assumed that he'd been in bed rather than having a shower. He leaned against the door frame and held the door firmly against his side, blocking any entry. If he recognised his visitors, he didn't show it.

'Yes?'

'Mr Hawthorne, we met earlier. I'm DI Foster and this is DS Matthews. We've come back as promised to see how Rosemary is.'

'She's fine, thank you. She's resting as you recommended.' He showed no sign of letting them inside, so Gill forced his hand.

'Can I see her? There are some points that we need clarifying.'

James sighed. 'Really? She's just lost her husband. She's

upset and confused. Can't you leave her to try to sleep, please?'

You're not getting rid of me that easily, thought Gill. 'If Rosemary is sleeping, maybe you could help? Could we come in for a few minutes?'

James stood for a moment, eyes flitting from Gill to Cara. Finally, he opened the door and stood aside. They went into the room where Gill had interviewed Rosemary earlier. James offered them a seat but no drink. He clearly didn't want them staying too long.

'How can I help?' he asked, trying hard to appear friendly.

'I understand that you and your brother were partners in the farm. Were you equal partners?'

'Yes.'

'And what was the arrangement? Did you share the jobs or was there specific roles?'

'I would imagine you've already worked out that I deal with the financial and administrative side of things. I am also the one who puts himself about touting for business. Look, we were both brought up on the farm, so can equally carry out daily duties. It's just that Steven was rubbish with paperwork, so was happy for me to take on that role. When you share a business, to make it work, and by *work*, I mean *profitable*, you need to work to your strengths.'

'So, did the business split all the money evenly?'

'Not that it's any of your business but, yes it was straight down the middle.'

'Were you surprised by your brother's death?' asked Cara, the change of direction unsettling James momentarily.

'I.... suppose I was, yes.'

'But he had threatened suicide in the past,' intervened Gill.

'He had, but they were just idle threats.'

'Idle threats? Why would he want to do that?'

James sighed. 'When things got too much for him, he'd get depressed.'

'Things? Such as?'

'Farm things, the running of the business.'

Gill could sense the irritation in his voice.

'But I thought you ran the business, Mr Hawthorne?'

'I never said that' said James, pouring himself a small whiskey.

'Have you any idea why your brother went beyond, *idle threats* on this occasion? Something must have pushed him over the threshold.'

James took a small sip of his drink as he pondered the question.

'I'm sorry, but I really don't know.'

'Where were you when you this morning when you were contacted?' asked Cara.

'I was away, on a short holiday.'

'How short?'

'Six days, look, what are you getting at?'

'Nothing, sir. I'm just trying to clarify the facts,' replied Cara. 'Now where did you take this small break of yours?'

'All over the place. I spent a few days driving wherever I fancied. Places of interest.'

'Such as?' asked Gill.

'I had a couple of days at the east coast, near Great Yarmouth, and spent a few days in the Peak district, in Edensor, walking.'

'Can you provide proof of your whereabouts? Such as names, addresses and places you stayed?' asked Cara.

'Why?'

'Routine, sir. We need to correlate all relevant information relating to your brother's death.'

James nodded, 'of course.'

'I'll be honest with you, Mr Hawthorne, it's not unheard

of, but unusual for a victim of a suicide not to leave a message of some kind to explain their actions. And now, we can't see how he could have got himself into that position on the branch of the tree without climbing up something or having help. Do you have any thoughts on that?'

James gave the slightest shake of the head. 'To our knowledge, he gave no explanation of his actions, note or otherwise. As to how he got up there, he probably climbed for all we know. It's not that implausible.'

'He left no note and there was nothing under the tree or moved by me when I found him.'

Everyone turned towards the direction of the voice. Rosemary stood in the doorway wearing a long silk gown with what appeared to be a fancy logo above the top pocket.

'Please,' she continued, 'I told you all this earlier.'

Gill noticed the swelling of her eyes to be less, but they were still very red. 'I apologise, but we have to ask these questions.'

'I know,' replied Rosemary, with a grateful smile. 'Is there anything else, because...' she left the sentence hanging.

Gill shook her head and thanked the Hawthornes for their time.

'So, what do you think, Cara?' asked Gill as she was driven back to the station.

'He seemed very jumpy. He's going to have to provide a few alibis.'

Gill nodded. 'He looked rather fetching in his dressing gown.'

'*Her* dressing gown, actually,' corrected Cara. 'It's the perfume. When he let us in the house, I smelt the scent on his gown. It's definitely "Obsession".'

'Are you sure?'

'Absolutely, It's my favourite. I'd recognise that fragrance anywhere. Do you think there's something going on between them?'

'I'm not sure. Maybe. Why?' asked Gill.

'I just had a feeling that we'd disturbed them if you know what I mean?'

Gill told Cara of her conversation with Deacon on the matter and their thoughts.

'That would make sense with what we had in there,' said Cara.

'James wearing Rosemary's gown hardly constitutes a rumble.'

'No. But when she walks in the room wearing his, it's a little coincidental, let's say. Did you not notice the initials embroidered on her gown?'

'I thought it was a logo, I didn't want to stare too much, or she'd think I was admiring her tits.' They both laugh. 'Still, it would explain why he wasn't keen on letting us in.'

'Rosemary probably listened to the entire conversation,' said Cara.

'Quite possible,' responded Gill, thoughtfully, 'It was funny that she only felt the need to intervene when we asked about the circumstances of the suicide. One of them knows what happened, I'm sure, probably even assisted. Then again, anyone with an ounce of common sense would know that we would be over it like a rash if there was no means of getting up the tree? I mean, talk about suspicious? It's encouraging us to dig deeper.'

'There's something else that's odd,' said Cara as she steered the car into the restricted parking area of the police station and parked up, 'if they're so cut up over Steven's death, why do they appear to be sleeping with each other hours after his body's found?'

After passing by the village of Skeffington, Deacon directed Karl towards Bakewell Farm. While they were out that way, it would be useful for them to revisit the scene and take a good look around the barn where Deacon believed they had initially tied Terry McGregor's body to the tractor. He'd phoned Susan frequently during the drive, but she didn't pick up, so he sent a couple of texts. The first was an apology. With the second he tried to explain why he didn't meet her at her mother's grave. That he received no response from Susan, an avid texter, said it all.

Police tape surrounded the barn and white screens covered the doorway. Only a few of the SOCOs remained operational there. After showing their ID, Deacon and Karl put on one-piece overalls and shoe covers to prevent any contamination of evidence. The building itself housed three tractors. The John Deere tractor stood impounded at the field. There was a CAT Challenger which kept pride of place next to a smaller red Forterra. Two large ploughs stood waiting to be used. Both covered by canvas sheets to protect them from the elements. Deacon knew the SOCOs would have the scientific side of things covered. What he was looking for was something different - a method. A way of getting Terry McGregor's body onto the farm and attached to the tractor without being seen or heard.

Deacon stood silently inside the building. It was a steel structure with eight large girders supporting a curved corrugated roof. A solid breeze-block wall filled the back of the building with the sides bricked to a height of about two metres. There was no visible light source save for the small shafts of light that revealed the cracks and holes in the roof. In the daytime, it was certainly bright enough inside with the open front and sides to allow plenty of light to spill into the place. It had been painted green all over by someone, but the spreading patches of rust suggested that it had been some time since.

The space around the equipment was limited, especially between the tractors, and that was something that made little sense. Why drag a body through here? It would be so awkward, especially if there's an accomplice as well. If Deacon remembered correctly, Dr Freestone had put Terry McGregor's weight at eighty-eight kilograms, a hell of a weight to manoeuvre through such small gaps, especially in the dark. The only access into the building was from the front, which was risky. So why here?

He walked outside into the afternoon sunshine, feeling the warmth against his face. He could clearly see the Timmins' farmhouse to the left, fields opposite and as he looked towards the right, he could follow the track that led to the field where the body was found. Once again, he asked the same question, why here? He made his way around to the rear of the building. To reduce the risk of detection, the murderer or murderers would most probably have brought the body here, the only blind spot from the farmhouse. Karl was already scouring the area.

'Anything?'

'Not sure, sir. Look at this.'

Karl climbed with ease onto one of a dozen oil drums that were lined up against the wall and surrounded by weeds and nettles. The guy was as fit as a fiddle and apparently runs five miles every morning in the early hours, and it showed. He was about five ten, without an ounce of fat on him. He had a strong jawed, tanned face and brown eyes which matched his short neat brown hair that he wore with a side parting. It would just be nice if he smiled more. Deacon followed him up onto the metal containers, a little slower, creating a rumbling sound that resonated as he did so. Karl pointed towards a wooden stake painted bright yellow.

'That post over there is the public footpath. It goes from that fence over to that gate in the distance.' He pointed to an identical post on the other side of the field, the pathway clearly visible in the long grass. 'So, nothing unusual there. However, if you look closely from the back gate to where we are now, you can see what looks like two tracks.'

Deacon had to look hard, but it was just noticeable, 'Tyre tracks?' he asked.

'Could be, sir. I've followed them up to that gate, and although the grass and weeds have re-established themselves, there are the odd spots that remain flattened.'

Deacon could see that it made sense to drive the body as close as possible to the location. The vehicle would also be out of sight of the farmhouse, lessening the chance of raising any suspicion. That would support Mrs Timmin's claim that she may have heard a car the night before the discovery of the body.

'I suppose there's no sign of a chain on the gate or lock?'

'No sign that there ever was one on there. There's a rope that loops over the post to keep it closed. And I've no idea which road it leads to. These country lanes all look the same, so I'll get onto that as soon as.'

Karl was right about the lanes. You need to know your way around the area, which suggested that the location wasn't random. Whoever brought the body knows the area–drove down a network of lanes, turned into a specific field and stopped at a spot hidden from view, which hinted a level of planning. Getting the body into the barn in virtual darkness, so as not to be seen whilst negotiating the gaps between the machinery must have been a challenge. And it still begged the question–why here?

The clicking of the latch echoed in the hallway when the door closed. Deacon made his way through to the kitchen and grabbed a beer from the fridge. After filling his glass, he walked through to the study. There was no sign of Susan downstairs, but he had noticed her bedroom light was on when he parked the car. In truth, he was glad that she was keeping out of the way. He needed time on his own to unwind, so could do without locking horns with her tonight. He would definitely speak to her in the morning, apologise and explain what happened—not that it would do any good. There was no way she was about to let this go easily.

He thought back to his conversations with the Timmins's earlier, and he and Karl's visit to the barn and their working theory of the route the murderer or murderers took to get the body to the barn. Mrs Timmins wasn't sure if she heard a vehicle the night before or if it was on the TVs news. Deacon reasoned that the mere fact she remembered it suggests that it was more than background noise on the television. She said it sounded like a smooth family car, but didn't know why? Neither of them had seen anyone that night, or indeed any other night. No people, no headlights. Although, hardly evidence, he believed what Mrs Timmins thought she heard, could indeed have been the vehicle that took the body of Terry McGregor to the farm. So, in the absence of any solid facts, he used his time based on that hypothetical start of events from which to work.

He finished his beer and impressed himself with his newly found resolve to not have another. Instead, he turned his attention towards the photograph in the gilded frame on the table. A ritual he'd followed most evenings since the death of his beautiful wife, Claire. The picture, taken in Barbados where they went for her fortieth birthday. Wearing that long figure-hugging dress that she loved so much. A big smile on her face as she held up her glass of champagne, lightly golden, matching the shade of her shoulder length hair. Deacon would often spend an hour each day staring at the picture, remembering the great times that they had together. Remembering what a beautiful person, wife, and mother she was - feeling her loss.

His mind took him back to the day when she told him the diagnosis, at the dining table during breakfast on a sunny Tuesday morning. How brave she seemed. How matter of fact she was as she told him she was going to die. That she only had weeks to live. She gave him that heartfelt, reassured smile of hers that said, 'no worries, you'll be Ok'. Even then she was worried about him. Not wanting him to be upset for her. Yet, it was like a truck had hit him. He remembered that feeling of hurt, numbness and helplessness.

'Don't cry,' she said, 'I need you to be strong for me and Susan.'

So, that's what he did. Even through the pain and the guilt - yes, he felt guilt. The guilt for surviving, was eating him up inside. He stayed strong because that's what she wanted so she got what she deserved. But now she's gone. He kept his side of the bargain so now he wants his time to cry.

It was sometime later that Deacon wiped the tears from his eyes and made his way to bed, swallowing to rid himself of the lump in his throat. Although he looked forward to the day when he didn't feel like this, he also, in a strange sort of way, enjoyed connecting with Claire. After climbing the stairs, he walked along the landing where a strip of light shone from beneath Susan's door, partially lighting up the carpet at his feet. There, he paused, ready to knock on her door and try to apologise and make amends but changed his mind. He wasn't ready to face her.

Although not averse to going into work early in the morning, even Gill had to admit that four-thirty was pushing the boundaries of reasonable, but she couldn't sleep. She was now on her third cup of coffee, the effect now kicking in and waking her up. She thought back to the previous day, which had been eventful. There was the suicide and the mystery that surrounded the scene, the distraught Rosemary Hawthorne and of course, the smooth, James. Something was not right there but she couldn't put her finger on what.

So, where do Rosemary and James fit into the picture, as grieving relatives, or murderers? Once again, more needed to be known about them, but Gill's initial impressions were confused. On the one hand she finds them to be conspiring over something - lying even. She suspects the only secret they may try to hide is an affair. After all, it wouldn't look good if their apparent relationship became public, especially in these circumstances. There was something about James that made him interesting to her. He was emotionally much stronger than he was trying to portray and less affected by his brother's death than she would expect.

After the visit to the Hawthornes yesterday, she and Cara had spent the day gathering information about the family. First, to check out James' alibis, of which he had provided locations and dates by email shortly after they'd left the house, before delving deeper into the business of the farm. Gill was also hoping to receive the results from the pathology report within the coming week. That should focus the investigation better. She looked at the clock, it was ten minutes to six. Time for another coffee and a read through her notes before Cara arrives. Pau had arranged a team briefing for later in the morning where both she and Deacon would update everyone on more recent developments.

Gill had not really had any dealings with Cara before. The odd greeting here and there, but she had to admit what she had experienced so far was good. Yes, Cara was a very good-looking young woman which probably created an unintended bias with Gill. Assuming her to just be a pretty face, rather than a serious detective. She has a very young-looking face. Long and oval, pale in complexion but smooth with a straight and flawless nose, thin lips, and soft green eyes. And even though she had her reddish blonde hair tied in a ponytail, it looked great. Matched with her five foot-ten-inch athletic frame, she could have been a model.

The team drifted into the office with tired eyes from long hours double checking information and chasing leads. But they were highly experienced at this sort of thing having been in this position many times before. As soon as Cara arrived, she and Gill discussed a plan for the day. Cara offered to follow-up on James Hawthorne's alibies, meanwhile, Gill focused on trying to gather some background on James and Rosemary. The discovery of a relationship would at least offer a motive to see Steven dead. Although, a somewhat extreme motive, she thought.

The team briefing came and went as efficiently as expected, with all relevant officers dispersed to take on their allocated duties. Pau invited Deacon and Gill to her office afterwards. Deacon had arrived only ten minutes before the briefing, so Gill had no chance to speak with him about developments. As a result, she assumed that some of the information was as much of a surprise to him as his update regarding Libby McGregor was to her and Deacon's theory in relation to the barn at the Timmins' farm.

Pau had produced miracles as she always seemed to do by negotiating a considerable amount of manpower. The Chief Superintendent had ended the meeting with one of her classic morale boosting speeches to pump up the egos of those present. Gill found it fascinating that no one seemed to notice their glorious leader, who told them in a very cloaked way that all leave was cancelled until the cases were solved. Gill and Deacon sat facing Chief Superintendent Pau, who sat behind her desk which was bathed in the light that shone through her large office window. Pau began.

'We've received a lot of calls from not only the Leicester Mercury, but a few nationals. It seems they've noticed we're using considerable resources on the McGregor's case and know the questions we're asking. I can only assume that someone has said something to the wrong person, you know how these things gain momentum. For that reason, I'm going to conduct a press conference, which as you know, I don't enjoy doing when we have so little to go on. But we need to gain some control over what they write. I'll give them Terry's name, before they discover that. They don't need to know the details at this stage, they'll make their own narrative up, anyway. However, this is an opportunity for us too. So, how do you think we should play it? Is there anything you want me to say that may help us?'

'Whatever you say gets sensationalised by the media so, it's hard to see how we could benefit,' offered Gill.

'We need to be careful,' said Deacon. 'Like Gill said, they'll spin it to sell papers and online space, and they're not stupid. A few of them can put one and one together and make two.'

So, what do you think we should say, Alex?' asked Pau.

Deacon Mulled over the question before answering. 'That we've found the body of Terry McGregor.... And we are also concerned for the well-being of John and Danny McGregor, whose whereabouts are presently unknown, and if anyone can assist with our enquiries, get in touch. No more. Yes, they'll fill in the gaps, but it'll be purely speculative on their part.'

Gill nodded in agreement.

'Fine, that's what we'll do,' said Pau. She focused her gaze on Gill. 'The Hawthorne suicide? I listened to what you said during the briefing. What's your gut feeling? Is it what it seems, or do you suspect foul play?'

'I don't know at this stage, ma'am. Certainly, things don't seem as straightforward as they should be.'

Pau thought for a moment. 'Unless something really dramatic comes up, publicly at least, we'll present it as an unfortunate suicide. Use the extra legs to get the background checks done, so we can clear it up. Do I make myself clear?'

Gill nodded.

'Good, I know these cases are in excellent hands. But promise me, if you need help, you'll speak to me because I don't want surprises.'

'Promise, ma'am,' replied Gill. She could not help thinking that this was the first time since moving to the station, that the Chief Super had spoken to her in such a way. As an equal to Deacon rather than his second fiddle, which made her feel good.

―――

'Here's as good a place as anywhere,' said Callum, helping Chloe down to the area next to the stream.

She let go of his hand and looked around her. It was perfect. Down from the derelict brick building at the edge of the field they stood in between two rows of bushes that had grown either side of the stream, and joined above them like linking fingers, creating a canopy of leaves. These filtered the daylight sufficiently making it dull but not dark, soft on the eyes. Odd sparkles of light appeared above them when the breeze ruffled the leaves.

'It's nice. We'll have to remember this place. Fancy a bite to eat, Cal?'

'Sure, but not what you're thinking, babe.'

He grabbed Chloe by the waist, turning her towards him. they locked lips. She felt herself getting aroused. As soon as Callum's hands reached up and touched her nipples, it was like electric shocks shooting through her body. Their kissing became more charged. Chloe could feel his erection pressing against her. She loosened the button of his trousers. He broke away from the embrace and reached for his backpack.

'Hold on, babes.'

He pulled out a blanket and laid it out onto the ground next to the stream. Chloe smiled. This is what today was all about. They had skived from school, to spend the day wandering across the countryside away from prying eyes. Callum was a year older than her at fifteen and had had sex with a few girls in his year. Chloe had done it for the first time with him two weeks ago. It was like affiliation to an exclusive club at school, with an ever-increasing membership.

She was tingling all over. She sat on the blanket and offered Callum her hand. He smiled and accepted it. She pulled him on top of her, once again locking lips as they took off each other's clothes. It was not long after when she felt him enter her and the lovemaking took Chloe to a very special place.

After sending Karl Goodman to Dudbridge Holdings to coordinate the interviews, Deacon passed his time trying to address the hive of thoughts that were buzzing around his head. He had slept relatively well last night, at least he thought he had. But his dreams were hijacked by thoughts relating to the McGregor's case. A family who seemed to have everything had simply, disappeared. Then one of them ends up dragged along a track like a dead animal carcass, with all dignity gone – a person with no value. He dreaded to think how they would find the other two.

There was Margaret Wilson, who he intended to speak with later in the day. Ignoring the death, the fact her employers were missing had shaken her up – really shook her up. There was much more to Margaret Wilson and her relationship with the McGregors, John in particular, of that, he was sure. Throughout the dream, Deacon had the impression that her relationships weren't only emotional or physical even, but she had control over the men. Orchestrating their moves somehow. But it was a dream and his brain made up whatever it wanted, blurring fact with fiction. Or was his brain subconsciously making deductions, creating connections from its own distorted perspective?

Every time Libby appeared in the dream, she was laughing hysterically at everyone. Her features were sharper, her eyes webbed with red veins. Her teeth longer and pointed. The more she laughed, the more it turned into a cackle. Even though Deacon was in a deep sleep, she scared him. He desperately wanted to wake up and get away from her but knew he couldn't. It felt like she wanted to keep him to stand as witness to the demise of those evil McGregors.

His dream moved on to the Three Gables house with furniture overturned in the room and the word SCUM painted in big letters on the wall. Libby stood in the corner of the room, cackling away, looking even more sinister than before with long witchlike fingers grasping an aerosol of red paint. He felt his heart speed up at the sight of her.

'They're all scum, I hope they rot in hell,' she kept saying.

The phrase kept repeating as if on a loop, getting faster and faster, louder and louder, becoming too much. Deacon woke from his sleep, heart pounding against his chest and sweating. His muscles ached all over. He reached for the alarm clock and looked in disbelief. He had overslept. Had the alarm not gone off? He had to rush to make the team meeting.

His plan for the day was routine, but he hoped to answer a lot of questions and shape a few theories. He wanted to take a proper look in the Three Gables, especially the living room where the disturbance took place. He also felt it was worth a more detailed search of the bedrooms. There were a couple of items that he was keen to find. Deacon also wanted to speak with Libby McGregor again, armed with more specific questions this time. There was an awful lot she didn't say yesterday, and now he knows she doesn't give a shit about her family, he can be far more pointed with his questioning and more demanding for answers without the risk of her accusing him of not caring.

With the sex over and their climax reached, Callum and Chloe laid on their backs holding hands in silence. They stared, mesmerised at the twinkling of the light above them that appeared as the leaves gently swayed with the light breeze above them, letting in the small flickers of sunshine, looking like stars. After a while and another kiss, they both got dressed.

Chloe sat at the edge of the stream, her feet dangling in the cold water, eating a sandwich she had made. Callum had gone to relieve his bladder in the old brick building above, which she assumed was once a stable but now a brick shell, the roof long gone. They would then both explore more of the countryside and no doubt find another spot to have sex - she hoped so, anyway. She thought about her parents and what they would say if they found out what she was doing. No doubt they would explode. Playing truant was bad enough, but if they knew who she was with and what they were doing, it doesn't bear thinking about. Still, her mum, like many others at the school, had made sure that her daughter was given the pill at fourteen by the doctor as a safety precaution. The irony was that what their parents consider a safety precaution was to Chloe and her friends, licence to indulge without consequences. And she was enjoying every moment and the sensation she felt whilst doing it. The first time they had sex, Callum used a condom. But now they prefer to do it without. That way they can really feel each other.

The bushes rustled as Callum stumbled and fell down the embankment, coming to a stop as he slid into Chloe's leg. She laughed at his misfortune until he lifted his head and she saw the look on his face. His complexion was pale and eyes tearful. His hands and arms violently trembling. He tried to speak but was unable amid laboured breathing.

'What's wrong, Cal?'

He stared at her, attempting to slow his breathing down.

'Call the police, babe,' he finally said between large gasps.

'Why? Look we can't…. we shouldn't be here.'

'Just ring the police, now!' he said between gritted teeth.

'Why, Cal? What am I supposed to say?'

'Tell them there's a guy in that building who's had his fucking head incinerated!'

―――

Turning into the driveway of Three Gables farm, his mobile rang. Seeing the name displayed on the screen, Deacon stopped immediately to answer the call, causing a loud crunching sound on the gravel.

'Hello?'

'Alex where are you?' asked Pau.

'At the McGregors' place.'

'Forget it. Another body's been discovered, so I want you there as quickly as possible. Now, where did I put that bloody address?'

It was only a short drive to the location. He parked behind a long row of cars, some he recognised, others marked police vehicles. He walked towards the entrance to a field where all the activity seemed to be. The metal gate propped open with an old brick and manned by a uniformed officer who he always acknowledged with a cursory nod, but never knew his name. There was a small brick building of some sort that from a distance appeared to Deacon as no more than ten by six metres in size. The roof was gone along with a window and doors. Weeds had somehow sprouted from the brickwork, a phenomenon he never understood. Judging by the height of the bushes and trees that it backed onto, he assumed there was maybe a small stream. As he arrived, he saw two teenagers wrapped in blankets. The lad was physically shaking and crying whilst the girl comforted him. Deacon assumed they found the body. Should they not be a school?

As soon as he walked into the small-bricked shell, the smell of burning flesh hit him. It wasn't particularly overpowering but seemed so with the taste that he got in his mouth, very similar to overcooked meat. He could only see the legs and the body of the victim lying on the floor with legs together and arms to the side, like a soldier standing, or lying in this case, to attention. Unnaturally neat. Temporary lights were rigged up to aid the photographer, who was taking pictures like it was going out of fashion. And standing next to the victim was the Pathologist, Dr David Freestone, who seemed quite intrigued with his new assignment. The bare brick walls had rusty hooks protruding randomly from them. It was cramped with just the four of them inside. Freestone acknowledged Deacon's arrival but held up his hand, signalling him to wait until he finished updating his report on Dictaphone. Eventually, he acknowledged him.

'Ah, Alex, welcome to my abode. A little bijou, maybe?'

'How are things, Dave?'

'If I was to offer a couple of clues, such as, hot headed or Coal miner, what can you make from that?'

'God knows, enlighten me.'

'If you are a religious man, which I very much doubt, this will test your resolve in humanity and God.' He moved to the side and held his hand out towards the victim lying on the floor.

'Jesus Christ!' Deacon couldn't believe what he was looking at.

'Yep, we've covered the big guys now, maybe the disciples next?'

Deacon moved closer to the body. The stench of charred skin and bone getting stronger the nearer he got.

'What happened?'

'It appears the victim has had a material of some sort forced into the mouth. And based on the result, I would imagine that someone forced a material of some sort into the victim's mouth, possibly using an accelerant like petrol or mentholated spirits. It was lit and as you can see, the head duly cooked. I imagine the moisture in the body prevented it spreading much further than the head. To be honest, if the perpetrator had wanted to barbeque the whole body, they would only need to soak it with petrol. I could be wrong, but I get the impression that they did what they intended.'

'Set fire to the head?' questions Deacon. 'But why?'

'That's your job, not mine.'

Deacon looked at the body. The face was jet black. It had shrivelled causing deep lines on the surface of the skin, reminding him of charred wood. The head shape looked more like that of a neanderthal. It was strange to see that despite the head being completely cooked, the closed eyelids and nose were still present in its form. Only coated in black skin. What did look terrifying was the wide-open mouth, some teeth still noticeable, creating a burned-out chasm; a cone shaped void where the main part of the fire had been. As Deacon's eyes scanned the rest of the body, he could see that from the neck downwards the damage was less and less– supporting the Pathologist's assessment that the intention was to only burn the head. But why? What kind of madman would even think of doing such a thing?

Dave Freestone broke his thoughts. 'Between you and me, Alex, there is something that's more disturbing about this that may interest you. To cremate a human body, it needs to be subjected to around eighteen hundred degrees for between an hour and an hour and a half. No way would this have been anything above eleven or twelve hundred degrees. Therefore, to completely bake the head, as it has, it would need to be topped up with fuel over a considerable period.'

'So, whoever did this would have needed to hang around to keep adding fuel to the fire?'

'I believe so.'

'And, Dave, do you think the victim was.....'

'Don't ask. I'll determine that when I cut him up.'

'Definitely, him?'

'Definitely. His manhood is unscathed. Although had the fire gone that far, it wouldn't have taken that long to burn, if you know what I mean.'

'Before you say it, I know it's my job. But just your thoughts. Do you notice any similarities from your perspective with the Bakewell farm victim?'

Freestone considered the question.

'Only that the attacks were both targeted at the head. Do you think it's the same person?'

'Or persons. Possibly. They're both pretty extreme to where the act is probably more symbolic than the death itself. That's a working hypothesis I have at the moment.'

'So, if I find our charcoal headed friend was alive when

the deed was started, it would be fair to assume that it was at the hands of the previous perpetrator?'

'I guess we could,' said Deacon.

He looked around the walls. Had the body been burnt there, he would have expected some evidence somewhere, be it scorching or soot. After all, the act must have generated considerable smoke? Even though the building was in an isolated area, it was hardly remote. A route linking the villages of Tilton on the Hill with Skeffington was a tarmacked single lane surface used as a route to access fields and farms. It also seemed popular with dog walkers and ramblers from what he'd seen so far. So, it would be foolish to commit such a deed here. It's something the SOCOs would determine, he reasoned. The way the body is laid out in the middle the floor struck Deacon as strange too. The fingertips looked rough and discoloured. Deacon bent down to inspect.

'What's this, Dave?'

'I assume that's where the rats have nibbled the fingertips. I've seen evidence of droppings on the floor.'

'So, you're not even free from attack when you're dead?'

'Afraid not. Trust me, if you lay long enough on the ground, there'll be some critter that'll have a piece of you.'

Deacon shook his head in disbelief as he stood up. He took in the full extent of the sight before him. The body would have been amusing had it not been so gruesome in its appearance. The head. A black burned-out mass that led to a badly blistered chest. Yet, from below the pectorals the body and clothing were in reasonably good condition, the trousers, socks, and shoes showed no sign of damage. Deacon also noted that the Rolex strapped to the left wrist still ticked away at the correct time.

'Can you give me a time of death?'

'I'm afraid not, Al. There are too many variables with this

one. I'll have to blow the dust off the abacus to figure this one out.'

'Ok, when?' asked Deacon impatiently.

'I'm back on shift later in the week, so if things are not too busy at death row, I'll make a start. But I'll warn you now, it'll be a slow and complex procedure.'

'I can appreciate that. Let me know as soon as you have anything, Dave.'

'Scouts honour, sir!' came the reply with a salute.

Deacon stepped outside taking a lungful of fresh air- although he could still taste charred flesh. He made his way to the two teenagers who were sitting together on the grass and crouched down beside them. The boy seemed calmer than he was when Deacon noticed them earlier, but still visibly upset. Deacon offered his hand.

'My name's Chief Inspector Deacon. I'm assigned to the case, and I'd like to ask you some questions, would that be alright?'

Callum grasped his hand with both of his and shook vigorously while Chloe looked on and smirked. Deacon signalled for the uniformed officer to step back to allow some privacy. Deacon eyed the two young people closely before offering a warm smile.

'So, tell me, why were you here?'

The two teenagers looked at each other, as if trying telepathically to agree on a reason. Chloe played with her hair, wrapping it around her finger and stare at the ground.

'We were on a walk,' said the boy.

'Ok,' said Deacon, 'before we go any further, how old are you?'

Again, the pair stared at each other, this time with more fear. Chloe looked as if she was about to say something but changed her mind.

'I'm fifteen and Chloe's fourteen,' replied Callum.

'Shouldn't you be in school?'

There was a considerable pause before Cullum answers, 'yes, sir'.

'And the school is?'

'Langford High', said Callum.

'Ok, I'm investigating the death of the person in the building there, so I'm not overly bothered why you're not at school because I need whatever information I can get. Do I make myself clear?'

The pair nodded in unison.

'However, I am interested in why you're here, what you were doing and how you came about to meet the victim. Now, because of your age we are going to have to get a full statement from you *officially* with parents and guardians present.' Deacon could see the panic in the couple's eyes. 'But, between you and me, it would be useful to get a general overview of events beforehand. As I'm sure you understand, what has happened in that building there is serious. So, I don't have the time to mess about. If you're going to insist that you were wandering the countryside taking in its natural beauty, I won't believe you. Now, I'd very much appreciate you telling the truth because I'm not in the mood to unpick riddles. Do I make myself clear?'

The teenagers stared at him. Chloe shifted uncomfortably.

'We wanted some time together, you know, to get to know each other better,' she said.

'And when did you arrange this day out?'

'A couple of days ago.'

'Today would be the least disruptive to our studies,' added Callum.

At least they have their heads screwed on regarding their education, thought Deacon. He continued.

I'm not too interested in the personal details but, by

getting to know each other better, I assume you mean talking and petting?' The couple nodded. 'Anything more serious?'

The couple stared at each other nervously before unilaterally, but reluctantly nodding.

'Listen, I will not follow that up on the legality front - others will, except to tell you off the record to keep safe, for God's sake.'

Callum stared at the ground whilst Chloe's mouth broke into a smile. Deacon continued.

'Now we're being honest with each other, I need you to focus on what I'm about to ask. It's quite possible that nothing you have seen today will bear anything on the death of the person inside that building. However, I want you to describe how you got to this place in as much detail as possible, giving me times where you can. So, let's start with the time and place you met up.'

Chloe and Callum told him they met at 8am at the bus stop at the local Co-Op store in Uppingham and caught the Leicester bus at 8.35am. They got off the bus at Tugby and made their way across country on foot. The lanes were quiet with only the odd car and tractor passing them. They mainly took the footpaths using a map that Callum had. Although some were overgrown and difficult to get through and to their knowledge, all gates to the fields were closed. From Tilton-on-the-Hill to where they ended up, they only saw a lady jogging along the lane with, judging by the moving patch of beige seen through the hedgerow, a dog.

When they arrived at the field, they found a spot next to the stream that was sheltered from the sun. They stayed near the stream for around forty-five minutes. Callum needed to relieve himself so went up into the field and into the small out-building. As soon as he stepped inside, he saw the body laid out on the floor, from which he ran back to Chloe to raise the alarm.

At this point Callum appeared upset by the memory, with Chloe hugging him as tears ran down his face.

Deacon remained silent for a few minutes, absorbing everything that the young couple had told him, noting every reaction. He concluded he was happy with what he had been told and was confident that it was truthful, and they had innocently but fortunately found the body. The reaction from Callum gave him the feeling that they had nothing to hide. Chloe apparently never went inside the building after seeing Callum's response. The pair gave Deacon a good idea of their timeline, but more importantly, an idea of the amount of activity in the area, or in this case - lack of it. Deacon thanked them for their help and arranged for an officer to arrange for a formal statement to be conducted involving the parents/guardians and for the teenagers to be driven home. The anxiety was clear in their features.

'What are you going to tell our parents,' asked Callum?

'I have to tell the truth,' replied Deacon. He stared intensely at them both. 'You were playing truant from school together, went for a walk through the countryside and discovered the victim of a horrific murder. You contacted the police immediately and provided an initial statement of events. Yes, you'll get some earache for bunking off from school, and rightly so. If they ask more awkward questions of what you were doing together, that's for you to deal with. However, it's surprising how proud parents are when their children discover something important. That'll take the edge off of things. It'll be a good story to tell at family barbeques. Now, I may want to speak with you again, but for now, there's a car over there that will take you back home.'

Chloe and Callum thanked Deacon and made their way to the waiting police car. As they walked, Deacon called to them.

'Hey. Remember what I said—keep safe.' They nodded.

Deacon could hear Dr Freestone instructing the medics who had just arrived to collect the victim, to take care in case the head came off. Although completely inappropriate, he imagined the head rolling off of the stretcher as it's carried towards the waiting vehicle, with Freestone, in full rugby kit chasing after it like he was going for a winning try.

He took a slow walk around the field to get a feel of the location. Opposite the main entrance was another gate. It was the same as the overgrown stiles leading to the field, with weeds weaving up between the rusty rungs. It showed no sign of disturbance with long grass and nettles still woven around it, leading to the conclusion the body arrived into the field via the gate that Deacon and the police had entered the field. A lane used by many other people–joggers, farmers and dog walkers alike. That gave a high risk of being seen by someone. He made a mental note to arrange for door-to-door enquiries in the local villages to see if anyone can offer any little snippets of information. It would also be useful to have a couple of officers talking to dog walkers, in case they come from a different village. If the same person who murdered Terry McGregor, which is possible, committed the crime, there was more of a risk of being seen moving or planting the body here than the previous location.

He looked back at the derelict building. The exterior looked neglected but not overly so. In fact, it was still in a reasonable condition for its age, which Deacon guessed was around fifty years old. What for he was buggered if he knew. But now it was a place of death. A cruel place of death. It's ironic it survived so long, but now it's tarnished by an incredibly foul deed–something it will now be associated with. And like most buildings that have been subject to such horror, it has the equivalent of a terminal disease. At some point it will have to be demolished to prevent it becoming some perverted attraction for human intrigue.

Deacon slowly circled, scanning the scenery, looking towards Tilton-on-the-Hill, the highest point in Leicester, so they say, he turned towards Skeffington Woods to the east. Deacon etched the surrounding area into his memory. There would have been smoke, and Deacon would expect it to be relatively dense, certainly with burning hair and skin, coming out of the building. Unless the body had been burned in the early hours of the morning, many in the surrounding area would see the smoke. But the location suggests, like the first victim, the murderer or murderers must have wanted the body to be found.

Deacon looked at his watch. There was little he could do now. He headed back to the Police HQ to support Chief Superintendent Pau in her press conference.

CHAPTER SIX

Pau's demeanour, tone of voice, and snappiness was clear. At the end of the press conference, she stormed out of the room and made straight for her office. Deacon, left sitting at the table beside her empty chair, realised he would need to do the same, to avoid being accosted by the remaining journalists who had not yet left the room. The last thing he needed right now was to be asked the same questions they had been asking for the past 10 minutes. He quickly rose from his chair and left the room, ignoring the calls for him to clarify any points the remaining hacks had conjured up.

He reached Pau's office and gently knocked on the door, before slowly opening it and walking in. Pau was sitting at her desk with her elbow resting on it and hand supporting her chin. He sat on the chair facing her. Pau's eyes stared piercingly towards the corner of the office towards the coffee machine. Every now and again she seemed to squint her eyes, like she was trying to look deeper into the corner. She slowly turned to him, eyes still piercing like lasers, not blinking. Finally, she spoke.

'What gives him the right to take that tone with me?'

Alex shrugged. 'About two-and-a-half million readers?'

'Oh, piss off, Alex.' The hand slamming on the desk causing her empty coffee cup to rattle in the saucer.

'I mean it gives him a lot more weight, and in his eyes, more of a right to ask such questions and be an antagonistic old sod.' He saw Pau roll her eyes. He continued, 'I'm sorry, I'm telling you how to suck eggs.'

Deacon knew some journalists were old hacks and would press for more details, read between the lines. Many of them have attended hundreds of press conferences, so get a sense of when they're being fobbed off or given what needs to be known rather than the full truth. They understand details need to be held back for a multitude of reasons - operational, victim safety, to mislead the perpetrator, to bide time. But unfortunately, it doesn't matter to them. All they're bothered about is the story, the scoop, the sensationalistic bullshit that they can add to sprinkle that extra fairy dust to make more people want to read their paper. And Pau knew that too. Yet, one journalist in particular - Jeremy Bentley - rattled her today.

Deacon and Bentley had crossed paths in the past. Bentley started his early career in journalism on fleet street working for *The Sun* news agency, following them as they moved to Wapping in 1986. He jumped ship to *The Daily Mail* in 1993 where he stayed for 10 years before having several shorter spells with most of the other major publications until he decided to semi retire and work for himself freelance. Thanks to his list of contacts and experience, there is still plenty of demand for the stories that he reports on. Unfortunately for Deacon and Pau, Bentley moved away from London and settle in the Midlands in a little cottage in Leicestershire.

He kept repeating the same questions, 'how was he killed?' 'Are the others suspected dead?' 'Where was the body found?' No matter how much Pau and Deacon stuck to their script of, 'it's believed to be the body of Terry McGregor and there is concern for whereabouts of his father and brother,' Jeremy Bentley kept firing back with the same three questions, 'how was he killed?' 'Are the others suspected dead?' 'Where was the body found?' Such questions triggered others to suspect that there was possibly more to this than they were being told, which made the briefing more combative than Deacon or Pau wanted. In the end, Pau ended the press briefing with the obligatory, 'That's all the information we have now, but as soon as we have any new information to share, we will let you know.'

'Listen,' said Deacon, breaking into her thoughts. 'Bentley and the others will go away now and report on what we've said.'

'Obviously!', said Pau. She massaged her eyes with each hand. 'And embellish it and add their take on things, I would guess.'

'That goes without saying. However, we have something which they're not aware of yet?'

Pau raised her eyebrows. 'The second body.'

'And with this other body in the equation, if it's one of the McGregors, and someone has mutilated it, it could very likely be the same sadistic killer or killers, which gives us a bit of time. They don't know about it yet, so while they're squeezing their story within an inch of its life, we have some freedom to push on with enquiries and investigate that one too whilst the vultures' focus is elsewhere. It may only buy us a few days, but we may get a break in that time.'

'Agreed,' replies Pau. 'The two murders are brutal to say the least. You can imagine how they're going to be played out in the media when they find out? Never mind the panic that'll develop amongst some of the public. Whatever, I'll see if I can draft in more support officers.'

'Thanks, that would help,' said Deacon. 'I'm also worried about stuff getting onto social media - true or not. We checked the mobiles of the two kids who found the body. You know what teenagers are like these days. Everything revolves around their mobiles and cameras. There was no evidence of them taking any photos or posting anything out. They were too scared to even think about it, I think. We told them and their families that we will monitor their online activity. That usually does the job. I also told the kids that I would tell their parents what they were doing, if any information comes out. That shit them up.'

Pau smiled. 'I bet it did. Good work and thank you for your support. Talking of which, how are you doing?'

'I'm fine. It's good to be busy again. Distracted, if you know what I mean? Right, I'd better get going,' said Deacon. He stood up and made his way to the door.

'By the way,' said Pau. 'Susan called me today.' Deacon froze. 'You need to talk to her. She is really hurting, Alex.'

He stood still with his back to Pau, his hand firmly gripping the door handle. Deacon thought back to the text Susan had sent him yesterday. The shock that went through him when he saw *that* word. The guilt he felt.

Pau continued, 'she has lost her mother, her kindred spirit, her true pillar of support. The person who was always there for her whilst you were out and about, chasing bad guys. But she needs you now.'

'She won't talk to me. She's locking herself in her room. And anyway, why the hell is she calling you?' Deacon remained facing the door.

Pau responded softly, 'She's calling me because she can. She's calling me because I gave her that option at your wife's funeral. She's calling me because she feels her dad doesn't care. Christ, I know you care, Alex. Let her know that!'

Deacon felt frozen, facing the door, gripping the handle

so hard his knuckles had gone white. His head was reeling. Confused. Angry. Ashamed? He didn't know. Finally he managed to open the door and left in silence.

DC Karl Goodman parked outside the address in the Northgate area of Oakham at just after ten o'clock. The drive through the countryside had been pleasant as always, with the fields covered in a thick layer of morning frost, giving a very wintery feel to the day. The sun was now burning brightly and during the last couple of miles, with steam rising from the grass verges at the side of the road as the rays evaporated the cold white powder.

Deacon got out of the car and stood outside the property, waiting for Karl to join him. It was a fairly modern detached house, only fifteen years old, he guessed. The tarmacked front garden area was small but opened up to the right side of the house where there was a garage and parking area, where a red Mazda MX5 convertible rested – its registration plate telling the world that it was the latest model. Behind was a two-metre-high brick wall, the top of which adorned with latticed black ironwork, and at the bottom several large clay pots filled with colourful plants. The two detectives were walking up to the front door as it opened, and Margaret Wilson greeted and guided them through the short passageway into the living room on the left.

Margaret was wearing casual bell-bottomed jeans, black Nike trainers and a white buttoned top. He noticed she seemed brighter than she did when they spoke last, at the Baker's Arms pub, although still quite dark around the eyes. Deacon politely declined her offer of coffee or tea. The room itself was bright with large patio doors that led to the kitchen area and a window on the adjacent wall letting in the sunlight.

Laminate flooring complemented high-quality furniture. It was modern looking and tasteful. The only thing that looked out of place was the cigarette packet, lighter and ashtray on a large glass-topped table.

'Thank you for sparing the time to speak with us, Ms Wilson,' said Deacon. 'As I said earlier, I want to speak to you to get a better idea about the McGregor family, the dynamics and of course, your role.'

'That's no problem, Chief Inspector. And you are?' She looked at Karl.

'DC Goodman, Ms Wilson.' Karl took his notebook and pen from his pocket.

'It certainly seems that you are important to the business and indeed the lives of the McGregor family,' began Deacon. 'Now, what do they call it in Government? A minister without portfolio.'

Margaret smiles. 'That's an interesting way in which you describe my job role. I think that's quite accurate, actually.'

'Ok, Margaret, let's start with you. So, what exactly is your role with the family?'

'I literally oversee everything. Think about it. You have three men working together in the business, and being typical men, they love the managing and deal making side of things and are very good at it. But with the more mundane side of life, they are absolutely useless. So, they need someone, you know, to keep the books right, organise meetings with clients, doctors, dentists, hospitals. In fact, I do everything they don't want to do. I'm going over to Dudbridge holdings later to ensure that everything is still going Ok.'

'Let's go back to the beginning. When did you join Dudbridge Holdings Ltd?'

'I started in 2001 as a PA for Mr. and Mrs. Dudbridge, David and Alison. They were a wonderful couple to work for. The pair of them had started the business not long after they got married. He was a very well-respected man, brilliant and driven. As a result, the business was growing year after year. From when I started, Alison had long since taken a back seat and let her husband run that side of things. But in 2006 David had a heart attack while working late at the office, and, when he didn't come home, Alison and her daughter took some food over to him and found him slumped over his desk. He was already dead, unfortunately. After the funeral, Alison knew she would need to take over the running of Dudbridge Holdings and did that for a while.'

'You say, for a while? How long, roughly?' asked Deacon.

'It was about a year-and-a-half. And I noticed she was asking me to do more and more. I could see she was struggling.'

'So, what happened?'

'That was when John McGregor became involved. Alison and David knew John McGregor, he used to deal with her husband, so she'd accompanied her husband to several corporate dinners and such like and they were friends. And I believe he offered to help run the business to relieve some of the stress. Since he was experienced with such things, I guess she thought, "Well, why not?" That takes a lot of pressure off of her. And as they started working together, they built up a relationship and you know, it turned into something more and they got married.'

'Did they get married before or after he took over the running of the business completely?' asked Deacon.

'I think it was after about three years into the relationship and by then he was pretty much in charge of everything, so it made sense. It gave Alison the opportunity to do her own thing. And from that point she enjoyed going on short trips, sometimes with Libby, and gardening because she was a very keen gardener, leaving the running of the business side to John.'

'Was Libby living in the house?'

Margaret seemed to pause for a moment. Almost surprised by the question. 'Yes, she was, she was she was still there.'

'How did Libby get on with the new family? Because she has two lovely parents, from what you say. She loses her dad. And then John McGregor and his two sons come on the scene.'

Margaret thought before answered. 'Typical stepbrother, stepsister relationship, I would say. I think there was some resentment from Libby when they entered her life. And there was John taking the role of stepdad, which was never going to be that smooth. Libby and her dad were very close, and it hit her really hard when he died. She grew really close to her mother. But I got the feeling she was very much against her mother marrying John, and definitely against her making John a partner in what she felt was effectively her father's business. The family business.'

'So, how did this all pan out, with John now married to Alison, and his two sons on the scene?'

'Libby became a real pain to the family. Very rebellious. Very argumentative and accusing various members of the family of bullying and such like.'

'Anyone in particular?' asked Deacon.

Deacon felt Margaret seemed a little uncomfortable with the question. Was it the pause? The eyes flitting around the room?

'Not really,' she replied.

'That you have mentioned it suggests that there was something that triggered your memory?'

She seemed to choose her words with care. 'Obviously John was not her father, and there was no way she was going to accept him in any shape or form in that role. She didn't seem too bad with Terry, just the odd arguments over nothing, half the time. I think that's because he kept himself to himself to a large degree, so didn't antagonise her. But Danny? They put up with each other at the start, but after a few months she absolutely turned on him. Don't ask me why, I don't know, and I got the impression he didn't know either. You know, for what it's worth, and I know because I've worked with them for the last ten years, John and his sons are three of the nicest people. Yes, I would imagine that you'll find some who will bad mouth them, because they are hard businessmen. But underneath all of that, they are very kind people.'

'It seems like you're trying to convince me.'

'I'll ignore that comment if you don't mind Chief Inspector. At this moment, I have lost my bosses, my colleagues, my friends. Decent, hard-working people who have been very good to me and whom I respect. I take offense at your comment.' Margaret's eyes welled with tears.

Deacon realised he needed to back off if he wanted more from her in this sitting. 'I apologise, Ms Wilson. It was a flippant comment that was not meant the way it came out. So,' he continued, 'John and Alison get married, Libby isn't happy with the situation. What happened next?'

'Do you mind if I have a cigarette? I will open the window?'

'Feel free,' said Deacon. Not wanting her to smoke at all, but it was her house. And after all, he was getting good background information from her.

Margaret opened the window as promised and lit up a cigarette. She took a long draw from it, eyes closed, before directing her gaze towards the open window and exhaling the smoke in that direction. It seemed to calm her, and she continued.

'Probably a year after they got married. Alison signed over the company to John.'

'Why sign it over? I thought it was a family partnership?'

'I don't know. But I would imagine John McGregor was doing a great job with it. His sons were doing a great job. So, it made sense, I think. And Alison could do her own thing.'

'Ok. And how did Libby take this?' asked Deacon.

'I don't know. I wasn't privy to that but imagine she wouldn't have taken it very well because as far as she was concerned, this was her dad's business that was given away.'

'To be honest with you, Margaret, it seems a strange thing to do. After all, Alison built the business up with her first husband. And I can understand bringing John in as a partner, but why sign it over completely? It just makes little sense to me.'

'It probably doesn't, but business can be complicated, Chief Inspector. Things don't always remain the same. They evolve.'

'At what point did Alison die?'

'Now that was a tragic accident. Alison went on a trip to York, and while she was there, she was the victim of a hit and run. I don't believe the driver was ever caught. She was dead at the scene, apparently. And that absolutely devastated Libby. I guess it was the straw that broke the camel's back, so to speak. She took her mum's death very badly.'

'How were John and the boys?'

'Obviously, they were devastated. It was John's wife after all. It was Terry and Danny's stepmother. They couldn't believe what happened. It was a really sad time for everyone. However, the funeral became marred with controversy and accusations. Libby wanted to bury her mother in a certain way. She had an idea on how that should go, and she wanted her mother buried next to her father. John didn't want that. He wanted her buried on the grounds of the farm. And that caused a lot of contention. Eventually, he decided to bury

Alison in the same cemetery as her first husband, David, but not next to him.'

'Why?'

'Why do you think? He was her husband at that point. He wanted her to be buried where he chose, so he could be buried next to her I guess.'

'Ok, so following the funeral, how long after that was it before Libby moved out?'

'I don't really know what happened. But I know that almost overnight, Libby packed her bags and left and vowed never to return. I don't know why. But that's what happened. That's what she was like. Fiery. Headstrong.' Margaret blew another mouthful of smoke towards the open window.

'Isn't she entitled to live at the farm? Doesn't she have some kind of stake in the farm and the business?'

Margaret became uncomfortable again. She thought carefully, 'To my knowledge, Libby has no stake in the business. That is John and his son's business, as far as the farm goes, I don't know how it all came about, but she ended with no stake, and she walked away from it. That was her choice, how I understand it, and right until the day she left, she was incredibly bitter towards the John and the boys.'

'Do you not find it strange that Libby, a true heir to the business, is being squeezed out?' asked Deacon.

'Maybe,' responded Margaret. 'But that was her doing.'

'In what way?'

'I don't know.'

Deacon bit the bullet and risked destroying any rapport he had with Margaret Wilson and ask the million-dollar question. 'You have been most helpful today in giving us a good understanding of the family. For that I thank you. However, I have one final question. Did you have a romantic relationship with John McGregor or his sons?'

Margaret looked offended and hurt by the question, but Deacon kept eye contact.

Margaret seemed to collect her thoughts before answering. 'No,' she said.

Deacon didn't believe that at all. He'd no idea why, but he felt she was lying. But for now, He'd let it go. He looked at Karl and stood up. 'I think that's all for today, Ms Wilson. I have a much clearer understanding of the family, the business and how everything connects, thanks to you. And believe me, it's really useful to have when investigating disappearances and the like.'

'By, *and the like*, I assume you mean Terry's murder. I saw it on the news before a nice police officer who was interviewing at Dudbridge Holdings mentioned anything. I think that, considering my involvement with the family, I should at least be told before the rest of the world, Chief Inspector. It was very distressing.'

'I appreciate that, but there are procedures. I'll ensure that if we have a new update, we will let you know as soon as we can,' replied Deacon, picking his words carefully, with the full knowledge of a second victim that could very well be another of the McGregor family.

As Deacon got into the car, Karl was staring at his mobile phone.

'That's a nice place, guv.'

'It is indeed.'

'She's obviously paid well. Look at this.' He held up his mobile. 'It's valued at six-hundred and forty-nine thousand pounds on Zoopla.'

Deacon let out a whistle. 'I think when we get back to base, Karl, it would be worth you doing some digging on Margaret Wilson.'

. . .

'I have the post-mortem report for Steven Hawthorne, Cara' said DC Gill Foster excitedly waving a file above her head.

'Aha! Let's hear what it has to say.'

They sat at an unoccupied desk in the office's corner, clearing the surface of a couple of empty coffee cups and wiping away the crumbs left behind from someone's lunch. Gill placed down the report and read its contents, flicking over the pages as she did so.

'So,' said Gill, 'The pathologist believes the cause of death to be suicide. The fatal part was the hanging, caused by Steven dropping from the branch with the makeshift noose around his neck. The doctor states it wasn't a noose in the traditional sense, with a sliding knot that tightens, but more of a loop made by wrapping the wire around itself. However, he emphasises it was effective as a means of death by the fact it was razor wire which pretty much cut through the neck simultaneously as causing hypertension. As a result, most of the kinetic force was applied to the spinal cord. Anyway, it says if that hadn't been the fatal cause, the severe bleeding because of the slicing of the neck and veins would have ended life quickly.'

'We guessed that.' said Cara. 'What else do we have?'

'Now let's see,' said Gill, skimming the text. 'There were no signs of any struggle or violence beforehand. No unnecessary bruising. There were several cuts and scrapes on the hands and around the face, which he attributes to the person handling, and putting the wire in place around his neck. Most of the eyeballs were missing but concludes that the tissues left, and the holes in the eyelids, were likely due to wildlife such as birds.' Gill read on ahead before raising her eyebrows. 'Now, this next bit is interesting, Cara. The contents of the stomach shows that he had eaten a ham sandwich a few hours before his death, which is partially digested. However, blood samples show very high blood alcohol concentration in the body that could have contributed significantly to the victim's state of mind and ability to make rational decisions.'

They two detectives looked at each other.

'Rosemary mentioned nothing about him drinking excessively, or being drunk,' said Cara.

'Coming to think of it, there wasn't a bottle lying about outside either?' replies, Gill. 'It's worth taking another look around there. And maybe having another word?'

'I'll grab the car and let them know we're on our way. Give them a chance to get dressed.' Cara gave Gill a wink.

During the drive, Gill and Cara agreed on the focus of questioning and who was going to do or say what. As she was driven to the location, Gill was thinking of how things had changed in a brief space of time between her and Cara. She was great company, good at her job and always willing to learn. She also thought about Deacon, and how he and Karl were getting on with their investigation. She certainly missed working with Deacon. He has such a clever inquisitive mind, and not afraid to explore outside the box. She has learned so much working with him. She was also worried about him.

Having him back is fantastic. And most of the time he is like his old self. But there are also moments when he doesn't seem right. Occasionally snappy. The decision to let Farmer Timmons work in his fields when clearly it was out of bounds, was a good example of that. And his reaction when questioned by her. The anger. That worried her. No, it scared her. Not because she thought for one minute that he would lose it and harm her, but because she fears he is not coping with the loss of his wife. And she knew from conversations in the past, he thought the world of her. But Deacon being Deacon would not openly admit an area of weakness. Cara turned the Ford Focus sharply into the driveway of the Hawthorne's farm.

Before going to the house, Gill and Cara again scoured the outbuilding for anything of interest, such as anything that could be used by Steven Hawthorne to access the branch of the tree. Although there were lots of random pieces of equipment in there, there was still nothing particularly that stood out. As they made their way to the house, they saw the dustbins lined up next to, what looked like an old stable. Cara opened the lids. She put on a pair of silicon gloves and pulled out three empty whiskey bottles and placed them on the floor.

They didn't have to wait long after ringing the doorbell for it to be opened by Rosemary Hawthorne. She looked much brighter than before and even offered a slight cursory smile. After inviting the detectives into the living room, she offered them tea, which they both agreed would be nice. Gill and Cara sat on the sofa and waited in the room before Rosemary returned carrying a wicker tray with a large white pot of tea in the middle surrounded by three mugs and a plate of biscuits. After pouring the tea she settled into the armchair opposite her visitors. Dressed casually in straight cut blue jeans and a 'University of Leicester' sweatshirt. She had her hair clipped back with a claw clip. She also seemed to wear a little make-up.

Rosemary took a sip of her tea. 'So, I presume this visit is an update on the situation with poor Steven?'

'It is,' replied Gill. 'We have received the pathology report, and it concludes that the unfortunate cause of death of your husband was suicide.'

Rosemary closed her eyes. Was that relief? thought Gill. And did she notice a wry smile on Rosemary's face or was she imagining it? She would exchange notes with Cara later.

Rosemary slowly opened her eyes, took a sip of her tea and exchanged glances at her two visitors. 'Can we now have Steven put to rest, and put this horrible event behind us?'

'As soon as coroner releases your husband's body, you'll be able to do that. There are certain formalities and procedures that need to be followed, and then you will be contacted. However, there are still some points we need to clear up here, which we obviously want to do as quickly as possible.' Rosemary nodded. 'First, and please forgive us for asking but we need as clear an understanding of events leading up to this terrible event. Had you and your husband argued on the night in question?'

'No, we hadn't,' said Rosemary, visibly annoyed at the question. 'So, don't go accusing me of making him do that to himself.'

'We're not accusing you of anything, Mrs Hawthorne. But you have to understand we need a clear understanding of the circumstances,' intervened, Cara.

Rosemary stared down at the carpet before making eye contact with Gill. 'We've been... were married twenty-years. Yes, it wasn't perfect and yes, we had our arguments, but they weren't that often and we got on well. Farming is a way of life. Twenty-four hours a day, seven days a week. So, the key to sanity is to have some time to yourself. I occasionally go on shopping trips for the day, and in the last few years, Steven would spend a day or the odd weekend going to places of interest to pursue his hobby of drawing. He was particularly interested in buildings. Pretty good at it too. He said that he preferred to draw the real thing than from a photograph. I used to go with him but ended up wandering around the places on my own while he was sketching away. So, going back to your original question, that "me" time that he and I had took any potential tension out of the equation.'

'Thank you,' said Cara. 'Secondly. Could you tell us if your husband in the habit of drinking? As in alcohol?'

Rosemary looked slightly surprised at the question. 'He wasn't a big drinker, no. If friends or family came over, he may have a few whiskeys, but that's all. The same if he had a stressful day, but only three. He couldn't cope with more than that.'

'Do you know if he was drinking the night, he took his life?'

Rosemary stared at Cara. 'No.'

'No, you don't know or no he didn't?'

'No, he didn't, to my knowledge anyway.'

'You told us previously that he used to get depressed? Did he drink then?'

'No' said Rosemary.

'Didn't you say he seemed depressed the night he died?'

Rosemary clasped her hands tightly on her lap. 'He was.'

'And did he drink that night?'

'No.'

'Ok, but you thought he seemed depressed that night?'

'He was bloody depressed, I told you,' Rosemary snaps.

'Do you think he may have had a drink? Did he seem drunk? Slurring his speech?'

'Not that I remember, no!'

'You see, this is where DS Matthews and I are getting confused,' said Gill, 'because Steven had a very large level of alcohol in his blood. And that's what's baffling us. Because you're saying that he didn't seem intoxicated and couldn't handle over three whiskeys. Yet the amounts of alcohol in his blood suggests that he was probably incapable of climbing up anything, let alone positioning himself and sitting on a branch long enough without slipping off to put the razor wire into position?'

Rosemary was clasping her hands so tightly now that they were visibly white.

'Let me tell you what we think, Rosemary. That he got himself up and onto the branch using something that has mysteriously disappeared, for now. And Steven either drank or continued to drink whilst sitting in position on the branch.

That would explain him being able to carry out the preparations for the attempt on his own life. Because there is no way he would have been able to function well enough to do that fully intoxicated with the amount of alcohol that was in his body. Now, can you seem why that seems weird?'

Rosemary nervously looked at her and nodded.

'Therefore,' said Cara, 'and with the information we have it makes sense, your husband must have drunk the alcohol in position, be it for Dutch courage or to calm himself down. Either way, there had to be a bottle with him which should be up on the branch, on the floor below or thrown within the vicinity. Either way, we have found none. Which suggests that someone cleared up after the event. Mrs Hawthorne, did you find a bottle and remove it and, maybe, put it in the bin?'

The closing of the front door broke the intensity of the interview and James walked into the room. He looked at everyone and gave a wave.

'Hello everyone. More questions?' he asked.

Shit! We were so close, thought Gill. Rosemary was getting twitchy, they were getting close to something resembling what had happened to Steven Hawthorne that night, and was certain that Rosemary and possibly James, were involved in the whole incident. Even if it was just clearing up evidence. The ladder? The bottle? And now that arsehole James comes in and kills it. She can already see Rosemary straightening her posture, gaining strength, feeling less cornered? Bad timing, but there we are. She could see Cara's face drop.

'We were discussing a hypothesis regarding your brother's death. I'm sure Mrs Hawthorne will update you. The coroner has concluded your brother's death to be suicide, but there are some loose ends that we need to clear up.'

'Loose ends, eh? whatever,' James said dismissively.

Gill looked at Cara and stood up. 'Anyway, thank you for

your time today. We really appreciate it at this difficult time. Also, I notice that picture of Steven on the mantelpiece there. I'm sorry to ask this, although we have a photograph of your husband but it's not very sharp and ideally, we need a clear picture for the records. Would you mind if we took that to copy? We'll take great care of it and return it in top condition?'

'Of course,' said Rosemary. 'By the way, when are you going to return Steven's belongings that you took from his study?'

'The team are still looking through his things to try to find a clue why he may have taken his own life. As I'm sure you can appreciate, it takes time. We have to be thorough. Is there anything you need, particularly, Mrs Hawthorne?'

'No, not at all. I was just wondering,' replied Rosemary, with a slight stutter.

'All he had in his study were a load of tatty history books and those stupid sketches of his, from what I can remember. There would be bugger all to do with the business, he left that to me. So, what takes so long?'

Gill was finding James Hawthorne a bit irritating and aggressive in his tone but bit her lip. 'I'm sorry, sir, but we will get the items of Mr Hawthorne's back to you as soon as possible.'

As Cara stood, she stumbled, falling to one knee. Her mobile phone bounced on the floor to the feet of James. He picked it up and gave it to her as she stood up.

'Thank you,' she said.

'Hopefully we can begin to make arrangements for my brother?' said James.

'I think we are about there, Mr Hawthorne.'

Gill and Cara left the house, stopping to put the empty whisky bottles into evidence bags, along with the picture of Steven Hawthorne and Matthew's mobile phone. When they get back to the station, they can get them dusted for fingerprints.

As they pulled away from the farm Gill looked at Cara. 'Oh, James I seemed to have dropped my phone.'

'Those drama lessons at school came in handy, don't you think, Gill? Eat your heart out Kate Winslet.'

They both laughed as the car drove along the country lane towards Leicester.

'I thought we were getting close with Rosemary until James turned up,' said Gill.

'There's definitely something she's hiding from us. But yet again, it's like he's waiting outside for the best moment to walk in and kill the interview dead.'

'Very good timing. Just a thought, Cara. When we told Rosemary that the coroner's conclusion for cause of death was suicide, Am I imagining it or…'

'…did she seem relieved? I thought so. She seemed to smile.'

'She became more guarded when the alcohol got mentioned and especially in relation to the high level in the blood.'

If there was one thing Gill was certain, it's that Rosemary knows far more than she is currently giving away. She was probably party to the death. Possibly helped? With James, maybe? One thing is for certain, they would get to the bottom of it. Rosemary is clearly the weak link, and they'll get another chance to talk to her, eventually. The burden of whatever involvement she has or knows is clear. It's a matter of time. Or with James' convenient interruptions, a matter of timing.

Driving home in the peak time traffic that seemed to go on longer each year, Deacon decided he wanted to have an evening where he could relax and maybe open a bottle of red wine. He certainly didn't fancy cooking, so, stopped on the way to pick up some fish and chips. He had texted Susan to see if she wanted anything taking back but had received no reply. As he pulled onto the drive, he could see that some lights in the house were on, therefore, assumed that she was obviously in and around the place. Once inside, he went straight into the kitchen to grab a plate and took the chips from the paper wrapping and put them onto it. He also felt that things needed to be sorted between him and his daughter, so he stood at the bottom of the stairs and called her name. Silence. He called again, louder this time. He heard the handle of her bedroom door turn.

'I have some chips for us to eat. Do you want to come down?' he asked.

'Not really.'

This whole situation was testing Deacon's patience. 'Ok, this isn't a question. I have some food. Come down and eat it, please? Now would be good?'

He went back to the kitchen to get another plate from the cupboard and put half of the chips from his plate onto it. As he sat down at the breakfast bar to eat, Susan came into the room. She sat at the chair opposite. She wore her grey track suit and flip-flops. He ate his food. Susan initially picked away at the chips before tucking into hers. She was saying nothing and avoiding eye contact. Deacon was about halfway through his meal before deciding to speak.

'Is this the way it's going to be from now on? You, ignoring me? Avoiding me? Not even looking at me?'

Susan continued to stare down at her plate and eat her chips. She finally gave a small shrug of the shoulders.

'Whatever you think of me Susan, and I think you made

that clear with your text a few days ago, this whole thing with your mum is affecting me too. I knew her for thirty years. We were married for twenty-seven, and I wouldn't swap that for the world. And you know what? She would have hated to see us like this.'

Susan stopped eating and stared at her remaining food. 'I just wanted you to be there with me,' she said, in a soft voice.

'I know,' said Deacon. 'And I wanted to be there with you. *For you!* This may not make sense Susan, but at the moment, I need a distraction. And I do a job that creates that. It doesn't mean that I want to forget your mum because I'll never forget her. And it's not because I don't care about you or your feelings because I care more than you will ever know. It's that I need to be strong for both of us, and that requires me to build up my own mental strength. And the only way I know is through my job, solving these complex puzzles. That doesn't justify me missing our meeting at the grave with your mother. No. I got side tracked and time ran away from me, and I have no excuse for that. I'm sorry. Really sorry, Susan.'

She stared at her plate in silence and gave a nod. A short while later she stood up and took her half-eaten plate of food over to the worktop. 'Thank you,' she said, and left the kitchen.

Deacon could hear her climbing up the stairs. 'Susan?' He heard the latch click as she closed her bedroom door.

'Well done,' he said to himself. He threw the rest of their chips into the bin. He grabbed a bottle of Merlot from the wine rack, picked up a glass and went into the sanctuary of his study. This whole thing with his daughter was stressing him out. He could see that the weekend was going to be a long one if the atmosphere was to remain like this.

It had been one hell of a return to work, and he felt exhausted. It was good to be back in the fold and using his brain again, but the weight of the investigations felt heavy on his shoulders. Two vicious murders. And even the suicide was off the scale using razor wire of all things. He supposed it was the shock to the body from looking after Claire at home, and afterwards, just moping about. And now full-on detective work again. To her credit, Superintendent Pau recognised the pressure the entire team were under and the amount of ground they had covered in the past couple of weeks. She suggested to everyone that this weekend would probably be the last free one for a while, so to make the most of it. Of course, there were a small number in the incident room and a number of the team, including Deacon himself would be on call if required. And of course, there is Susan, for whom he carries so much guilt. Letting her down again. He is such a shit father to her but if only she knew how much he doesn't want to be that. And if he's honest with himself, he just can't handle the emotional toil at the moment.

The wine seemed to warm his insides. He could feel it working its way through his body. He was thinking of Susan. The tension between them was getting too much for him. He can see she needs him for love and support, and he wants nothing more than to give her that, but he don't know how. What to say or do. It's tearing him up deep inside. What would Claire have done? She always knew how to deal with such things. She had the right words to say. But he was fighting his own emotions and reeling from the loss of his beloved wife. So much so that he didn't know where to start with Susan. She needs him more than ever, yet he is failing her miserably. He looked towards Claire's photograph - that gilded frame that seems to be his window of comfort these days. 'What can I do?' he asked. He picked up the picture and clenched it close to his chest. Slowly, his mind wandered back to the day he said goodbye.

The service was as close to perfect as it could have been. She was given a wonderful send off. There was nobody in the church who wasn't made aware, if they didn't know already, what a fantastic and beautiful human being she was. How caring and loving she was to her daughter and family and proud of their achievements. And how much she her friends and the wider community loved her company, support, and that wonderful infectious giggle that she had that made everyone smile. But to him, she was more. Claire was his lover, his wife, the mother of his child, the rock of support that he often needed. She acted as his confidant, his sounding board and conscience. As a person, she was just wonderful. And now she was gone.

There was a moment in the chapel, just before the curtains closed for the very last time to allow her to slide into the cleansing flames of eternity. One magic moment when the large stained-glass window seemed to fill with light. Rays of sunlight sliding along the ceiling from the back of the chapel towards the front, eventually resting on the casket, creating an eerie glow around it. Was it the sun revealing itself from behind a cloud or her saying goodbye? That moment will stay with him for the rest of his life.

CHAPTER SEVEN

At Petals Garden Centre, Deacon made his way to the cafe area, passing a kaleidoscope of colours and fragrances created by the plants and flowers. This time he was on his own, allowing Karl to conduct a few of searches and checks, to discover more about John McGregor. Before leaving the station last night, he'd called Libby to arrange another chat to delve deeper into the family. Although she seemed annoyed to have to waste more time talking about people she didn't like, she agreed to meet here before the place opened to the public. She was placing an orange juice and a hot cup of coffee on a table as he arrived.

'Good morning, Libby. Now, this is service.'

She smiled. 'Careful what you say, or I'll charge you.'

They sat at the table.

'Thank you for finding the time to speak to me,' said Deacon. 'I appreciate this isn't necessarily a good time. But then again, in these cases, there rarely is. But I need to get an understanding of your family to enable us to build up, not so much a profile but a picture of who the family members are and the dynamics.'

'That's fine. Not that I think it'd help.'

'It can often prove useful, believe me. Are you Ok to make a start?'

Libby gave a slow nod of the head. Deacon guessed she'd been at the centre for some time preparing for the customers. With her hands covered in soil, she sat down in her black leggings; muddy Doc Martin boots and grey hoodie. Her hair tied in a ponytail.

'From what we understand, your parents were married in nineteen seventy-six. They started Dudbridge Holdings in nineteen seventy-eight, which deals mainly in property, farms. Am I right so far?'

'Yes. Farms, small holdings, and the like,' said Libby.

'Ok. You were born. Do you want to take it from there?'

Libby took a small sip of her orange juice and placed it on the table. 'So, I was born in nineteen eighty-two. I was an only child, and I had a great life. Loving parents. They spoilt me rotten, I suppose. And then Dad died.'

'And when was this?' asked Deacon.

'Friday June the sixteenth, two-thousand and six. That date's forever etched in my brain. I saw him in his office. Me and my mum went over to take some sandwiches for him to eat as he was working late at the office. So, we thought we'd go over and surprise him. We found him sprawled across his desk. I thought he was asleep at first because he'd been working long hours for months. Mum realised straight away what had happened. He'd had a heart attack. God knows how long he'd been there on his own. I was nearly twenty-four. And from that point, my heart was broken.'

Deacon thought he could see the sadness in her eyes. 'You were very close to your father?'

'Yes, I was. A daddy's girl. He treated me like a princess.' Libby stared at the glass of juice as she spoke.

'Ok. Please, in your own time.'

Libby gave an enormous sigh. 'After that things were different because Mum was doing a lot of the work at the office, trying to keep it ticking along the best she could. Although I don't think she knew much about the management of the place. She left that side of things to dad. I would help when I could, you know, photocopying and filing. Stuff that didn't involve any specialist knowledge. Anyway, at this point I was concentrating on my studies. Not long after, probably a few months, mum employed someone to help with the management of the company. He was from a similar background, so could do the more client-based stuff. That was the arsehole himself, John McGregor. Mum kept him at arm's length at first, which was great. But he kept offering to do more and I think in all fairness, the workload was drowning her. And with his background he knew the way things needed to be done, and I think he kept things afloat.'

'Sorry for butting in, Libby. But am I right in assuming your mother employed him at this point?'

'Of course. Anyway. He started worming his way into her affections. I mean, it was blatant. Embarrassing, but he was persistent. I think he grew on mum a little, although I found him creepy. He'd be very polite to me when Mum was about, otherwise he hardly acknowledged I existed. I'd feel him staring at me, undressing me in his mind, behind my back. I don't know why, but that's how it felt.' She took a gulp of her juice. 'Anyway, after the chase, mum fell for it, hook line and sinker and they got into a relationship and eventually married. When that happened, he moved into our place with his two sons. And that was the first time I'd ever met them. Both as thick as shit, by the way, but a chip off the old block. So, I'm about twenty-six or twenty-seven, Danny was thirty ish and thought he was God's gift, and Terry was about thirty-two. Anyway, I realised John was playing away if you know what I mean. And that started happening quite early in the marriage. And I think it was with that tart Margaret Wilson, his PA, who was obviously willing to give him a blow job, if asked.'

'Can you just stick to the facts rather than the insults, please, Libby?'

She slammed her empty glass onto the table. 'If you want the background story, I'll tell it my way, Chief Inspector. If you don't like it, there's the door.'

Deacon didn't want to blow the interview while she was being so cooperative, so put up with the snipes. He held up his hands. 'Ok, please continue.'

'*Anyway*, I know mum suspected as well. She occasionally mentioned stuff to me when we were on our own. Mum was certain John and Margaret Wilson were getting it on, but even if not with her, she knew he was playing away. She said it was a woman's intuition.'

'Did she confront John or even Margaret about this?'

'I assume she said something to John, because occasionally, they would have the mightiest rows, and for weeks after things would be frosty between them and his sons'.

'Why his sons?'

'Oh, they would always pull together. You take on one, you take them all on. It didn't matter how wrong they were because they were always as thick as thieves and in it together.'

'That seems really odd behaviour,' said Deacon.

'Maybe. As a team, they were intimidating, threatening and nasty. Anyway, the next major life-changing incident occurred in twenty-seventeen when someone killed mum. Things were already pretty unbearable in the house, so she went to York for a few days to meet a friend and do some shopping and stay over a few nights. While there she was killed by a hit-and-run driver. She was apparently dead at the scene. And they never found out who did it. And still to this day, I think those bastards had something to do with it.'

'What makes you say that?'

Libby paused before answered. 'Before mum died, we started going out more together, for a coffee or wine, a bite to eat. She was spending less time at home. John had taken over the business - I think she'd signed it over to him. But I would guess that was because of pressure on his part because the guy was manipulative and a complete fucking bully. She would tell me about her feelings and what she suspected about John. But ironically, she'd found solace in a new friend she absolutely thought the world of. That's who she'd meet in York. Whenever she mentioned him, her face lit up, and she'd smile. I felt so happy for her because as the marriage to John dragged on, she was getting more miserable, a shell of her old self.'

'Who was this friend?'

'I don't know. She never gave a name. I knew it was a male because she always referred to her *friend* as he. And I never pushed it. She'd tell me in good time. Anyway, after her death, if not before, things were completely signed over to John when she passed. So, it became impossible for me to stay. There were many crossed words and I upped sticks and left in the one hope that they'll rot in hell. And it seems to me like my wishes are coming true. So, there is light at the end of the tunnel, you could say.' She smiled.

Deacon mulled over what Libby had told him. 'What I find it difficult to understand, is the sheer hatred you have towards your stepfamily. I get the animosity over them taking over the business, and the resentment regarding your mother's treatment by them. And I recognise how invasive it must've been having these guys coming into your home - your dad's home. But I just feel that there's something more, something that you're not telling me. Did something happen to you? Did they do something to you, Libby?'

'Nothing happened to me.' She stared down at the table.

'Are you sure?' asked Deacon. 'I can arrange help.'

'I said, nothing, happened.'

There was a silence before Deacon spoke. 'All I want is an understanding of the family and their relationships, good or bad. You have to understand I'm looking for two missing persons along with one found dead, from the same family. Now, I know your feelings regarding them, but you have to understand my job is to find out what's happened to them, and if necessary, who's responsible and bring them to justice.'

'I understand,' said Libby. 'But bringing back the memories of my parents is difficult for me.'

'I appreciate that, Libby, and I'm sorry to put you through this. But if there's foul play, if there are people out there who could cause harm to others in society, it's my job to find them.' Deacon finished the last of his coffee and stood up to leave. 'I'll leave you to get on with things as I'm sure there's a million and one things to do to keep this place running.'

'There is, Chief Inspector.'

'I will most likely need to speak to you again. But meanwhile if you remember anything that may be useful, call us.' He gave her his business card. 'Do you have a photograph of your mother that we could use as part of our investigation?'

'I'll email you one.'

Deacon sat in his car and tried to process the interview. Libby certainly helped fill in the gaps or at least confirm what he learned from Margaret Wilson. Still, he couldn't help thinking she was holding something back. Was there a painful experience she had? As hard an exterior she likes to present, he honestly believes that deep inside she is more delicate, vulnerable even. Is she scared? After all, she said that the McGregors were nasty and bullies. Does she know something that could help with the investigation - in which case, why hold back? Or is she involved? Maybe she took revenge. She seems to have enough reasons to. More pieces to the puzzle. Pieces with no form or colour, yet. But they have value and gives him something to mull over in the coming days and weeks.

Deacon steered the Audi onto the main road. His next stop—the Three Gables. Now the primary activity had wound down with the SOCOs, he wanted to have a good look around the place. He'd texted Gill last night with the offer of her joining him if convenient. He knew she was busy with the Hawthorne case, but it would be good to have her alongside to bounce thoughts and hypotheses around. Karl would drive down south sometime today to get more background on John McGregor. He called Gill after leaving Petals and she promised to meet him.

As he turned into the drive of the Three Gables, he could see Gill standing next to her car tapping her watch. He parked next to her.

'Good morning, Gill. How the devil are you?' he asked.

'All good and interested to have a nose around the place. It's like one of those weirdo dates, don't you think?'

Deacon laughed. 'Yes, I guess it is.'

The uniformed officer at the door waved them through after seeing their ID.

Gill lifted the blue and white police tape set across the doorway to give them access. The house was cool but not uncomfortable. Deacon touched the radiator in the hallway which was lukewarm. The thick dark grey carpet of the living room seemed to spring as he walked on it. They slowly scanned the surroundings, trying to take in the scene's enormity before them. The furniture strewn all over the place is how it they found it, he presumed. Yet it looked unusual, probably because the furniture and what he assumed to be ornaments and vases also laid alongside, did not appear to be damaged in any way—probably cushioned by the thick carpet as it fell. He remembered his thoughts the last time he was here when he could only look through the open doorway. But now in the room and among the mess, he felt even stronger that the furniture disturbed as an afterthought. It looked too carefully placed.... Done to mess the place up rather than the result of a fight or struggle. Vases laid on the floor with most of the flowers still inside. Chairs rolled forwards or over on their sides. More suspicious was the large glass display cabinet that was face down on the carpet with its contents of miniature porcelain figures, lying against its glass doors, mostly unbroken from what he could see. He would have thought it impossible to achieve even if tipped with care. There were no signs of anything thrown across the room and certainly no damage or scuffs on the walls or curtains pulled down from their rails. In fact, to an experienced police officer, it was a neat mess.

'If it wasn't because we have the body of Terry McGregor and a second victim that may be his brother or father, you'd think it was an amateur attempt at an insurance scam,' said Deacon. 'Add a small broken window, something that doesn't cause too much damage, and insist that it was broken when burgled,' Deacon said. 'Then tell them a few grands worth of jewellery was missing.' Unlikely to convince insurance companies these days but he'd seen it all when he was in uniform, back in the day.

'Unless they knew the person or people they willingly left with, and I'm assuming they did, they would be forcefully taken. In which case, it would have needed a small gang and surely made a lot more mess, if they'd put up a fight?' said Gill.

'Unless they were armed. And there's this.'

He stared at the large words painted on the wall. When shown the image by the police photographer, he'd assumed it originally painted with a brush, because of the runs that rolled down from the letters like blood. But on closer inspection it was done with a spray can, which would be quicker. "SCUM". It's such a powerful a word that carries such gravitas, especially in this setting.

Opposite the bay window was an equally large mirror which made the space seem bright and enormous. On the far wall, there were a couple of original watercolours. He looked closely at them but couldn't really read the signatures. There seemed to be nothing of interest lying around the room, although, again, he knew that the SOCOs would have already taken everything that may be of value to the investigation, be it an artifact or fingerprints. As testament to their hard work and toil, a faint layer of powder remained.

Deacon led Gill into the kitchen. It was a vast space. Deacon couldn't help thinking that it was probably close to half the footprint of his entire house. A dark tiled floor supported brushed chrome appliances all around the room. In the centre stood a large breakfast island supporting a highly polished black granite work surface. Very classy, and expensive. Every appliance, pot and pan looked high quality to Deacon's untrained eye. Hardly purchased from Asda or Amazon like his own.

The ceiling was painted black but peppered with twenty or thirty small spotlights, which gave the effect of stars in the night sky. Very calming and very effective. He flicked on the wall switch which lit the room. He followed Gill to the large patio doors at the far end of the kitchen. Outside was a beautifully manicured garden worthy of any golf course he'd been to. Which, in truth wasn't many, he hated the game.

He strolled around the room opening cupboard doors to see what was inside. Nothing unusual. No different from anyone else, except the quality was exquisite. God knows what the kitchen would have cost to fit out.

They made their way up the stairs to the first bedroom which they believed to be Danny's, with the big bed and where they'd found the explicit pornographic magazines, when last here. There was now an obvious area on the desk where the computer once stood, taken by the team for analysis. Gill opened the bedside drawers and smiled at Deacon. The SOCOs had been as thorough as always and removed everything for DNA testing, including the used condoms and cigarette packet. As much as Deacon he had a problem with the head SOCO, Trevor Jardine, he had to admit that they were meticulous. They moved to the next room.

Deacon believed this room was the main bedroom, so likely to be John MacGregor's. He looked more closely at the photographs on the wall, hoping to recognise a face, a place or something of interest - a tiny clue that would help the case. Gill, meanwhile, conducted a more thorough look around the rest of the room than she did on their previous visit. Again, wearing her gloves and carefully inspecting every loose object she could find for something that would help them.

Deacon stared intensely at each picture, face close to the glass of the frame, sometimes so close it steamed up with his breath. Staring deep into the soul of the photos he tried to understand what their purpose was—what were they revealing? Or just as importantly, what are they not showing? He still struggled to get his head around why someone would want to surround themselves with superficial photographs of themselves? The odd one, yes, maybe of a family holiday or a birthday or a loved one. Was John McGregor such a narcissistic and shallow prick he needed to admire himself and the fruits of his success again and again?

'What I don't understand is that his wife was killed in a hit and run. Yet, there is no memory of her. Don't you find that odd?'

'Very,' replies, Deacon. 'But ignoring this display, have you seen any reference to her existence in the house at all? He was married to her for God knows how many years, yet there isn't even a wedding photo in the place. And he had a stepdaughter, Libby, and again, no sign that she was ever part of the family. How strange is that? You would have thought that there'd something. Yet, they seemed to be erased from existence. It just feels wrong.'

'Alison and Libby effectively cancelled. No one to my knowledge has ever been socially cancelled in whatever shape or form, unless they've pissed someone off,' said Gill.

'Maybe. If you're right, whoever that person or persons is, could be the key to solving the case? We know Alison died in a hit and run, which is suspicious, but Libby is still alive and kicking. Hopefully, she's not in danger. Then again, if it was John and the boys who did it, why would they be missing or indeed, deceased? That's makes little sense in my head at the moment, Gill. I still think there's more to this family than we know so far. Especially with their business dealings. I'm sure we can learn more about them from Margaret Wilson because I don't think she's told us anywhere near what she knows.'

'I got the impression she's told us just enough. And if she's that loyal to John McGregor to withhold information, when she knows he's missing and possibly come to harm, she must have something to hide. She was sleeping with him or knows where he's hiding.'

'Or both?' Suggested Deacon.

The remaining rooms offered little more insight. As they left, Deacon was still grappling with why anyone would feel the need to want to remove the existence of a loved one. He thought of his wife and the memories that are melted into all areas of his house. And the photograph that he needs to hold close to his heart as he sits alone at night when the memories are at their strongest. Didn't John McGregor have any feelings for his wife? And even if the feelings were gone, would there not be at least one photograph of Alison? A wedding photograph, maybe?

'What are your thoughts, Gill?'

She shook her head. 'We came here hoping to learn more about the McGregors, but we've learnt nothing. I wonder if the erasing of Alison and Libby's existence is significant, though.'

It was just after lunchtime when Deacon got back to the station. The small pile of paperwork neatly placed on his 'overspill' table next to his office desk had become a not so small pile. Every time he walked out of the office, the admin fairies added another load of bureaucratic crap. He switched on the computer and put his coffee on an old coaster with a colourful print of a matchstick man drawn in crayon by his daughter, when she was in primary school. How time goes by. She must have been six or seven, now a nineteen-year-old young woman. He felt a tingling sensation in his body thinking about their current difficulties with each other. Was it guilt? Whatever the feeling was, he needed to find a way of resolving the issues between them - especially now they're on their own. He was so out of his comfort zone trying to deal with the situation. He knew her. But knew he'd have to face it, eventually. The meal the other night was a start. He'd try to talk to her again tonight.

There was a post-it note placed on the base of the computer monitor asking him to phone Dave Freestone asap regarding the post-mortem of the second body. He dialed immediately. After a friendly receptionist put him on hold for what seemed like an eternity, the phone clicked, and Dave spoke.

'Good afternoon, Al. I have just put another of our satisfied customers in the fridge.'

'Five-star service as always, Dave. You spoil them.'

'I know, but I'm always there to please. Anyway, because of the urgency of this, I've allowed your client to jump the queue. But I'll tell you now, don't expect that again. I've completed the PM on our hot-headed friend, and thought you'd like the main points up front, because it'll probably take me a week before I complete the report.'

'I appreciate that, Dave.'

'Ok. this was always going to be a rather time-consuming process because of the death and the damage caused. Fire is a great cleanser. It destroys a lot of the evidence I normally extract from tissues, so I've had to hypothesise to some extent and where possible, try to triangulate with what data and information I can to validate, so here we go.'

Deacon completely understood the doctor's position and appreciated him sharing his method with him up front. Dr Freestone was a great pathologist, a true gentleman and unofficially, a great comedian. Freestone continued.

'Judging by the degree of burnt tissue in the lungs, he was alive when the material entered his mouth and set alight. The accelerant used would need to be a low flash point substance such as petrol or kerosene, for example. I would imagine that the fumes from the liquid would have rendered the victim unconscious depending on how long the perpetrator waited to light it. But what I can say categorically, he was breathing, though not for long I would imagine, as the inner lungs are well and truly cooked.'

'Whoever's done this is one sick bastard,' said Deacon, after taking a moment to process what he'd been told.

'Indeed. You know, I deal with death all the time. As I've said before, our jobs are very similar, except I'm the detective who investigates death. Like you, I gather the evidence, follow the clues, and find out what happened to my patients and hopefully determine why. In my years in medicine, I have seen the results of disease, and what cancer can do to the body, for example. I have worked with war and bomb victims. Industrial and agricultural accidents can occasionally be as damaging and severe as the two bodies we have looked at. But what makes this particularly alarming is this seems to result from a person or people doing it *on purpose*. It's not an accident. Not collateral damage. It's pure evil.'

Deacon noticed how Freestone's manner had changed. The lighthearted, sarcastic demeanour that he normally exudes had gone. He had never known Freestone to be like this. The cases had clearly affected him. Freestone continued.

'I've checked again and can confirm there is no evidence of the body being restrained on the arms, wrists, ankles, or legs. No bruising at all. It is unlikely that a person wouldn't put up some sort of fight, so no one would leave their arms and legs free. I can't tell for sure because of the heat damage, but someone could have held him down by chest. What does that suggest? And this is where I hypothesise, I believe, from a sound base of reasoning. The victim needed to be unconscious to be moved around and "prepared", if I may use the term? Now, I have found no evidence of a blow to the head. In fact, there's no evidence of impact, which suggests purposely laying the body on the floor. The toxicology doesn't support him being drugged. Or he breathed in a chemical vapour of sorts that rendered him unconscious. There are a number available. In the movies it's always chloroform, but in truth, that doesn't work that quickly and lasts if it's held over the mouth and nose. I would imagine if the victim was unconscious, it would be an anaesthetic, like that in a hospital operating theatre. So that would need to be kept on the mouth as there's no trace of any intravenous activity.' Freestone paused. 'However. What I can reveal with certainty is traces of skin under the nails. Most of it is his own, so I assume he scratches himself a lot, but we separated another sample. We've run it through the database there are no matches.'

'That's a shame, Dave. But you've given me plenty to think about.'

'Now, Alex. Do you think I'd offer you so much information without delivering a good, tongue down the throat finale?' replies Freestone excitedly.

'I'm all ears.'

'The teeth were in a bit of a state. But there is something along with the medical records that enable me to confirm it's the body of John McGregor.'

'Oh my God,' said Deacon, more in relief that they had found him rather than surprise.

'To be honest, we only had five teeth we could work with, but they matched his dental records. The false hip on his right side and scarring from an old Achilles operation were more than enough to confirm. We had a sample of some blood taken from the leg that confirms. So, John McGregor is your man.'

Deacon felt a little overwhelmed with everything he'd learned from the pathologist. He thanked him for his time and bringing the PM forward. He sat for a while massaging his temples as he processed what Freestone had told him. If Terry and John McGregor had succumbed to such horrific deaths, he reasoned Danny would die, or has died in a similar fashion. Unless he was the murderer. Either way, now knew he had a psychopath or psychopaths on the loose that needed to be caught quickly.

Gill washed down the last bite of her tuna and sweetcorn sandwich with the remains of a lukewarm coffee. After leaving the Three Gables Farm, she'd nipped into the supermarket to pick up some lunch and a pint of milk. During the drive back she thought about the McGregors and how weird and dysfunctional they seemed. It was like a takeover. John McGregor and his sons had muscled in on the business, the estate, staked their claim and metaphorically at least, cast Alison and her daughter into the wilderness. Weird. This led her to think about the Hawthornes and how weird their relationship seemed. The tormented and depressed Steven. The broken-hearted Rosemary... allegedly, and the smug overly confident James, who she's certain is shagging his sister-in-law. Then again, that's hardly an offence in British law. Morally wrong and considering the current circumstances, reprehensible, yes, but legal.

She was confident that Steven hung himself, possibly because of depression. His doctor confirmed Steven's prescription of Sertraline antidepressants. However, why is something she'd find out? According to Rosemary, he'd threatened to end his life before, which is why she took little notice of his threat the other day. Yet something must've happened for him to go through with it. And of course, there was nothing at the scene that enabled him to get into position and drink alcohol from which Rosemary forgot to mention. Hopefully they'll get some prints from the bottles. And there's the general secrecy that seems to surround Rosemary and James. It's just weird.

Gill put on her silicon gloves and sifted through the

contents of a box she'd signed out from the Exhibits room earlier. Ted, the Exhibits Officer, only let it out of his sight because it is to be returned following the suicide verdict from the coroner. It contained various papers retrieved from Steven's study. She carefully looked through them. Utility bills, fuel receipts, a trade magazine, and a washing machine service plan. Nothing of any significance. The rest of the papers were sketches, mainly of buildings, which didn't surprise her as she'd seen several books on architecture around the Hawthorne's house.

The sketches were very good for her untrained eye. In the bottom right-hand corner, Steven has signed them. There were some that were partially completed, but the ones with the signature were very detailed, sometimes, he even included people walking, pushing prams, riding bicycles in the foreground which must have taken ages. A few of the buildings she knew, such as King's College in Cambridge, York Minster, and Pulteney Bridge in Bath. There were others she recognised but couldn't remember the name. There were about fifty of them. Most were of specific buildings, about ten were village or town scenes, and there a couple of a woman, probably Rosemary, although the facial features were not so good. Clearly his talent was with bricks and mortar rather than life drawing. She placed them neatly back into the box. Art was Steven's escape.

Cara was calling in at the lab later today to speed things up regarding the prints from the whiskey bottles and her mobile phone. Mainly, because she wanted her phone back. If they found evidence that would question whether there was an assist in Steven Hawthorne's death, they could follow it up and she'd feel better. If not, it remains an unfortunate suicide. She'd have to deal with it. She took the box back to the Exhibits room. While Ted seemed in a good mood, she was hoping to ask a favour.

Deacon sat down in the lounge's corner and took the first swig of his pint. Pedigree bitter, his favourite, and always kept well here at the Royal Oak. A good way to end a week like this. He placed his glass on the table and took his mobile from his pocket to call Gill. She came through the doors as if on cue and joined him, dumping her handbag and a buff-coloured wallet on the red felt covered seat. Taking off her coat she sat by Deacon and scanned the table.

'Do I have to buy my drink? You invited me.'

'Don't you worry your little cotton socks, DC Foster? I'll get you one.' Deacon stood up and walked over to the bar.

'Thank you. A double, please,' she said.

'You get what I buy,' he replied.

Deacon soon returned and handed her a double gin and tonic. She drank half of it in one go.

'That's better.'

'What took you so long?' asked Deacon.

'I had a look through Steven Hawthorne's stuff. Nothing particularly of interest, but he's a bit of an artist. He'd travel to visit different places, with the sole intention of drawing landmarks, buildings, towns, things like that. They are great. According to Rosemary, his little sorties kept things good because it gave them both space.'

'Interesting. The PM report has registered the death as suicide. So, is this a passing interest or are you still uncomfortable about something, Gill?'

'It's just not sitting right. I don't know what it is, really, which is why I took another look. *Anyway*, when I took the stuff back to the Exhibits room, I thought I'd ask Ted if I could see anything found in the attic at the Three Gables.'

'And knowing Ted, he said no?'

'Well, you know how anal he is with evidence. However, what he does now is photograph and scan everything, so he always has copies of the evidence for us to look at, while the actual stuff is safely under lock and key. That way, if we want to see anything for reference, he can send us a photograph or two. Which is what he did. There were a couple of boxes in the attic that just had old ornaments and pictures, you know pictures of fields and things like that, which I assume had been on the walls in the rooms before being removed as tastes changed. But there was also a zipped-up suitcase, which is where it gets interesting. There were photographs, wedding photographs, and holiday snaps by the looks of it.'

'Of Alison?' asked Deacon.

'Photographs of *all three of his wives*. I'm guessing here because I don't know what they look like. There are old passports in there. Marriage certificates for all the wives, and their death certificates. I noticed several letters from solicitors who were dealing with what looks like business matters. Takeovers, maybe, I haven't read through all the details. But it certainly looks like John McGregor legally had the business transferred over to him. Now don't you find that strange? It's a family business. Why bother?'

'If that's such an important document, why's it in a suitcase in the attic?' asked Deacon.

Gill grabbed the buff folder from the seat and handed it to him. He flicked through a few of the documents. This was indeed a potential treasure trove for their investigation. He will certainly spend some time over the weekend sifting through the contents.

'That's brilliant work. Thank you, Gill.' He finished his pint. 'And to celebrate your industrious work, you may buy the next round.'

Gill shook her head and went to the bar to fetch their drinks.

'Is Cara joining us?' asked Deacon as Gill returns with their drinks.

'I don't know. She's been out following up on some stuff

today. I've been trying to call her, but of course, she hasn't got a mobile at the moment. Although I emailed on the off chance that she logs on.'

'She's lost her mobile?' Deacon was concerned. If there is one thing no officer wants to do is lose their mobile, encrypted or not. There are too many people out there who can unlock them.

'It's in the lab. She got James Hawthorne to handle it, so we bagged it to get prints from it. We did the same with a photograph from Rosemary.'

'You're teaching her bad habits.' He took a large gulp of his drink. 'Anyway, why the prints?'

'Me and Cara still think that there's more to this. That a third party was involved somehow. What we know from the PM is he was very drunk. So, he wouldn't have been capable of climbing into position in such a condition. Therefore, he must have been drinking while in position on the branch, yet there's no sign of a bottle. But when we went to the house yesterday, we found a few whiskey bottles in the bin. So, we've got the lab to check for dabs. Hopefully, Cara will let me know if....'

Her mobile began to ring and vibrate. She looked at the screen. 'Talk of the devil.' she picked it up to answered.

Deacon finished his pint and checked for any new emails on his own phone while Gill took the call. Judging by her responses, he couldn't tell if it was good news, bad news or indifferent. Eventually, he heard Gill suggest that she and Cara meet up tomorrow for a coffee somewhere. When she finished, she turned to Deacon.

'Well. That's an interesting development,' she said.

'Please tell.'

'So, there are two distinct sets of prints on the bottles. And Steven's is all around the neck and shoulder as you'd expect if he was drinking from it. But there's another set of prints that are very dominant around the base of the bottle.'

'Rosemary's?' asked Deacon.

'You'd think. No. They belong to James.'

Deacon stared at Gill, surprised. Gill and Cara's gut feeling about the suicide and the suspicion of external involvement was absolutely valid. James Hawthorne, who apparently arrived at the farm *after* his brother's death, is now placed at the scene *of his death,* and all because of a bottle or two. But more to the point, why did he and Steven's wife lie about his arrival? What did they have to hide? He turned to Gill.

'This, as far as the Hawthorne's case goes, changes things.'

———

It felt good to be at home in his study, relaxing with a nice glass of Cabernet Sauvignon. Only the corner lamp was used to light the room enough, so it was not too bright and made the atmosphere feel warm. He asked Alexa to play Kate Bush's debut album "A Kick Inside," because it was Claire's favourite album and "Them Heavy People" had been stuck in his head all day. He remembered how he, along with his teenaged friends were all into her music and particularly this album because she was so original. And sexy. He looked at her picture in the gilded frame, smiled and raised his glass. "The Man with the Child in His Eyes" was now playing. Absolutely beautiful.

He took a sip of the wine and smiled as he thought back to him entering the kitchen and finding a note on the worktop from Susan. It was instructing him to switch the microwave on for three and a half minutes to heat the spaghetti bolognaise that she had made him. Things were moving forward slowly. He knocked on her bedroom door to thank her but there was no answer. She probably had the headphones on. Still, small steps, as they say. Sadly, he sent her a WhatsApp message to say, thank you. But at least he could see that she'd read it. He didn't know what, but he would build bridges.

The folder given to him by Gill sat on his desk asking to be opened. He did so and emptied the contents. He set them into small piles. Wedding photographs, other photographs, passports, marriage certificates and letters. As he stared at the wedding photographs, he realised he didn't know what any of John McGregor's wives looked like. So, using the logic of how young or old John looked in the photos he could put them in chronological order, or wife order which is probably a more accurate term. He will get one of the team to confirm next week. The first two looked like Church weddings, the third, he presumed to be Alison Dudbridge, was at Leicester's County Hall. A place he knew well, having visited frequently for his job and the odd marriage ceremony. He looked at the three women. All very different in their looks and build. Therefore, he assumed that John McGregor didn't go for a type.

He lined the three marriage certificates up on the desk. Mary Lockton, September 27th, 1975. Isabelle Burton, 14th February 1998 and Alison Dudbridge, June 14th, 2008. He was now getting a broad idea of the timeline of John McGregor's life. He placed the Death Certificates alongside their respective names. His mind was trying to make connections that most likely didn't exist. Mary Lockton, died of skin cancer on 15th March 1992. Isabelle Burton drowned on 15th February 2005. And Alison Dudbridge lost her life via a hit and run on 18th June 2017. His mind was wandering all over the place trying to find something from nothing. The title track, "The Kick Inside" finished, so he sat for a while in silence, trying to solve something that probably is not there to be solved.

At least there were faces with dates. Ok, not useful on their own, but offers a perspective of thought. An opportunity to consider, to rearrange and reconsider what he thinks he knows. He poured another wine and considered what he could listen to next, more as background music, but couldn't decide on anything, so continued to work in silence. Although decided he was too tired to do more, anyway. He turned to the photograph of Claire. There she was, smiling at the camera. Smiling at him.

His thoughts moved back to the wake. In contrast to the subdued atmosphere of the funeral service, the gathering afterwards was a very different affair. As the people gathered, the volume in the room increased considerably as the mourners talked more freely and feel more confident to laugh and joke. A wake has a habit of doing that. Loosening the tethers and releasing people from sombre memories, inner reflections, and what ifs to the sharing of funny stories and anecdotes regarding the deceased, to help them prepare for a new future in a world without their loved one or friend. And as the drinks flowed the mood of the room lifted more.

He remembered how the tears began filling his eyes, so he slipped away from the crowd and stepped outside where the biting winter air quenched like pins and needles on his warm face. He stood a while, eyes closed, letting the cold air blow against his face. As he opened his eyes, he saw a red-tailed kite with wings fully extended gliding effortlessly, spiralling upwards higher towards the clouds. If he was a spiritual man, he would probably view that as a portent of sorts. He buttoned up his coat and walked away, the noise and the laughter fading into the distance. He returned an hour later. Finally able to take control of his emotions and rationalise his thoughts sufficiently to face the people celebrating the life of Claire Deacon.

His daughter, Susan was constantly circulating the crowd.

Thanking them for finding the time to attend. Taking on board people's pity and sincerity. Making her mum really proud. Making him really proud. He knew she'd be hurting inside yet she did this in homage of her wonderful mother. Yet, he cowered away, not prepared to engage, heartbroken. Useless. He remembered Pau and Gill were there, both catching his eye occasionally, but he could not speak to them. Two people who were very special to him, yet on that day, he couldn't face them.

He soon found himself lost in the memories of his last goodbye to Susan, and the long days and stresses of the past week soon wrapped their tentacles around him, and his eyes slowly closed.

He was standing in front of the Judge.

'So why did you kill him? Why did you set him alight?' The Judge pointed at the man sitting in front of him, his body wearing a pin stripped suit, white shirt and blue tie with a head that was charred and an enormous gaping mouth that had burned away.

'It wasn't me,' pleaded Deacon.

'And why would I believe you after what you did to him,' he pointed at another in the crowd, smartly dressed, this time with a grey three-piece suit accompanied with a white shirt and small red bow tie?

'Yes, look what he did to me,' he said with a huge hook inserted in his eyes clinking as he spoke. 'The guy is SCUM,' he shouted, to cheers in the gallery.

'I will take that into account,' said the Judge. 'And you, sir! Stop engaging in sexual activities in this court!' Danny McGregor turned to the judge whilst still coupled with a female partner.

'But we need photos for the magazines,' he said.

'But you're all scum,' said Libby, standing up at the back of the court, 'so it makes no difference. You all deserve to die.'

'But I did nothing,' pleaded Deacon. But no one was listening. 'I did nothing. I did nothing. I did nothing.'

'Dad!' The sound of Susan's voice jolted him from sleep. He opened his eyes to see his daughter with a hand on his shoulder shaking him. He felt momentarily confused where he was.

'Sorry, I must have dozed off,' he said.

'I could hear you upstairs. You were shouting, I don't know what, it was all mumbled. I thought you'd caught a burglar or something. That's why I have this with me.'

'Ah, my truncheon. It's been a long time since I have had to carry that,' he said.

'It's lucky the light was on, and I saw you, otherwise I may have wrapped it around your head.'

They both smiled at each other at the thought.

'Anyway,' she said, 'I'm going back to bed.' She walked towards the door.

'Thank you,' said Deacon. But she didn't acknowledge him and continued up the stairs to her bedroom. He looked at the clock. One-thirty am. 'Time for me to go to bed too,' he whispered to himself.

―――

The light emanating through the open window from the streetlamp was enough to change total darkness into a shade of grey which made it possible to make out the outline of the furniture in the sitting room. On the table were two empty bottles of wine, and one with probably a glassful left in it. A small orange glow lit up her face as she sucked on the cigarette, ash falling from the end into a full pile of stubs in the ashtray placed on the table beneath her. The air was still outside so offered little to draw out the smoke from the room, but she didn't care. It was just possible as she took another drag of the cigarette to see the glistening from around her eyes and down her cheeks.

The past week had gone from bad to worse. When she visited the Three Gables and discovered that John and the boys were missing, Margaret feared that something terrible had happened. And now, John and Terry are dead, and she would put money on Danny being found the same way. She loved John. They'd been close for a long time. Shared memories, shared experiences, and shared beds. Her hand shook, and more ash dropped toward the ashtray as she recalled the detective, Chief Inspector Deacon, asking if she and John were linked romantically. That can never get out. It will complicate things significantly. The extra payments he gave her, the minor share in the business and the house he bought her. All he wanted in return was loyalty and sex when he felt like it, which suited her fine. She benefitted very well from the arrangement. Hopefully the police won't look too deeply into things.

Margaret gulped down the wine from her glass and poured the remaining contents of the bottle into it, spilling some on the table. Who could have killed them? From a business perspective, it could be several people. They were hard businessmen, and she'd heard rumours about some things they'd done, but that's all it was—rumours. Yes, there had been times when she'd been involved in some of the less kosher dealings. But John was always gentle with her, and the boys always behaved themselves in her presence. Margaret stubbed out her cigarette and lit another. No matter what, she would remain loyal to John and the boys and their legacy. She held up her glass in a silent toast and drank the last of the wine.

Deacon felt well-rested this Saturday morning. He'd slept like a log after going to bed and woke just after nine. Following a shower and a cooked breakfast, he felt good and refreshed.

He poured himself coffee number four and sat at his desk in the study to look again at the stuff collected from the McGregors' attic. The three piles of papers sat on the table as he had left them last night. He fired up his laptop to check for any work emails needing immediate attention. It was something he didn't particularly like doing when at home, but at the weekends he liked to make sure he missed nothing urgent. He logged into his account and scrolled quickly through the unopened emails. One name of interest stood out, from Libby McGregor. He opened it immediately. "FYI– Mum", was the message. He opened the attachment, which was one of two women, smiling at the camera in what looked like a pub garden, judging by the two drinks in front of them and the battered ashtray. One was clearly Libby and Deacon presumed the other was her mother, Alison. He compared the image to that on the wedding photograph. It was a match. Now he just needed confirmation of the first two wives. He would scan them and send them to the incident room at the station to have their identities confirmed.

There were twenty-three legal documents and letters. Some he understood, others he had some idea what they were about, others he found confusing. However, what was interesting is that in all three marriages, the wives had businesses in their own name, but at some point, his name got added as a partner. And in all three businesses he took over the running of the operation initially, before legally given ownership of the entire business. Tragically, all three of his wives died. One naturally, although Deacon was now interested in finding out more about her and the cancer diagnosis, and two following tragic accidents. Which, again, it would be interesting to get the full details of their deaths; especially following the opinion given by Libby. But the absolute gem which made him feel even better than he did earlier this morning, is that all the legal business representation from

McGregor's first wife to his last, were all conducted by Francis Marshall Solicitors. They claim to specialise in personal and business solutions. This could be about trust. Knowing from experience they are professional, reliable, and effective solicitors, why not use them again and again? However, Deacon's not that trusting. Why use solicitors based in Bristol when there are lots of reputable legal beagles locally? He could be wrong, but it stinks. And, although this seems to point a rather accusatory finger at the victims of these murders rather than the murderer or murderers themselves, he firmly believed this to be the key to finding the person or persons responsible. He would prepare some action for the team for Monday.

It was around eleven o'clock when Gill and Cara left the coffee shop to have a wander around some shops. Following Matthew's news last night identifying the fingerprints on the whiskey bottle, they'd now linked James Hawthorne to the scene of his brother's suicide. For that reason, Gill thought it would be a good idea for the pair of them to have a catch-up. So, they agreed to meet at the Caffè Nero on Market Street in the city centre at nine-thirty.

The layout of the place was ideal for them to talk freely without being overheard by other costumers. They sat in a corner on sofas on the first floor. The place was pleasant enough to be in and not overcrowded as such places often become—especially on a Saturday. They spent some time talking about the Hawthorne case, their suspicions and where to go next. Once they'd talked through what they had, what they knew and what they suspected, it seemed pretty obvious to them both what they needed to do next. And that was to find out more about James Hawthorne. And possibly to look at his alibis again regarding his trip that he had been on prior to his brother's death.

Gill was really enjoying Cara's company and felt she was getting to know more about her. Since being paired up on the Hawthorne's case, Gill had certainly gone from acting a little dismissive of the woman, probably because she was relatively new into CID, but maybe there was a bit of jealousy. After all, Cara was very attractive, and she could see the guys in the station casting a not so glancing eye her way as she walked by them at the station. This was the first time Gill had seen Cara with her hair loose. At work she always had it tied back. And she had to admit that Cara is unbelievably blessed in terms of her youthful looks, but with her wavy reddish blonde hair loose, she looked stunning. Over the past week, she had realised her initial perception was wrong and she should not have been so judgemental, because Cara had been proving herself to be a good detective who takes no shit.

The sun was shining from a clear blue sky which seemed to make everyone happier, well, in Gill's eyes, anyway. She and Cara spent some time sat on a bench in the town hall square facing the iconic fountain that, if she remembered rightly was about one hundred and fifty years old. She never tires of looking at the bronzed structure. In her mind it's one of the most beautiful and relaxing things to look at, with its central pillar, that sprays water from the top into a small bowl below, which spills over into a larger bowl that has a kind of floral decoration. The water then cascades over the edges into a stone circular pond below, passing the fountains real focal point, the four large, winged lions. They also spew water from their mouths into the pond below, in which a huge amount of coins lay, where people had thrown in their loose change for a wish. Very magical.

'Are you enjoying your time with us?' asked Gill.

'I am actually. To be honest, I enjoyed uniform too, but

this is interesting in a different way and has an element of excitement. But like the other role, it's the variation that I like in the job, I guess.'

Gill knew exactly what Cara meant. 'However, on the flip side, it can be very routine and mundane. But hey, that's the police for you.'

The two shared stories from their time in uniform, and some calls they had been sent to, and weird and funny situations they had to deal with in the line of duty. The pair of them were crying with laughter during some recollections. Gill found it interesting when they started talking about their current position at Leicester HQ, and Cara's experience when stationed in Derby.

'It was very similar in culture to when I started in uniform. Very much a man's world, and I felt intimidated by them to a degree. I had to work twice as hard as the male officers to gain any respect. It could've been because I had just been promoted to CID, so there was a lack of trust, and the need to prove yourself.'

Gill understood that mentality completely. After all, isn't that exactly how she was towards Cara?

'I'm now happy working in Leicester, because the culture is completely different,' said Cara. 'Here you're part of the team, new or not, female, or male. What also helps is the Chief Superintendent is a woman and an Asian woman at that, who's slight in build but powerful in stature.'

Gill had to agreed. It certainly made her life easier when she arrived. 'As a woman, I cannot imagine the barriers Chief Superintendent Pau must have faced on her climb to such a senior position. But she's done it, and from what I've experienced so far, has done a good job. She commands respect and has metaphorical balls the size of church bells.' They both laugh at Gill's analogy. 'I'll tell you who definitely made my transition into the team easy, Deacon. He supported me every step of the way. Yes, if you did something wrong, you'd get bollocked. But even now, he does it in private, which I respect. Yet, when you do something that's good, and moves the investigation forward, he congratulates you in front of the team. I've met no one like that. He never claims credit for anything that's done by anyone else.'

Cara agreed and recalled a conversation with Deacon after her first month in the team. 'He asked me how I was, if anyone was unhelpful or unfriendly, and if there was anything he could do to support me? I appreciated that. He then told me that we are all just one team, pushing in the same direction but using different tools depending on our job roles. And that all he was technically, was the team mascot. Praised by those above when it goes right and blamed when it goes wrong.'

Gill recognised everything Cara had said and added that she has always felt at ease with him and appreciated. And he's not a womaniser by any stretch of the imagination, and absolutely thought the world of his wife, but he seems to enjoy having females around him.

'He certainly communicates well with us,' said Gill. 'In fact, there is often a playfulness when he talks to us but it's not in a flirtatious way. He can be a bit like a naughty schoolboy, trying to say things to see how you to respond. Whereas with some of the male colleagues, Karl for example, he can be a bit more formal.'

Cara asked Gill about the death of Deacon's wife. She had only been working for him for around six months when he took absence of leave to look after her. Gill told her how devastated he was when he learned of his wife's diagnosis. How he seemed to go into autopilot, coming into the station each day and trying to carry out his duties as normal. She thinks it was Pau who forced his hand and convinced him to take an extended leave of absence to be with his wife and care for her in her last weeks. She mentioned the funeral. Both she and Pau attended, and they actually spent the service and the wake together, which made it easier on such occasions among strangers. Gill recalled how Pau seemed to know most of the Deacon family well, which surprised her, but felt that she got to know Pau a little and found her interesting to talk to, although of course, she remained incredibly guarded. Deacon definitely saw them there but chose to keep his distance.

'That's sad,' responded Cara. 'What's your assessment of him since he's been back, Gill?'

Gill had not really given it much thought, but on reflection she had to start with the caveat that it had only been a couple of weeks.

'There's been so much going on, Cara. The Hawthorne suicide and the oddities associated with it. The murdered and missing McGregors and the extremities of the murders. Everyone has been on full on, working long hours, compiling lots of evidence. And with such a weight of responsibility and expectation, anyone would forgive him if he buckled. But this is like Deacon of old. He's constantly processing the information he's got and finding different ways of approaching the cases to solve the puzzles. I have to admit, I've never worked with anyone like him since joining the police. However, and this is just my view. I'm concerned that it's all a front, and I'm not sure if he really is coping as well as he likes us to believe. There's something lost when you look in his eyes. That brightness, that naughtiness that fun side, seems to have gone. Yes, he still cracks the odd joke and yes, he's still as sarcastic as ever. But something is definitely missing. And, I'll be honest with you, I feel sorry for him because I think he's still in mourning and using the job to distract himself from the truth. I'm certain that Pau knows that too. But he's a complicated and stubborn man. He won't allow anyone to help.'

'That's so sad,' said Cara.

They had spent an hour wandering around the shops, trying on clothes they didn't buy and sampling perfume they couldn't afford. Realising the time, Cara suggested they go for something to eat before making their way home. So, they decided on an Irish themed pub that they both knew, which was close by and did decent food without charging an arm and a leg for the pleasure.

They had an enjoyable meal in which Gill had spaghetti Bolognese and Cara went for the fillet of salmon in butter sauce and new potatoes, both washed down with glasses of Chardonnay. As they were part way through their second bottle, one of them, although Gill can't remember for the life of her, who, suggested that each reveal something about themselves that no-one else at the station would know. Gill opted to go first, telling Cara something she did when she was at college, which she shouldn't be proud of, but in truth, she don't know many people who did it.

'It was a threesome with two very drunk and willing classmates. Yes, it was a great experience, what I remember of it, and it is a very personal naughty badge of honour.' Both she and Cara screamed with laughter. 'I would absolutely die if my parents were to find out even now, and I had to explain myself.'

Cara eventually stopped laughing, wiping the tears from her eyes.

'Your turn,' said Gill.

Cara then revealed her secret. She was gay and was currently in a relationship with another woman, a beautician called Christie. Gill sat with her mouth open. She would never have thought that in a million years. This beautiful woman, this person who every man seems to drool over is actually in love - with a woman. Amazing!

'You're a lesbian?'

'A *lesbian*?' repeated Cara, laughs. 'You sound like my mum.'

'I'm sorry, and also, I'm sorry if I appear to be smiling. If the guys back at the nick knew, they'd be devastated.'

'Why?'

'Because you're the station's pinup,' replied Gill.

'Why?' asked Cara, looking surprised.

'Because your young and beautiful...... don't you see them staring at you when you're there?'

Cara seemed quite perplexed at the question. 'Well, no. And why would I? Men are just men. Colleagues. I have no feelings for them. It's like if Pau kept staring at you. You'd hardly get off on that, would you?'

They both laughs and promised each other that their secrets were safe. While they were polishing off the last couple of glasses of the second bottle of wine, Cara stopped Gill during their conversation and pointed out of the pub window. James and Rosemary Hawthorne were walking along the other side of the street, looking in the shop windows, hand in hand. Well, what a surprise, thought Gill.

CHAPTER EIGHT

THE INCIDENT ROOM was bustling on this sunny Monday morning. Deacon had called a team briefing to update everyone on the overall progress so far in the McGregors' case. Officers and support team members were talking among themselves and sharing the fruits of their enquiries thus far. Be it evidence or intelligence, it would all be inputted into the HOLMES computer system, a great asset to large and complicated investigations the McGregors' case had turned into. Hopefully HOLMES will soon flag up patterns and inconsistencies.

Karl had spent Friday on a trip down south at Deacon's request, to find out more about John McGregor, and was glad to have the weekend to recover from his sixteen-hour day. He was hopping about as if standing on hot plates when Deacon waved him over.

'Good to see you back in one piece. Hopefully a worthwhile trip?' said Deacon.

'Very. I have some interesting stuff, guv.'

'Good. Sit down and tell.' They sat at a table in the room's corner.

'I spoke with some old acquaintances of John McGregor down in Devon, to get a better understanding of him.' He took out his notebook and opened it. 'I think I've more of an idea of who the man was, or the type of man, anyway. As you know, he was born and raised in Bristol and attended the university there on a business degree programme. He dropped out halfway through year two. He's been married twice before. The first wife, Mary Lockton, who's the mother of Terry and Danny, and John had a business providing student accommodation in the city which was doing well. However, she died of skin cancer when they were ten and twelve, respectively.'

'I suppose living down south, at the coast, they're exposed more to the sun?'

'Except she didn't. She hated the sun according to friends. So, I did some research online and found that stress can contribute to the condition—and inorganic arsenic poisoning.'

'But that didn't show in the post-mortem?'

'No, guv. But if it's used to trigger the condition and stopped long enough before her death it can be difficult to detect. Although, in truth, I don't know.'

'But you're throwing it into the mix?' said Deacon.

'As a hypothesis, yes. Anyway, he was still living in Bristol at this point. But here's where things get interesting. A couple of years later he meets his second wife, Isabelle Burton, who owned a very successful estate agent and letting business down south. And sure enough, John McGregor not only wormed his way into her life, but the business until eventually, he was pretty much running the whole thing, lock stock and barrel. Sound familiar? I spoke to a couple of her old friends, and they can't understand why she'd do that, because she loved her work. But they said he was charming when they met him, and Isabelle became besotted with John. And guess what? She died in mysterious circumstances.'

'I've seen her death certificate; it was accidental death caused by drowning.'

'Yes, but it's not as black and white as that.'

Deacon felt the hairs on the back of his neck rise. 'Ok, you have my attention.'

'They lived out in Woolacombe, North Devon. She'd go out for an early morning swim if the weather was Ok. But apparently one day the current got her and swept her out to sea, and she drowned. But here's the thing, guv, her friends found it strange for a couple of reasons. First, she was a fantastic swimmer and swam at county level when she was younger and regularly competed in competitions. So as far as they were concerned, it made little sense. And second, she'd been swimming in that stretch of water since she was at school. She grew up in the area and did the early morning swim since she was about ten years old. So, she knew how the tides and the currents moved like the back of her hand.'

Deacon digested what Karl had told him. 'He seems to have a lot of bad luck with his wives. That's good work, Karl. What're your thoughts?'

'Gold digger? Ok, they weren't millionaires, but the last two wives were successful–and single.'

'And how did he find them, I wonder?' said Deacon. 'It can't always be luck, a chance meeting. He must have sought them out somehow?'

Deacon glanced at his watch - a couple of minutes to eight. After thanking Karl, he prepared for the briefing. Although not specifically assigned to the case, Deacon had asked Gill and Cara to attend, if possible, now the Hawthorne case was nearing its end. Although the prints found on the whiskey bottles could change things a little, he was confident it could be tied up relatively quickly. The two detectives would then become available on a more full-time basis on his investigation.

'Ok everyone, can I have your attention, please.' The volume and activity in the room died down and everyone looked towards Deacon as he stood by the large glass wipe board that was full of notes, thoughts, and photographs. 'Chief Superintendent Pau will join us, so as soon as her Highness arrives, we can get into the details.' Deacon heard the door close behind him before he finished the sentence.

'Her highness has arrived, DCI Deacon,' said Pau as she walked past him and stood behind the team at the back of the room.

Everyone stared at Deacon in silence. He could see that they wanted to laugh but remained stone faced.

'Ok, let's start with our major investigation into the missing men. I can now confirm, if you haven't heard already, that we have a second body which is John McGregor's. Like his son, Terry, the cause of death was again horrific. This time the murderer set fire to the victim's head–or to be more precise, his mouth.' Several officers in the room shook their heads in disbelief. 'Now, that clearly leaves us with Danny.' He tapped his finger on Danny's photograph on the wipe board. 'Thinking out aloud, he could have killed his father and brother over some family squabble. But my gut feeling is he's lying somewhere, dead.'

Cara raised her hand. 'I suppose there is a third option, where he's held captive by the murderer or murderers?'

'Fair point, and it would be great if we could find him and help piece the whole thing together,' replied Deacon. 'But the reason I don't think that's the case, is because Terry and John were killed within a few hours of each other. We believe all three men were taken together, so it would be fair to assume that if two of them have been killed around the same time, surely the third was too. If I'm correct, unless we get some information or have a bit of luck, we're going to have to wait for Danny's body to be found. Any questions so far?'

There was a general shaking of the heads by the team.

'Interestingly, we still know very little about the McGregors. The interviews that you conducted have not really been as fruitful as we would have hoped. The McGregor's seemed to have been very guarded about their private lives. If I remember rightly, two girls found Danny a bit of a charmer, and that's about it. John has a stepdaughter, Libby, whom we've spoken to on a couple of occasions. She left home a few years ago, and to be fair, can't stand the guys. And of course, there's their PA, Margaret Wilson. Or is she more than a PA, we need to find out. We've conducted a couple of informal interviews with her and if I'm honest, I believe she can offer us far more information than she has so far, so, again, we need to revisit.'

'Do you think the daughter, or the PA could be involved in their deaths, sir? Came a question from someone at the back of the room.'

'Good question. I think not. But we're not ruling anything out. Margaret Wilson is far too attached and protective to the McGregors to harm them. And Libby? Again, my gut feeling is no, but she's still a suspect. Finally, I'd like to thank DC Goodman who made the long journey down to Devon last week, following up on information that he gathered on John McGregor. It makes interesting reading and will be available to you all for background purposes. If you have any thoughts about any aspects of this investigation, please contact me. We have several lines of inquiry we need to follow that DS Buxton has allocated, which are in the action book. Do you wish to add anything, ma'am?'

Pau made her way from the back of the room and stood next to Deacon.

'First, thank you for the hard work. It isn't going unnoticed. As DCI Deacon has explained, there's still a lot we need learn about the victims and of course, we still have a missing person to find. As you know, there's a lot going on and the condition in which we've found the bodies is unusual and disturbing. Therefore, for obvious reasons, I expect you all to remain professional at all times and divulge this information to no-one. Do I make myself clear?' Those present dutifully nodded. 'I believe the public would be petrified if they found out about what we've discovered. And, please, take care. We don't know who we're dealing with. Let's hope for a productive day. Thank you.'

The team went back to their duties and the incident room became a noisy hive of activity again. Pau looked more closely at the information presented on the wipe board.

'I'm intrigued with what DC Goodman uncovered,' she said to Deacon. 'Do you have thirty minutes for a coffee and catch-up with Her Highness?'

Pau was processing all that Deacon had told her regarding Karl's trip down south and what he'd discovered, as they sat in her office with a fresh coffee each.

'He's done well,' she said. 'And how do you think he's developing?'

'Very well. He's taking responsibility for his part in the team and is becoming.... dare I say it.... Likable.'

'Big praise indeed, from you. So, what's your gripe?'

'There's no gripe. I need players - loyal players. Like Gill. Cara's also on the same wavelength. Karl? He's still proving himself. But I believe he's close. His enquiries are effective, as we've discussed. He considers the information he has well and makes rational assumptions from it. He hasn't gone off on a limb yet, which is good. And he's learning to smile, which is an enormous improvement. He's not there, but he's progressing well.'

'But he's new to CID, and you know it's quite a culture shock. And I would imagine that your reputation precedes you, so you would expect some apprehension on his part?'

'I take it you mean my charm and wit?'

'No, I don't. Ok. And you? It's been a challenging couple of weeks. How're you coping being back in the thick of it?' Pau stared at Deacon intensely.

'I'm good.'

'Bollocks. Tell me the truth, Alex.'

Pau's question was not unexpected considering his circumstances, but her reaction was more confrontational than he expected. And as is often the case with him, his brain clicks into fight-or-flight mode–generally fight. He didn't really think before answering.

'OK. The job is shit. I'm expected to achieve the impossible. So, why am I still here? Because I love my job, it gives me purpose and I honestly think that I'll find the answers to the questions posed. I'm good at what I do. I can get results from the little I'm offered. Why? Because no matter how complex a case seems, it's about simple elimination. And I still get a buzz from that.'

'That's good, Alex,' said Pau. 'I do like it when you're rattled. I always feel you give an honest answer rather than the bullshit you want me to hear. Now let's talk about you. Not the job. *You.*'

Alex was not one to bare his soul. He was what his late wife, Claire, referred to as a man's man–a bloke's bloke. Someone who keeps his feelings and emotions to himself. Stiffer upper lip, as they say. In fact, it wasn't until Claire's passing that he lost some of that self-control. It was like the invisible shield he hid behind had become damaged. He never liked people asking him about his feelings. It wasn't because it made him feel weak. No. It made him feel uncomfortable, vulnerable even, and the reason he refused the offer of counselling after losing Claire and spent weeks unable to sleep. He was in no doubt it would have helped, but inner emotions are not something he wants to share. But if there was one person, he could express some elements to, it was Pau.

'How are coping within yourself,' Pau asked.

Deacon stared down at Pau's desk. 'From a personal perspective it has its moments. When I'm at home, it's difficult sometimes and lonely. There are still memories that become overwhelming when I'm in the house on my own. But I'll get through it, I know I will. I've considered moving house, but then I think, why? Our place has so much of Claire's personality in it. And of course, there's Susan who I know is going through worse. Christ, she lost her mother. We should be there for each other, but I think we both recognise that we are very different people. I realise now, it was Claire who gelled us together as a family unit. She had a way of bridging the gaps. But we're slowly beginning to at least talk occasionally, and eat the same meals, although not necessarily at the same time, but small steps.' Deacon looked up at Pau. 'Being back here and investigating a case like the McGregors, gives me something to focus on while at home. It's a welcome distraction.'

'Thanks for your honesty. If you need support in any form, just ask. And keep working on your relationship with your daughter. That's more important than any job.'

James Hawthorne drove the black Range Rover out of the farm gateway onto the road to Leicester. As he sped by Cara, she continued to read through the news on her mobile phone for another ten minutes before driving into Hawthorne farm.

Opening the door to the farmhouse, Rosemary Hawthorne seemed surprised to see Cara standing there.

'Morning, Mrs Hawthorne. How are you today?' Cara gave a big grin.

Rosemary seemed momentarily confused before composing herself. 'Good morning DC Matthews. I'm afraid James has made his own way to the station. He didn't realise you were going to pick him up.'

Cara thought quickly. 'Really? I'm so sorry. There was obviously a mix up. There're so many things going on. Anyway, how are you?' she asked.

'Yes, I'm fine. You know, considering.'

'Good,' answered Cara, sympathetically. 'Actually, while I'm here, would it be Ok to have a quick chat to clarify some last points?'

'Yes, of course,' replied Rosemary reluctantly. She opened the door and led Cara through to the sitting room where she sat while Rosemary made them both a cup of tea.

About five minutes later, Rosemary carried a tray into the room with a steaming teapot, cups and a small jar of milk neatly placed upon it. Once settled with their drinks, Cara took out some papers from her bag. 'If you wouldn't mind, I would like you to talk me though some points from your initial statement?'

'Why? I've told you everything?'

'I'm not sure you have, Mrs Hawthorne. There are some things which don't quite make sense. I just want you to help clarify them. It's probably a misunderstanding on our part, so we need to clarify them. Do I make myself clear?'

'But James is at the police station now. Can we not wait until he comes back?'

'I'm afraid not. Mr Hawthorne is to be interviewed by my colleague who will ask similar questions. So, I'd just like you to be as honest as possible with me. You're not necessarily in any trouble. But by not telling us the truth, makes us very suspicious.'

Rosemary looked uncomfortable but kept eye contact as she took a sip of her tea.

'We thought you'd be more comfortable here. If you wish, we can go to the station and conduct the interview under caution? And no, you wouldn't be interviewed with Mr Hawthorne, I'm afraid. So, are you Ok to talk here?'

'Yes.'

'Ok,' I'll get straight to the point. You said you found your husband in the garden at 4.15 on Wednesday morning?'

'Yes,' replied Rosemary in a whisper.

'We have the bottles. The whiskey bottles, that Steven was drinking from on the night he died. We've taken prints from it, so we know who was there. As you know, he wasn't on his own.' Rosemary stared at Cara. 'So, would you like to tell me what really happened?'

Rosemary gave a deep sigh. 'It was as I told you. He was depressed and was threatening to kill himself, which he often did but never went through with it. But this time he was different.'

Rosemary kept her stare in Matthew's direction, the detective got the impression she was not looking at her but relieving the evening–her memory replaying the events like a movie.

'He was angry and abusive and calling James all sorts of things. I'd never seen him like that before. In fact, he was scaring me. So, I called James. I didn't know who else to speak to. He was staying somewhere in the Peak district but said that he'd make his way down to us and speak to him. By the time James arrived, about an hour or so later, Steven was already on the branch with a bottle of whiskey and the razor wire around his neck. I honestly don't know when he'd put that up there. I can't remember seeing it earlier. Anyway, he was drinking heavily.' She began to cried. 'He was shouting at James, but it was mostly incoherent. We were trying to calm him down. James tried to climb up the ladder to get Steven down, but he was kicking out at James and nearly lost his balance, so James backed off to allow Steven to calm down. But Steven was getting more irate and drunk. So, James suggested I went inside the house, as he could see it was upsetting me, and he'd try to calm things down and talk some sense into Steven. So that's what I did.'

'How long were they out there together?'

'I don't know. They seemed to be out there for ages. Maybe a few hours. Then James came into the house about 11.'

'And Steven was still outside? Was he alive?'

'Oh, yes. I heard him shouting. He was shouting and singing and abusive, although most of the time he was incomprehensible.'

'What happened then?'

'After a few hours, me and James went outside to see how he was, because he was quiet, so I thought he'd calmed down. And that's when we discovered him.' Rosemary paused. Cara guessed she was reliving the image of her husband hanging by the razor wire.

'And the ladder? Who moved it? Where is it?' asked Cara.

'It's in the hay barn where it came from, out in the south field. I don't know why I moved it. We were both in shock. James was upset, I was hysterical. We were panicking.'

'About what?'

'That's the point. I don't know.'

'And the whiskey bottles?'

'James thought it would look bad if they were there because people would want to know why we didn't call for help if we knew he was drinking. So, he moved them. I was about to call the police when James suggested he went away and turn up later.'

'Why?'

Rosemary raised her eyebrows. 'Why do you think? How would it look?'

'Did you sleep with him that night?'

'No. And that's exactly what James worried about. People's impressions.'

'Tell me, how long have you been having an affair with James?'

'As I've just said, I haven't...'

'...How long have you been having an affair with James?'

Rosemary sat silently for a while, fidgeting, before answering. 'A few years. Steven and I seemed to lose that connection married couples share. We always wanted children, but I was unable. I know that hurt Steven, but bless him, he said it didn't matter, and we had each other. We used to joke that we had a thousand sheep every year to look after, so wouldn't have time for children of our own.' She smiled as tears rolled down her cheeks. 'He became more distant and would go away some weekends to do his drawing. And I was finding myself alone more and more, and one thing led to another and that's how it came about, I suppose.'

'So, James would come round at the weekends. When Steven was away?'

'Something like that.'

'Thank you,' said Cara. 'There's no law against any of this. Ok, morally it's questionable. There's nothing you've told me so far that suggests you caused Steven's death. You could have done more to prevent it, such as call the police. I just don't understand why you didn't tell us this in the first place?'

'Because I'm scared.'

'Of what?'

'I don't know.'

'As I've said,' said Cara, 'my colleague is speaking with James at the station. Is there likely to be a difference in accounts?'

'Why would there be? I've told you what happened. And what I've said is the truth.'

According to the website, the Dudbridge Conference Building, referred to as the "DCB", with a matching logo, is located at the south end of Dudbridge's car park. It has three rooms that external businesses and organisations can hire for training, planning days and conferences. All rooms are tastefully decorated with light ceilings and walls and grey doors with matching carpeted floors. The rooms, named 'Fuchsia', 'Tulip' and 'Orchid', are identified by a square wooden plaque at the side of the corresponding doors. Each has a long French polished table with several chairs each side and a ninety-five-inch screen at the top end of the room. There are some smaller desks either side of the entrance door, most probably for breakout sessions. Wireless keyboards sat on the tables and flip chart pads on portable stands.

As Deacon and Karl entered the building, both men buttoned up their jackets. Clearly the heating is switched off when the building's not in use. However, the overall impression when entering the place was positive. It's bright, clean, and modern. It certainly gave the impression of a professional business environment, making those who hired it feel comfortable.

They opened the door to the 'Fuchsia' room. The lights automatically switched on. Everything within the room was as expected with the long table and accompanying chairs neatly laid out. It was clean and prepared for the next booking. Karl noted the lack of natural light, which Deacon found interesting, considering it was a meeting room. They walked along the corridor to the next room, identified by the plaque next to the door as 'Tulip.' Again, it was a similar set-up to the first room. However, this had light spilling in from the wall of windows offering a view of the meadows. But again, there was nothing of interest.

Deacon was finding the experience wasteful, time wise, but knew he needed to close things down from an investigatory perspective. He and Karl made their way to the third room, known as 'Orchid.' The lights switched on as Karl opened the door. The smell and the scene hit the two detectives simultaneously.

The room, like the others, was neat and bright with water colours on the walls themed around the room's name. Someone had stacked the tables and chairs against the wall under the display screen at the opposite end of the room. The only focus of attention being the man sitting in the chair. From a distance, his posture looked good with his back straight, legs together, bent at the knees and the shiny black shoes placed perfectly on the floor. The perfect ergonomic position, thought Deacon. The arms were at his side and bent at the elbows, allowing his forearms to rest on the wooden arms of the chair, both hands tightly gripped around the edges. His grey three-piece suit gave the air of a business manager, although the open collar shirt made things more casual.

The only actual signs that maybe something was wrong were the closed eyes and red stains on the collar of the shirt and jacket shoulders. The wide-open mouth stretched the lips and showed the bottom half of the teeth. And then there was the long drill that was protruding from each side of the head. The shank sticking out of the left ear and the tip breaking out just above the right ear. There remained a clump of body tissue stuck to the tip. Several flies were buzzing around, flying in and out of the mouth. Laying more eggs in the warm rotting flesh, guessed Deacon. As Deacon moved closer to the body, the more rancid the smell became, suggesting some decomposition.

Deacon turned to Karl who looked a little pale, staring at the sight before him, but under the circumstances was holding up well.

'Call in. Tell them we want the surgeon over pronto, uniforms to seal off the place and it's worth getting the pathologist on standby, by the looks of this.'

Karl nodded and began punching in the numbers of his mobile and walked outside of the building to arrange things in the fresh air. Deacon took a few steps closer. He was still a few meters away, but didn't want to contaminate any potential evidence. He stared in disbelief.

James Hawthorne walked into interview room 4 at around 10.30am by the duty sergeant and asked to sit at the desk next to a tape machine. He looked overdressed for the occasion in his blue blazer and white shirt. Sitting cross-legged, he looked up at the camera fixed in the ceiling, from which Gill was observing, and tapped his watch.

'Arrogant, prick,' said Gill to herself.

She made her way to the interview room and entered.

'Mr Hawthorne, I'm glad you could make it. I hope you don't mind, but I would like to record this interview.'

'Do I have any choice?'

'Not really,' replied Gill.

'In which case, should I have legal representation? I had the impression that this was an informal interview. And I would like to say for the record that I came here voluntarily, yet feel I'm treated like a criminal. Why your colleague had to take my fingerprints, I don't know.'

'In answer to your first question, not unless you've done something wrong. The second, at this point in time it is an informal interview because I'm trying to gather information, but you still have your rights. As far as the prints go, that's normal procedure, so you're treated the same as anyone else. And third, had you not agreed to come here, I would have arrested you and brought in under caution. And that may also be the case if you decide to end the interview at any point. So, do you want a solicitor?'

James considered the question before answered. 'No. Not yet.'

'Good, let's get started.' Gill gave a big smile and sat at the table facing Hawthorne and switched on the recorder, introducing herself, James Hawthorne, the time and the date for the record.

'Thank you for coming in and speaking to us today. The reason for this chat is to enable us to tie up a couple of loose ends regarding your brother's unfortunate death, and allow you and your family to move on to the next chapter of your life.'

James nodded.

'Mr Hawthorne has nodded,' said Gill. 'Ok, as you've told us previously, you spent a couple of weeks travelling around the country, staying at various locations, of which you provided us a comprehensive list, which we thank you for. Everyone confirmed you arrived, stayed and paid in advance. Then on Wednesday the eighth of March, at about 4.15am, your sister-in-law discovered your brother hanging. Is that correct?'

James sighs. 'Yes.'

'And you arrived later that day?'

'I did.'

'Were you due to arrive on the Wednesday anyway, or was it because Rosemary called you?'

'As you know, I was on holiday, so no, I was not planning to go to the farm at that point. Rosemary called, and I came straight over from Edensor, where I was staying.'

'What time did she call?'

'About 5am, if I remember correctly.'

'And where were you when you received the call?'

'I've just told you. I was in the Peak District, in Edensor.'

'When was the last time you'd visited the farm?'

'A couple of days before I took my break. Look, I can't see what you're insinuating here. I've lost my bloody brother, and I feel like I'm being treated as a suspect in his death?'

Gill ignored the outburst. 'Mr Hawthorne. Let me tell you what's niggling us. Rosemary finds Steven on the Wednesday morning. Now, following informal interviews and conversations with both Rosemary and you, there was never any suggestion that Steven was drunk the night before, which we find strange?'

'Why? Rosemary probably didn't know he'd been drinking if she was in bed. And as you know, I didn't arrive until later that day, after driving down from the Peaks.'

'That I might understand in different circumstances. However, we have some odd anomalies. Let me explain. First, according to the toxicology report, Steven had so much alcohol in his system, he wouldn't have been able to climb up to the branch. Yet, there were no steps or ladders anywhere to be seen, so someone must have moved them, suggesting someone else was there. Now, ignoring the access issue, he must have been drinking whilst in position on the branch, which means he probably had the razor wire around his neck long before he became intoxicated. And you never know, he might not have gone through with the attempt if he wasn't drinking? It was possibly an accident. He became so unsteady he fell off of the branch. But there was no bottle? So, again, that suggests that someone else was there to clear up before the police were called.'

James fidgeted. 'Ok, so someone was there and murdered him, and made it look like a suicide. But as you know, Rosy was in bed, and I was on holiday. And if that's a possibility, I would like you and your colleagues to do your job and find out who's responsible.'

'And that's exactly what we're doing. And we found the bottles.' Was that a slight stiffening of James's body? thought Gill. 'And our great forensic team has pulled some prints from them. And guess whose fingerprints they found?'

'Don't play games with me.' James seemed more aggressive in his tone now. 'It could be anyone at the house and you know it. Any of ours could be on it.'

'Yes, they could. But they're not just anyone's. Predominantly, around the neck are your brothers, which is no surprise if he was drinking from it. And the other prints are yours.' James sat motionless. 'And, Mr Hawthorne, what is interesting is that one of the last prints, which lays over your brothers, is yours. Which places you at the farm the day before you said you arrived?'

'I want my solicitor,' barks James Hawthorne.

'I think that would be a good idea,' said Gill. 'Interview ends 11.50am.'

It had been around three and a half hours since Karl had made the call. And as expected, the building, the car park, and the small area of land around the building were now officially a crime scene, with police officers keeping access to a minimum. The Divisional Surgeon had been and gone, officially declaring life extinct. Now the police photographer was getting as much visual evidence as possible to capture the scene. As he snapped away, the tall figure of the pathologist, Dave Freestone, walked into the building looking like a model for a catalogue. He wore a dark blue pinstriped two-piece suit coupled with a light blue shirt and yellow tie, and topped off with brown Chelsea boots. He carried two large black leather bags containing his 'tools of the trade'. Deacon got the impression that this man could dress in ill-fitting overalls, splattered with paint and still look good. As he got closer, he stopped, closed his eyes and took large breaths of air through his nose.

'I recognise this vintage, Alex,' he said. 'It's a good week old.'

Karl looked at Deacon and slowly shook his head.

'You'll get used to him.' Deacon whispered. He turned to Freestone and shook his hand. 'We keep meeting, Dave.'

'It all feels a bit "Midsomer Murder." Since you've returned, you seemed to have brought out the worst in people.'

'I sometimes think that, Dave, but I worry that you'll have nothing to do. Anyway. We'll leave you to get on and I'll try to catch-up with you later.'

'Of course.' And with that, Freestone placed down and opened his bags and circled the body and get his first impressions of his 'patient.'

'Interview with James Hawthorne and his legal representative, David Willis, starting at 3:15pm. As an overview, Mr Willis, Mr Hawthorne and myself were discussing anomalies in the sequence of events from the statement that he gave us at the start of our inquiries and the disparities we've uncovered following our investigation into the death of Steven Hawthorne. The point in which Mr Hawthorne asked for legal representation was when I revealed we had found three empty whiskey bottles at the farm, in the recycle bin, that we believe Steven Hawthorne drank from on the night of his death. He consumed a considerable amount of alcohol that may have contributed to his death. Most of the fingerprints on the bottles were those of Steven Hawthorne. However, we discovered another set of prints which are identified as those belonging to James Hawthorne, which are layered on top of Steven's. This suggests that he was most likely the last person to touch the bottles. I would guess to place it in the bin.'

David Wallis laughed. 'That is completely circumstantial. Pure speculation. You're just guessing and changing the narrative to suit your own mickey mouse theory.'

'If you let me finish, Mr Wallis. Before the police arrived, someone had removed the bottles from the area. Therefore, and more significantly, it places that person, *you* Mr Hawthorne, at the farm, around the time of the tragedy - the day before you claimed to have arrived.'

'This is complete nonsense. You cannot seriously expect to build a case from that,' interjected Wallis.

Gill ignored the solicitor. 'Hear me out, please. So, this is what we believe happened. Steven Hawthorne was feeling depressed and was threatening to kill himself. He's abusive and aggressive. After climbing up to the branch of the tree in the garden, he's wrapped a length of razor wire around several times and formed a loop at the other end to act like a crude noose. He puts that around his neck and threatens to jump. He's drinking bottles of whiskey, the ones we have recovered and have fingerprints from. His wife, Rosemarie, gets worried and calls you for help. So, you cut your break short and actually arrive on Tuesday in the early evening to calm the situation and get him down. How am I doing so far, Mr Hawthorne?'

James sat stone faced in silence. His solicitor whispered in his ear.

'I'll continue. You spend a considerable amount of time

trying to get your brother to see sense, but to no avail. So, you leave him up there hoping he would calm himself down over time or the alcohol subdues him a bit, and he comes down by his own accord. You go to bed for a few hours, but when you check on him in the early hours of the morning, you find him hanged. Whether he jumped or fell, be it deliberately or accidentally, we'll probably never know. You put the bottles in the recycle bin for whatever reason, because we were always going to find alcohol in his body during the postmortem. Maybe you weren't thinking rationally. And you cleared off so it wouldn't look bad that you were sleeping with Steven's wife when he needed help.'

'Let's stop right there,' said Mr Willis, getting to his feet. 'How dare you insinuate such tripe? You ought to be ashamed of yourself. Mr Hawthorne has lost his brother in a tragic suicide, and you throw tawdry comments and accusations at him during this time of grief. I think we'll end the interview here. Come, Mr Hawthorne, you don't need to be subjected to such cheap allegations and slurs.'

James was about to stand.

'I wouldn't go just yet. Sit down, please.' Gill looked towards the camera. 'DS Matthews, would you like to join us?'

Both men looked up at the camera and back to Gill. Mr Willis sat down. Cara entered the room with a document, which she gave to Gill.

'For the record, DS Matthews has entered the room. This is my colleague, DS Matthews, Mr Willis, and I know you've met her on a number of occasions, Mr Hawthorne. She held up the hand-written document. This is the amended statement of events that Rosemary Hawthorne volunteered earlier this morning. The series of events I shared with you corresponds with what she said. If you disagree with anything I've said, that's fine, please say so. That includes, to use your words, Mr Willis, the "tripe" and the "cheap allegations and slurs." Obviously, if your version of events differs, we can work through those if we decide to charge you both of perverting the course of justice. So, is there anything I've said that's inaccurate, so far, Mr Hawthorne?'

Mr Willis whispering advice for some time into his client's ear. Meanwhile, James Hawthorne sat motionless. He gave an occasional nod of the head. The solicitor turned to Gill and Cara. 'Mr Hawthorne believes the information you've presented aligns with his recollection of events. However, other than removing the bottles, which were not intentionally done to hide evidence, he had no part in his brother's death.'

'We're not saying you have Mr Hawthorne. But we need to know what happened, no matter who it embarrasses. Do I make myself clear?'

'Yes,' said Mr Hawthorne.

'What happened after you asked Rosemarie to go inside the house? You stayed outside with your brother for a few hours. What did you talk about? Why was he so angry?'

Hawthorne seemed to collect his thoughts. He shook his head and began.

'In truth? I honestly don't know the root of his anger that day. We never got to that. He spent a lot of time mumbling incoherently to himself. There were clearly some demons inside his head. He called me every name under the sun. He didn't like the direction the farm was moving in. I've been trying to streamline the place and change the way we do things, but that needs investment. Whereas Steven wanted to do things like he always had, like dad always did, and was accusing me of embezzling the farm's money. And believe me, you're welcome to look at the accounts, I take as much from the farm as a salary as he does, and to be honest, we're eating away at what capital we do have tied up, because of rising costs and lower profits on livestock sales. But to be honest, these weren't new arguments. We've been at loggerheads over the way the business should run for a long time - years. But he was furious that night.'

'Did he know about you and Rosemary?' asked Cara.

'No. Or if he did, he never said so.'

'Why did you not call the police?' asked Gill.

'I considered it. Why didn't I? I don't know.'

'Didn't you think he could lose his balance, especially with him drinking?' asked Cara.

'Again, it never crossed my mind. In retrospect, it was bloody stupid of me to not even consider it, but what can I say? That's something I'll have to live with. Maybe we could have got him help.'

'Why did you leave him outside on his own?'

'He was far too irate. We were going in circles, arguing about the same stuff, so I thought if I left him, he'd have time to calm down on his own without me acting as the punchbag. I didn't intend to go to sleep, but after bouts of him shouting stuff or bursting into some nondescript song, I suppose with the long day and the travelling, I nodded off. Anyway, I woke up a few hours later and... well, you know the rest.'

Gill turned to Cara in case she wanted to ask something. She shook her head.

'Thank you for your time, Mr Hawthorne, and for the legal support, Mr Willis,' said Gill. 'Interview ends at 4.26pm.' She stopped the recorder. 'You're free to go.'

Hawthorne and Willis looked at each other, surprised at the abrupt ending, but rose from their chairs and followed Cara out of the room. She returned a few minutes later to where Gill was sitting at the table.

'What are your thoughts, Cara?' asked Gill, rubbing her eyes with her palms.

'I think we have as much as we can get from this. James is the only person who really knows what they said and what happened while he and Steven were together. And to be fair, he appears to have been alive when James went inside the house because Rosemary heard him shouting and singing too.'

'Although I can't help thinking that there is more to Steven's beef with James than just farm stuff. As Rosemary told you, her husband was very abusive towards James from when he arrived. It would be interesting to know what they talked about, or argued about for, what, three hours?'

'Conveniently, he asked Rosemary to go into the house,' added Cara. 'So, there could have been a private conversation, but that's what it'll always be—private.'

'We'll see what DCI Deacon thinks regarding charging them for perverting the course of justice, but they have lost a brother and a husband, so in the scheme of things, it seems a little petty.'

'Was there negligence, Gill? Rosemary and particularly James could see how precarious the situation was, what with Steven with a makeshift noose around his neck and drinking himself stupid?'

'I think there was, but is it our place to go there? They have to live with the consequences. No. I think we're done. One last thing, Cara. At one point James referred to his sister-in-law as "Rosy".'

'Did he indeed? How romantic.'

'Thank you for making yourself available for a quick repartee, because I really need to get back to the hospital and work with more satisfied customers, like my friend here,' said the Pathologist Dave Freestone after calling in Deacon and Karl. 'We haven't met, have we?' he said, pointing to Karl.

'No, sir. Only when you arrived.'

'Well, if you're going to be spending time with the death

magnet, here, I'm sure we'll be seeing a lot more of each other. So, for the sake of formalities, I'm Dr David Freestone. But of course, you can still call me "sir" as it's good for my ego.'

Deacon wasn't sure if Karl was grasping Freestone's sense of humour, so let things run. Both he and Karl waited in anticipation for the summary of the pathologist's initial findings.

'Right. There are certain things I can tell you for definite at this stage, some I can surmise, but will need to be confirmed during the Post-mortem, and, of course, there will always be a speculative element. So. first, it is a male. He has good taste in clothing, and upon initial inspection, hypostasis, and bruising, I believe he died in this chair.'

'Killed in this room?' asked Deacon.

'I never said that,' said Freestone.

Deacon was trying to get his head around this. 'Ok. So murdered elsewhere and moved here in the chair?'

'I think nothing. Where the death happened is your area. "How" is mine. There are marks, bruising and burns on the tops of the wrists and the front of the ankles. This suggests some kind of restraint. Maybe tying with rope, but forensics will discover that. And as you can see, our victim was gripping hard on the arms of the chair. Let's move on to the star of the show. The drill. It's a twelve-millimetre diameter drill, two-hundred millimetres long. It entered our friend's head from the left ear and exited around the area of the right. From a speculative perspective, I believe that the intention was to go ear to ear. However, even using sufficient restraint, that would still be difficult to achieve. You're drilling through bone and soft tissue. And, according to people I know who do that dirty engineering nonsense, drills wander. Any questions, so far, chaps?'

Karl shook his head. Deacon raised his hand.

'Ah. Al. Before you go to the time of death, let me finish. Judging by the skin and flies, and overall smell of decay, I believe at this stage the person died about a week ago. Again, I can be more specific at the PM. What I will say, and I don't normally engage in this speculative stuff, but I suspect the person who committed this murder is likely the same as the previous two. And the reason I say that? The extremity of the murders is obvious. But also, the inventiveness. I don't want to praise the culprit. But he, she, whoever, like before, there's nothing in the killings that's spur of the moment. The person or persons have put in time to conduct the acts in the way they're staged. And to be frank, to think that someone has the mental capacity to do this is scary. And finally, and I stress I cannot confirm this until the post-mortem, if this *is* the same person who committed the other murders, the victim was probably alive when this happened.'

With that statement giving pause for thought, Freestone picked up his bags, said goodbye and left the room. Deacon and Karl stood in silence for a moment. Deacon was certain that this would be the last of the bodies they'd find. The McGregors were the target; he was sure. But what if the people who committed these crimes had initially done it as a once in a lifetime action to avenge the McGregors? Why would they stop? They probably enjoyed it in some twisted way. He turned to Karl.

'Could you wait for the SOCOs to arrive? Ask them to pay attention to the chair. Assuming the murder took place elsewhere, as Freestone alluded, we need to know if there's any incriminating evidence on it. And if it belongs here, who removed it and how?'

'No problem, guv,' said Karl, with a nod of the head.

Following a lengthy conversation between Deacon and Pau regarding his findings at the Conference Building, and the comments of Dr Freestone, Pau thought it wise to pull together a press conference. She explained to Deacon that they needed the media to be on-side. The downside would be that she'd have to speak with them, which she didn't pretend to like. They would also work on the assumption that the third body was that of Danny McGregor. Absolutely unprecedented, but Freestone was positive based on the MO and the creativity applied to the cause of death, that it was likely to be the same person or persons involved, so it would be fair to assume that Danny would be the victim. She got her press officer to arrange a rushed gathering with the distinct instructions of not making it seem rushed. But it would be really useful if they did it in time for the six o'clock news bulletins to show live on tv to have as much coverage and impact as possible.

The press conference would be in Room 3B. Mainly because it was the most recently decorated, so would represent the force well on television. With soft pastel blue walls and gold framed portraits of the late Queen and King Charles, and nostalgic black and white framed photographs of the police force from the nineteen fifties and nineteen seventies, it was perfect. And finished with a beautifully crafted crest of the Leicestershire police force. Just inside was a table set out, again with the Leicestershire police crest printed front and centre. On top were about half a dozen microphones. A large seventy-inch screen TV screen was on the wall behind the table, with the contact telephone number for the investigation team. Deacon and Pau entered the room, which was bustling with around fifteen reporters and press teams who were noisily talking with each other. Almost immediately, the conversations stopped.

'Good afternoon. Thank you for coming on such short

notice. For those who don't know, my name is Chief Superintendent Pau. The person sitting to my left is Detective Chief Inspector Deacon. As promised, I want to give you an update on our investigation into the death of Terry McGregor and the disappearance of his brother Danny and father John. I can now confirm that we have found the bodies of Terry McGregor, whom I spoke to you about the other day, and his father, John McGregor. Preliminary tests strongly indicate the third body is Danny McGregors. The victims were in different locations around the south of the county. The information gathered so far suggests that an unknown person or persons took them from their home on the fifth of March and killed them shortly after. We offer our sincere condolences to family and friends at this difficult time. I think it would be worthwhile to hand over to the Investigating officer, DCI Deacon.' Pau turned to Deacon.

'Thank you. A lot of police work has gone into this investigation. As a result, we've been able to get to this point quickly, and put together a timeline which led to the men's unfortunate deaths. The investigation is ongoing, and we're pursuing many lines of enquiry, using all resources available to find the perpetrator or perpetrators responsible and bring them to justice. We are confident there is no danger to the public. We firmly believe that someone targeted the men. Why? We'll discover as our investigation progresses. We will, of course, release information as we see fit, but want people to appreciate that this is a complex investigation, but of the highest priority. If there is anyone with information that would be useful in our enquiry, please contact our team on the number shown on the screen behind me.'

Deacon could see some reporters vigorously typing away on their laptops to send for an updated front page. Others were still holding up their digital recorders and mobile phones. He continued.

'Again, reiterating what Chief Superintendent Pau said, this is a murder enquiry. And someone killed the men in a quite brutal manner. But I don't want to go into any further detail at this point. All we ask is you all allow us to get on with our investigation. And if any details change, we will inform you. Thank you, any questions?'

A rather unkempt man at the front raised his hand. 'Jonathon Thompson of the Daily Mail. You mentioned the deaths were quite "brutal." Could you elaborate on that, please?'

'No.' said Pau. 'Let's say they were done with an element of visceral aggression. Next question, please.'

In stark contrast to the first questioner, thought Deacon, a well-presented lady in the third row of the room raised her hand. 'Channel Four news. Do you think that there is any need for the Leicester community to worry that there is a murderer loose in the streets?'

Deacon always found these gatherings annoying. It was like no-one listened to anything that was said. But he duly obliged with an answer, because she seemed nice and maybe because she was attractive.

'No. As I said, we believe this to be targeted at the family. As to the reasons? We're still investigating.'

Pau sat quietly, tapping her fingernails on the table. A tell-tale sign to Deacon, who had known her for a long time, that she was getting either bored or frustrated.

'One more question, please?' she asked.

'Yes. Do you have a suspect for the murders yet, and if so, could you offer any other details? And if not, what makes you so sure that the public is not in danger?'

Deacon recognised the voice straight away and was hoping to close the question down before Pau bit. But she was fast out of the blocks to deal with Jeremy Bentley.

'That obviously makes no sense. Why? Why would I

possibly jeopardise the investigation to answer what is frankly a disrespectful and provocative question like that?'

The slight smirk that Bentley had on his face disappeared. Deacon thought Bentley was about to say something, but Pau was in charge and went for the submission.

'And may I say, *Jeremy Bentley*, that this isn't the place or the occasion to score points and go for a sensational headline. Three men have lost their lives. A family murdered. And they deserve the respect of us all. And that includes you. The purpose of these gatherings is to inform you of what we have discovered and what we can tell you, so that you can inform the public. That's the prime purpose of this press conference. I'm not interested in you furthering your career. I am interested in you doing your job professionally, in the correct manner and with respect for the victims and the public, like most others in this room.' Pau paused to good effect. The room was silent. She slowly scanned the room from left to right. 'Thank you.' She tapped Deacon on the arm as she rose from her chair.

Deacon could not help but smile as they left the room. He followed Pau along the corridor. She didn't turn around or speak but marched to her office. Deacon went to his office, still smiling about the belittling of Jeremy Bentley, while the red lights of the TV cameras and digital recorders were still brightly lit. Captured and stored for the public to witness. A proper dressing down. Pau at her cutting best. It would probably only be a matter of minutes before it's shared on the internet and social media outlets.

The voices in his office were far too happy as he walked through the door. Gill and Cara turned to him with big smiles on their faces. Either they'd won the lottery, or they've good news to share.

'Ladies. Sorry, team! What do I owe such joviality on such a long day?'

'The Hawthorne case is closed,' said Gill. 'We're as satisfied as we can be that there were no suspicious circumstances.'

'That's good news. So, your approach of interviewing James and Rosemary separately worked, I presume?'

'It corroborated their stories,' said Cara. 'In truth, only James will ever know what happened when he and Steven were alone, but we're satisfied.'

'Good,' said Deacon. 'If you're satisfied, I am. Have you completed the report?'

'It'll be with you in the morning,' said Gill. 'We've just watched the press conference on TV. Hopefully, that'll trigger something from the public.'

'I hope so. Actually, I'm glad you two are free. I'm holding a briefing tomorrow at eight-thirty? It would be great if you could be there?' They nodded. 'So, if you are going to celebrate your result today, maybe tone it down,' he winked.

Gill and Cara smiled. 'Of course! Our coffeeshop gathering will be purely a backslapping event, no alcohol,' said Gill, tapping the side of her nose with her finger.

Deacon laughed. 'I wouldn't expect anything else.' As Gill and Cara left the office, he said, 'By the way. A fantastic result. Well done.'

They acknowledged him and disappeared. His mobile rang. Pau's name lit on the screen. He answered.

'Hi, ma'am, it's a pleasure to have you call me. How can I help?'

'Shut up, Alex. I've just realised the significance of today.'

'Yes, it was an excellent result from Gill and...'

'Stop,' shouted Pau, so loudly that Deacon pulled the mobile away from his ear. 'Alex,' Pau continued in a calmer voice, 'what's the date today?'

'I don't know. What is it? It's...' the penny dropped, and,

not for the first time recently, he felt a surge of guilt burn into his heart.

Pau let out a sigh. 'I'm sorry, Alex. A phone call is hardly the best choice of communication. What are you doing?'

'I need to prepare for the team briefing tomorrow.'

'You don't,' responded Pau. 'You need to go home to your lovely daughter, who, I'm sure, will know what today is. The rest can wait.'

Deacon walked into the kitchen, placing the laptop on the worktop. He called Susan's name. There was no response. He called again and listened intently for an answer. Nothing. His heart began racing as he quickly climbed the stairs, two steps at a time. He approached Susan's bedroom door and knocked. There was no reply. He called her name again and waited for an answer. No response. He turned the doorknob and walked into her bedroom. She wasn't there, which was a relief, although he didn't know why. Was he expecting her unconscious with a bottle of pills spilt onto the bedside cabinet? He didn't know.

He looked around the room. Everything in it seemed to be clean and sparkling, absolutely spotless, with a really fresh smell. He was not sure what he expected, but what he realised is this was the first time he had probably set foot inside the room in over a year. Is that normal? After all, she's a young woman. It's her own private space. But it's his house, he reasoned. Then again, surely a father would have a conversation in her room. But he can't remember doing that for a long time. Since she was small, when they played with her toys. Is he really that bad a dad? So, disconnected from her? The self-reflection was too much. His head was spinning. His chest felt heavy. He was feeling emotional, teary. Why?

He felt anxious. He couldn't understand why. For Christ's sake, Susan had every right to go out. Long gone is the need to ask her parents for permission. She's probably in town with friends, gone for a drink. Or probably at the university at a late lecture? But he was panicking. Susan has been acting strange lately. Combative. Deep down, he was worried about her mental health, and how the death of her mother was affecting her and if she might harm herself. But what had he done to help? Nothing. He'd ignored her because he wasn't sure how to cope with this. Claire knew how to deal with these things. She always was great in such circumstances.

Deacon reached into his pocket and frantically searched for his daughter's number. He found it and dialled. It rang but soon went to answerphone. He cursed to himself as he hung up. He raced down the stairs and into his study. Claire stared at him with her big smile from within the gold gilded frame. Tears streamed down his face.

'I don't know where she is. What am I doing wrong?'

He checked his mobile again for a message but accidentally knocked the gilded picture onto the floor. It landed with a crash, the glass fragments breaking in front of Claire. The sight of it felt like he had stabbed her in the heart. The shards covering her beautiful smiling face.

'I'm sorry,' he cried. He stared down at her. The magic broken by the glass. His portal into her spirit. He dropped to his knees and picked up the pieces of the glass and put them on his desk alongside the hollow picture frame. He tried to compose himself.

'I've got to find Susan,' he said, staring at the frameless photograph. And then the thought came into his head. He grabbed his car keys and left the house.

. . .

The carpark was empty save for a few randomly placed cars, so he parked close to the path. He walked by the neatly pruned trees and the colourful beds of tulips and roses that flanked the stone pathway. He'd walked this once before a couple of months earlier. Only then there were few flowers, little colour and he had a heart that felt like lead. He turned onto a smaller paved area leading to the remembrance garden. In the distance, he could see the black marble headstone of Claire Deacon, surrounded by an array of blooms. And on the bench to the right of him, facing the flowers, was a person sitting absolutely still. He knew who that was. Deacon quietly approached and put his left hand on her shoulder. He felt her body jolt. She turned and stared at his hand and touched the wedding ring on his finger before holding his hand. Susan turned and looked up at her father, a face filled with both sadness and joy.

'Thank you,' she whispered.

'Can I sit with you?'

She smiled with teary eyes. 'We'd like nothing more.' She tapped the space on the bench beside her.

'I see true to form, you've forgotten a birthday present for mum.'

'As I always said....'

'I know...,' said Susan.

'...what better present could there be than me?' they said together before bursting into a mixture of laughter and tears.

'You must have said that every year,' said Susan.

'But it was true!' said Deacon as he gave his daughter an enormous hug.

They both turned towards the headstone in silence to reflect on happy memories with a wonderful mother and wife. And there they stayed for the next forty-five minutes. It was Susan who broke the silence.

'I saw you on the news earlier. Well, my friend called me to say you were on, so I watched it back on my phone.'

'Ok,' was the best Deacon could muster, not really knowing how to respond.

'You said the murders were really bad. Extreme? Brutal? I can't remember the exact word. What did you mean?'

'Let's say they were more violent than normal. Anyway, don't worry about it.' Deacon really didn't want to get into a conversation with Susan about the murder investigation.

'I realised after watching it that I've never seen you do one before. So, I searched on the net and there are quite a few. Even from the time when you had a decent amount of hair!'

'Whatever,' joked Deacon, 'I just have it cut shorter now with slight grey highlights added to make me look distinguished.'

'But seriously. What I realised is that mother here, obviously used to switch channels, so I wouldn't see them, and I was wondering why? But I think I know why?'

'Enlighten me, young lady.'

'To protect me. So, I wouldn't worry about you getting into danger. And as the head of the investigation, any of the bad guys could target you for vengeance or to just get you off their trail.'

'Susan, it's not like the television shows. I'm not tailed by bad guys everywhere I go.'

'Dad, be serious. You know it could happen. You deal with dangerous people, it's you or them.'

'Susan, please don't worry about it.'

'All I'm saying is that's what mum protected me from it all. The school plays you couldn't attend because of your job, and presentation evenings and such like? She always used to say that your job is very important and you're a hero to everyone in the city because you keep us all safe. And that used to make me feel good because I didn't know anyone else whose dad was a hero. Yet, you know what, it wasn't until today and seeing those press conferences and interviews that you'd done, that I fully realised just *how* important your job can be and *how* potentially dangerous.'

As Deacon listened, he could imagine Claire doing that, to protect Susan. But calling him a hero? He felt a lump in his throat. She'd said that to him lots of times—he could hear her saying it now. My God, she was special. He turned to Susan.

'Doctors are heroes, nurses, soldiers, fire rescue. Believe me, a lot of my job in a nutshell involves research, solving puzzles and admin. It's just time consuming.'

'Look, dad, I'm sorry,' said Susan, grabbing his hand. 'I'm getting angry at you for not being with me, for not coming here each week to remember mum and share my grief. Yet, while I'm acting like a selfish cow, you're taking my crap while spending all hours trying to find a mass murderer, which in the scheme of things is....'

'As important as our loss. I may not show it, but I feel it. Believe me, I feel it.'

'I know. I saw you the other night—in the study?'

Deacon felt embarrassed and decided not to acknowledge it. 'I'll tell you what? We're celebrating your mum's birthday. What did she love to do on her birthday?' he asked.

'Go for a pizza!'

'So why don't we carry on the tradition?'

'Great idea, dad. I take it you're paying?'

Deacon slowly shook his head. 'Yes, as always, dad will pay.'

CHAPTER NINE

DEACON ENTERED THE CROWDED ROOM. The noise was initially deafening before they realised he'd arrived, when it drew down to a whisper.

'Good morning, all. As you know, Chief Superintendent Pau and I conducted a press conference yesterday, which has obviously generated a lot more interest in the case. Clearly, we need to get things moving and solve these horrific crimes. For all the work we've done and all the avenues we've pursued, there're still too many, not necessarily dead ends but loose threads. Now, that's not any fault of ours. We've been following whatever lines of enquiry that are presented to us— but we need to close them off. Could we be looking in the wrong places, speaking to the wrong people, or asking the wrong questions? I don't know, I'm just throwing that thought out there. Think hard about those we have spoken to and whether we need to talk to them again.'

'Now we've made a specific appeal for information. I hope someone will get in touch with that golden nugget of information that will help us move forwards. The work and time that you have given to this investigation has been outstanding, so thank you. They say you're only as good as the team around you, so we're obviously fantastic! Talking of the team, I would like to welcome back into the fold DI Foster and DS Matthews, who have successfully brought the Hawthorne case to a close.'

The team clapped.

'Now, everyone's back. Let's put some focus on where we need to go. We need to revisit any evidence we've got so far. Whatever you're looking at, double check it, go back and see if we can press people further. I don't believe for one minute that no-one knows anything. It may be a good idea for you to look at evidence colleagues have got so far, like a critical friend, and maybe consider approaching it from a different angle? Karl, I want you to look again at the interview transcripts from Dudbridge Holdings. You'll be able to approach them from a more objective perspective. See if anything jumps out that's worth a follow up. As I've said, I'm sure there're people out there who know more than they're letting on, for whatever reason, and it may be quite innocent. They may not realise what they know, but we can't wait for them to come forward. We have three brutal murders, and you all have access to the details. Someone *must* have some twinges of a conscience in relation to them. We also need to think of motives for these murders. Let me remind you of what happened.'

'There was Terry McGregor, dragged along a farm track thanks to a hook through the eyes. So, someone clearly wanted him to be seen. The supporting information from the post-mortem says that he was alive when that happened. Now, I think you'll agree that's frightening. Whoever felt the need to do that, indeed, whoever can inflict such horror and pain on another human being beggar's belief. With the second murder, we found the father, John McGregor. Here, he had a material placed in his mouth along with an accelerant that was set alight. And guess what? The pathologist is pretty convinced that he was alive when this happened. Finally, and this may be new information to you, we now have a third body that we believe is Danny McGregor. And the reason we believe it's Danny and the same murderer is because when found, he had a drill through the head. Let's be honest, these murders are not normal. But there must be people out there who will know who did this. Now, I'd like to say to anyone here, if you have any thoughts on a potential connection or theory, I am open to your thoughts.'

There was some discussion within the room.

'A final point.' Deacon looked around the room at each person. 'Do not let *anyone* know what we know. Because if this gets out, it has the potential to cause absolute panic. Remain professional throughout.' Deacon paused for effect. 'Thank you all for your time. You know what you need to do and keep up the good work.'

As the team dispersed and went about their duties, Deacon asked Gill and Cara to meet him in his office.

―――――

Having got himself a coffee from the vending machine which unusually tasted coffee (ish), Deacon opened a box file that contained general case notes and thoughts. He was sorting papers on his desk when Gill and Cara entered the room, drinks in their hands.

'Ah, good to see you both, and thank you for the coffee,' said Deacon.

The pair looked a little guilty for not thinking of buying one for their boss.

'Anyway, I wanted to speak with you both out of the meeting because I want you to focus on a couple of people because I don't believe we've peeled away at the skin enough.

Margaret Wilson. As you know, Gill, we spoke with her not long after she raised the alarm at the Three Gables. Karl and I paid her a visit at her home last week, which is a very plush and expensive place in Oakham, considering she's not a business partner - allegedly.'

'So, you suspect that she's more involved with the business than she's making out, or providing *extra services* to her boss, if you know what I mean?' asked Gill.

'Suspicious, cynical me does think that, yes, but we've no evidence—yet. Maybe a long-lost aunt left her money. But I think not. She offered a lot on that visit, but we felt she was holding back, feeding us just enough information. She needs squeezing a bit more, I think.' Deacon faced Gill. 'So, I'd like you to concentrate on her, read through her file, and go from there.' Gill nodded. Deacon continued.

'There's Libby McGregor. The stepdaughter and stepsister to the dead men. Again, I've spoken with her on a couple of occasions, and she's a very interesting. She's quite a complex character. I think there's more to why she walked out of the family house and the business.'

'Do you think something happened to her personally? Something traumatic?' asked Cara.

'It's crossed my mind, yes. And the hatred, the absolute venom that she has towards the McGregors is off the scale. I'll continue talking with her because she seemed to open up a little more the last time we met.'

'Do you think she could be involved with the McGregors' deaths?' asked Gill.

'Possibly. I don't know. She believes that they're responsible for her mother's death. And in her mind, they stole the business from her family—her dad's business. Maybe they did something bad to her, but, deep down, I doubt that she'd murder the men. She certainly wouldn't be able to do it on her own, even if she was involved. No, I think her way of dealing with it is to walk away and cut that period from her life. There's a possibility that she knows something that she doesn't think to be relevant that could prove important to the investigation—it's just a feeling. And finally, we have Libby's mother, Alison McGregor, previously Alison Dudbridge. We know very little about Alison except for the vague profile that came mainly from Libby.'

Deacon continued. 'a hit-and-run driver during a trip to York killed Alison. The police never found the driver. The North Yorkshire Police have sent over the case files. I glanced through the file and couldn't see anything in there of importance to us we didn't know already. But I wonder if there is a connection between Alison's death and that of the McGregors? Libby thinks that her stepfather or stepbrothers were involved. But that's not based on no evidence. So, I'd like you to focus on Alison, Cara. Keep Libby's thoughts in the back of your mind, but don't spend hours trying to find a connection that isn't there. Now, Libby seemed to think that her mother was seeing someone—a man, a companion? A boyfriend? In fact, Alison told her so, but stopped short of saying who he was. If you read the York file, Cara, you'll notice that there's a mention of a male, but no statement. So, if he existed, why didn't he come forward? Once again, look through her file and familiarise yourself with what we know, so we can find out what we don't.'

'No problem, sir,' said Cara.

After Gill and Cara left his office, Deacon blew out a long mouthful of air, which had the effect of relaxing him. He felt good today. More rested and alert. Lighter, because of a large weight being lifted from his shoulders following his evening with Susan. They went to their favourite pizza restaurant, the Pizza Palace, where they always went with Claire and had what he can only describe as an enjoyable, no, it was better than that; it was a fun father and daughter evening. Susan was relaxed and seemed to enjoy herself, and Deacon finally felt more connected to her. It was so good to see her smile. He even challenged Susan to a pizza eating race, like they did when she was young—which he won, to the disgust of some of the other diners. Susan pointed out it was because he had a big mouth and ate like a pig! They eventually returned home and shared memories and funny stories about Claire, her mum, his wife. They both needed that. Therapy, maybe. Whatever it was, had lifted the atmosphere in the house and simmered the tensions between them. They both made their way to bed around midnight, but not before Susan saw the broken picture frame of her mother laying on his desk. She didn't ask how it got broken, but carefully picked up the glass pieces and told him she would buy a new one in the morning.

Deacon believed the return of Gill and Cara to his investigation would be a big lift. Gill Foster is a police officer he trusts, and they work well together. She has good instinct and is meticulous in her investigations. Cara Matthews has come into her own in the past couple of weeks. Her attitude is great, her work ethic is unquestionable and her sense of humour fits in perfectly with that of Deacon and Gill. And of course, there is Karl. Deacon has warmed to him significantly on this investigation, having watched him close hand. In the absence of Gill, he and Karl had to pair up quite a bit. Karl is growing in confidence all the time and giving him the lead at Dudbridge Holdings is Deacon's way of letting Karl know he is trusting him more and giving him the extra responsibility. He just hoped he didn't let him down.

———

Cara uploaded the documents from a range of files relating to Alison McGregor. She and Gill had spent the previous two hours reading up on the case and talking to various colleagues to get up to date on the developments so far. In truth, although consumed by the Hawthorne's case, both she and Gill had also monitored this investigation. But it was really useful for them both to read through the documents in the case file and talk it through with each other. Following lunch at the local coffee bar, they were now sitting at their desks, wearing headphones to cut out the office noise and concentrating on their allocated tasks. Cara loves music but plays none when working. She likes silence. Cara was savvy enough to recognise that Deacon chose her to conduct something that he considered important and something that she did well, which made her feel accepted as part of his team.

The professional relationship between her and Gill had come on by leaps and bounds. In many respects, they were opposites. Gill could be brash and muscular, built like a Russian shot putter, but had a heart of gold when you got to know her and is very 'naughty'. Cara knew fully that she was lucky in terms of her looks and figure. But in this job, it can work against you. And she believed it had because she had not taken seriously in the past and had lost credibility. For God's sake, she can't help how she looks. But it certainly seems if Gill had a problem with it, she doesn't anymore.

Cara uploaded a picture of Alison, the one sent by Libby, she assumed. She stared at the face. A good-looking woman. Far younger looking than her age. Cara wondered what Libby looked like—if she shared her mother's looks, her genes. Alison McGregor had a face that was a stranger to Cara, yet familiar. Reading through the report of the accident that took Alison's life, Cara could see why some people might view it as suspicious. Hit and runs are often accidental, and involve, for whatever reason, the driver to take off. That's what happened in York. But it seemed different. Alison's body lying on a minor road off of the beaten track. Planned or coincidence? She was also unconvinced that a woman who, along with her husband, builds a successful business, and then allows her second husband take that from her. It just didn't seem the thing you would do, even if she only wanted to hold on to it for sentimental reasons. No. There are several things that seemed odd. Cara jotted down some thoughts on in her notepad to determine her next actions.

Deacon sat trance-like in his office, trying to find a connection in his brain that could trigger a chain reaction of sorts to get the case moving. Things were pretty static at the moment. Yes, they had the bodies, and he was still waiting for the pathologist, Dr Freestone, to conduct the post-mortem and hopefully confirm the identity of the third body to be that of Danny McGregor. But as always, nothing moves as quickly as he'd like, and he knew well that Dr Freestone had responsibilities to more people than just himself. Nonetheless, in Deacon's world, his was the most important. The sudden noise of the phone ranging jolted him from his thoughts. He picked up the receiver.

'Good morning, sir. It's Katie from the Incident Line. We've received a call from a lady. She specifically asked for you, said she saw you on the news and has some potential information about the McGregor family. Are you Ok to take the call?'

Deacon could feel his heart pounding. 'Of course! Put her through.' He gathered his thoughts and kept the receiver to his ear until he heard the click of the transfer. 'Hello?'

'Hello,' came a soft, nervous sounding voice at the other end. 'Is that Chief Inspector Deacon?'

'Yes, it is. Who's speaking?'

'I'd rather not go there yet. I'm calling because I may have some information for you about the family - you know, the

McGregors? It's not about their murders. I know nothing about their murders. I need to make that clear. But there's something I know about them which may give you some background of what they were like. My experiences of them and why people may have wanted to kill them. Could we meet somewhere to talk?'

'Of course. Where? Do you want to come to the station?'

'No, no. I don't want to go there. You never know who's watching. They used to have people everywhere.'

'Ok,' replied Deacon, wondering what she meant by that. 'Where do you suggest?'

'Do you know Bradgate Park?' she asked.

'Of course.'

'The Hunts Hill carpark?'

Deacon had to think. It was not an entrance to the park he had used, but remembered reading about issues the Park Trust was having with vandalism and fly tipping. 'Is that the one near the Old John Tower and the War Memorial?' he asked.

'That's it. Can we meet there? I have a red Mini One. If you can make it, we can walk, and a talk is that Ok?'

'That's fine. When?'

'Two o'clock today. Is that too short a notice?' she said.

'I'll be there,' replied Deacon. And with that, she hung up.

He held the phone receiver to his ear long after the line went dead. It was intriguing, and he was more than a little excited that this could prove a valuable call that moves the investigation forwards. Whoever this lady is, she has a strong enough conviction to reach out to him with something she believes to be important. He felt confident his trip to Bradgate park this afternoon would be worth his while.

Deacon guessed that the drive to Bradgate park would take no more than thirty-five to forty minutes. He drove further from the city into the countryside. The openness of the fields had a magical effect, making Deacon feel more relaxed. As he got nearer the park, the road became more winding and scenic, with the low hedgerows that lined the lane revealing the open space, the green fields, and small woods. He drove over a small bridge that seemed mystical, with bellows of smoke rising from each side as the Great Central steam train passed underneath. A little further, he drove through a dark tunnel, a result of tree branches and new season leaves meeting high above, forming a canopy, starving the road below of light. Small specks of sunshine made brief appearances through occasional gaps in the leaves like twinkling stars, making the experience special.

Deacon thought back to his trips here as a child with his parents. His friends would talk about the place and the special days they had there with their families. It was a cheap day out when money was tight, and life seemed simpler. They would explore all corners of the park, yet each time they visited, would discover something new. Playing in the open spaces, having picnics, looking for the deer that roamed the park and running up Old John hill, trying to be first to reach the tower. Deacon smiled to himself. He was pretty certain if he tried the run now, he'd require medical treatment and a considerable amount of oxygen before he even reached halfway.

A sign finally directed him into the parking area. There were probably thirty cars neatly parked in random bays. He spotted the red Mini One parked to the left of the parking meter. He pulled into the space next to her. As he punched in his registration details at the parking meter, the lady from the Mini joined him.

'Extortionate, isn't it?'

'I've paid less for more,' replied Deacon with a smile.

'Chief Inspector Deacon, I presume?' she said.

'It is. And you are?'

'There's plenty of time for introductions.' She looked around the carpark. 'Put your ticket in your car and we can walk.'

He placed the ticket on the dashboard of his car and caught up with the young woman as she walked around the side of the closed metal gate, used to prevent vehicles going any further along the tarmacked pathway.

They initially made their way in silence, walking past dog walkers returning to their cars and joggers in spandex garments - some wearing them well, others would have been better with something looser. The path became loose stone, which led to the entrance to the park. And there in front of them was Old John Tower.

Walking in the park grounds towards the Tower, Deacon used the time to profile his companion. In old money, she was around five feet eight inches tall with an athletic build. She had a long attractive face that was tanned with sharp features and straight brown hair that was just below the shoulder. The blue three-quarter slacks with cream leather sandals showed her neatly manicured and painted toenails. She completed the look with a tight-fitting black Ramones tee-shirt, accentuating her large, rounded breasts. The gold band on her finger showed she was married, and the two small names tattooed on the back of her hand near her thumbs were probably children's names, although he couldn't read what they said.

After navigating a few metres up some rocks, they arrived at the tower; she barely broke into a sweat, whist he was glad they'd actually made it. Around the wall of the monument was stone seating where you could lean back against the tower and stare out at the scene before you. There were miles of green land and trees unspoiled by modern technology. Innocent, silent and safe, which Deacon surmised was why she wanted to meet him here. They can see everyone around any approach. There's no chance anyone could surprise her. That's exactly what she wanted. And he fully understood.

She turned to him. 'It's beautiful, isn't it?'

'It is. But I know you haven't brought me all the way out here to admire the view, as lovely as it is. Are you ready to talk?'

Her body seemed to stiffen before nodding. For a few seconds, she stared at the scenery before her and placed her hands on her lap, turning her wedding ring on her finger. She took a deep breath and began.

'I worked at Dudbridge Holdings for about three years. I really enjoyed it. The people were great and like a big family. I looked after the accounts, along with another colleague, Margaret Wilson. To be fair, she was like the team leader, I suppose, so was in charge. Just about everything business-wise went through me. Although there were some "special clients" that only Margaret dealt with.' She signified the "special clients" with her fingers. 'I didn't know who they were, but assumed that they were high profile, or their cases were more sensitive. Anyway, after about a year of working there, Danny McGregor appeared more in the office and seem to take a shine to me. He would come in almost daily to talk to me and flirt, I guess you could call it, putting on the charm. This went on for a few weeks before he eventually asked me out on a kind-of date. I wasn't sure at first because he was one of the bosses, but eventually I thought, why not? So, we started seeing each other regularly, and we'd go to the cinema or to a restaurant or to a pub, and we seemed to get along really well and have so many laughs. He was great fun and lovely, at the start at any rate. Things between us developed and then, you know, it became a more serious relationship.'

'So, I spent odd nights with him at his place. We never stayed at mine because lived with my parents in a cottage they rented and it was just too small And to be honest, I didn't feel comfortable about us doing it there anyway, if you know what I mean. My parents really liked him. He used to come to our house regularly to pick me up, so would talk with them while I was getting ready. Like I said, he was great, absolutely charming.' She went quiet and stared directly in front of her.

'Are you Ok?' asked Deacon.

The young lady nodded and continued.

'But you know, as time went on, he got a bit too much, really. He'd come in the office and sit next to me and put his hand up my skirt while people in the office, you know? And the sex started getting really rough. He was getting more masochistic, like he was trying to hurt. One day, he tied my wrists to the frame of the headboard, and we did it that way. When he finished, he put on a dressing gown and left the room with me still strapped to the bed. As he was walking towards the door, I was telling him to untie me, but he just kept walking and closed the door behind him. Anyway, the next thing.....'

Deacon could see tears rolling down her cheeks. 'Do you want to take a break? We can go for a coffee?' he said.

She pulled a tissue from her pocket and wiped her eyes. The whites now tinted red as she looked at Deacon, shaking her head.

'It's alright. I don't think I've ever spoken about this before. The emotions.... I didn't expect. Shall we walk towards the river?'

She stood, and they both walked down the hill along a dusty path.

'Where was I? So, I'm left in his room and the door opens, and I assumed he'd got himself a coffee or such like. But no, he entered the room and, to my horror, called his brother to show me lying there, naked, tied to the bed. Absolutely embarrassing. And Terry stood in the doorway with a big smile on his face and said something like, "nice lay, Danny". I felt like shit. And then he called his dad to see what Danny had got himself. By now I was crying, hysterical, hurling abuse at the perverted bastards, and I think I was begging them to go away. But John turned up and came up to the bed, inspecting me. I was kicking and screaming at this point. I felt absolutely humiliated. John was laughing at me and turned to his sons and said something like, "oh, the poor little whore seems upset about something". They found it hysterical. Eventually Terry and John cleared off.'

Tears flowed from her eyes, and she began to breathe heavily. She wiped her eyes, this time with the back of her hands. Deacon touched the back of her arm as an offer of comfort. She held up her hand, determined to continue.

'I was screaming abuse at Danny, but he just smiled at me and undid his robe. He got turned on and climbed on top of me. I was kicking at him, but he grabbed my legs and have his way. While he was raping me, because that's what it was, he was saying through gritted teeth how much he loved a bit of rough and told me to keep resisting because when I'm tense the sex was even better. It finally ended. And, like nothing had happened, Danny went for a shower and left me tied to the bed. I felt cheap, naïve, abused, and humiliated. When he came back, I shouted at him to untie me. Eventually, after God knows how long just laughing at me, he did. The first thing I did when my hands were free was slap him across the face as hard as I could and told him what a complete bastard he was. He just smiled at me as if he felt nothing. It must have had some effect because the side of his face turned bright red and his nose started bleeding. I got dressed as quickly as I could and left. I had my purse with me so caught a bus to town and then home.'

'That sounds like a terrifying ordeal,' said Deacon.

They stopped, and both leaned against a rock wall, staring

out into the park area with lush grass and brambles. There were some deer in the distance, slowly wandering about, chewing the grass. A peaceful sight, he thought, in contrast to what he'd just heard. The pair of them stared in silence at the landscape.

'That's just one aspect of who they were. Give me a minute and I'll tell you the rest.' She pointed towards the Deer. 'Look at them. Serene, beautiful free spirits and with the rangers, safe from predators and danger. I suppose that's all we really want, isn't it?'

Deacon nodded in agreement. 'Although confined. As big a space as it is, this area is the only world they'll ever know.'

'I think we all live in a confined space when you think about it. Most people may go further afield for a holiday, but in our day-to-day lives, we exist within set parameters; self-imposed maybe, but confined all the same.'

Even though Deacon could argue the point on a number of fronts, he found it an interesting concept. He turned to the lady next to him. 'Would now be a good time to ask your name?'

She gave a wry smile. 'It's Jessie. Jessie Ryan. Mrs. Back then I was Jessie Bateman.'

'Thank you, Jessie,' said Deacon. 'Why didn't you want to give me your name before?'

'I needed to meet you first. To know if I could trust you.'

'And I presume I've passed that test?'

'Yes. But then again, as you've probably realised, I'm not a great judge of character. Shall we walk?'

They made their way back to the footpath. There were very few people out on this side of the park, except for the occasional dog walker.

'So, tell me more, Jessie.'

'Right. Following that day at the Three Gables, I'd taken a week off from work, claiming to be sick. I just couldn't face the place and especially the thought of Danny being there, near me. During that time, I never contacted him, and he didn't contact me. But I knew I'd either have to face him at some point or leave the job, which I didn't want to do. When I did return, he seemed to keep out of the way. I'd see him walking by the office and occasionally look my way, but didn't come close. I don't know if my colleague Margaret knew anything, because she acted weird and, as I've said, she was like the designated boss.

After a couple of weeks, a box of chocolates appeared at my desk one morning. And then the next day, Margaret, who was sorting out the end of months' accounts with me, disappeared from her desk and who should come over and sit in her place but Danny. As you can imagine, I told him what to do with himself but, at the end of the day it's his family's company so he could do what he wanted. I tried to ignore him, but he kept bugging me and his voice was getting louder so people in the office were beginning to glance over. I told him that if he lowers his voice I'd listen, just to stop him embarrassing me in front of my work mates. He asked me if I wanted to go out. No apologies for what he'd done—not that an apology would ever be enough after what he did to me. I just kept saying no, but he kept asking. In the end I was getting angry and frustrated, and I told him that he had some cheek to even speak with me after what he'd done. He just smiled and said that deep down I should admit that I enjoyed it as much as he did. That lit the fuse for me. I turned to him and whispered in his ear, something along the lines, "I'm going to do what I should have done a few weeks ago. I'm going to the police and report you for rape". Now I don't know if I imagined it, but his face dropped, and that smug smile on that bastard's face disappeared. He got up and walked out. And guess what? Ten minutes later Margaret conveniently returns to her desk. Coincidence? She was staring daggers at me, so I guess not.'

'Do you think she knew about the rape?' asked Deacon.

'I don't know. But she knew something, I'm sure.'

'Did you report the rape, because I can't recall seeing anything in his file?'

'No. Let me explain why. The same day I told Danny I was reporting him, something happened. I left at the end of the day as usual. As I'm walking through the carpark, John McGregor pulls up beside me in his black Range Rover. The tinted window of his door winds down. "Hello Jessie," he said. "How are things." As you can imagine, I must have gone beetroot red knowing the last time he saw me I was tied to a bed, naked as he inspected me and referred to me as a whore. My mouth was dry, but I didn't want to be intimidated by him, so I told him all was well. "Do your parents still rent out that lovely cottage in Liddington?" he asked. So, I said, "Yes." "It's a beautiful place, lovely views, very picturesque," he said. I agreed and told him that Mum and Dad love it there and to them it was the perfect life. "I can see why," he said, and closed his window and drove off to park his car. That unsettled me, I don't know why. I suppose him not mentioning what had happened at the house; don't get me wrong, I would have died of embarrassment if he had, but I don't know. I assumed he was playing mind games. How wrong I was.'

There was an empty bench on the grass off from the path.

'Do you fancy a sit down for a while?' She asked.

'Why not,' he said. They made their way over to the wooden bench and sat down to face more glorious views. Jessie again seemed lost in the scenery for a minute or so before continuing.

'Everything seemed to go quiet over the following couple of weeks and work was getting back to how it was before, enjoyable again. Even Margaret seemed cheerful and happy and nearly fun to work with. But one day I got a call from my mother. She was hysterical. I'd never heard her like that before in my life. My parents had received an eviction notice. There were new owners of the cottage, and they wanted mum and dad out of the place within a month. The family who had owned it were getting on a bit, I suppose, and had sold it. Apparently, a buyer came from out of the blue and offered a substantial amount of cash, above the value of the property, so it was a no brainer. My parents were devastated. They never had a great deal of savings, and the owners of the cottage let them rent at low rates on the condition that they kept it in a fit state of repair, which they did. They were distraught, and it was causing so many problems trying to find them somewhere to live at a price they could afford at such short notice. We eventually had to settle for a small bungalow on the outskirts of the city, but it was chalk and cheese for them. They were never really happy after that.

Anyway, a while later, I was at my desk and Margaret was away from hers, probably checking on the other girls in the office. She left a pile of files on her desk, so intrigued, I looked. There were some high-profile names and landowners, along with more unscrupulous ones. And then I saw it. Mum and Dad's dream cottage, and guess who the buyers were?'

'The McGregor's?' said Deacon.

'Yes. It's not the type of property the company purchased. We dealt in farms and smallholdings. They bought it out of spite, and I assumed as a warning for me to keep my mouth shut. And that really angered me. When Margaret returned, I slammed the file on her desk and asked her if she was in on it and what she knew. She looked terrified that I'd seen in the file. She picked it up and scuttled off somewhere out of the way. Obviously to tell her beloved boys. I was seriously considering walking out of the job there and then, but, you know, I wasn't stupid. I needed the money until I could find something else. Although, that changed.

The next day, Margaret Wilson wasn't about at the start, which was unusual because she was always checking up on us first thing in the morning. I assumed she was keeping out of my way. I was expecting some response from John, a disciplinary of such. But what happened was worse. John, Terry and Danny McGregor walked into the office around ten am with Margaret towing along behind. John told us all some money had gone missing, and, although they don't suspect anyone, as such, they would need to check everyone's desk. So, they were going to conduct a search. Obviously, none of us would have dreamt of stealing anything from the business, so were quite happy for them to search our desks. But, when they got to mine...hey, presto, guess what they found?'

'Was it money, by any chance?' said Deacon.

'Yeah. Absolutely stitched up. And they marched me out in front of everyone as a thief. Bastards. Before they threw me out of the door, I told them I know why they had done this, and I was definitely going to the police to report Danny now. And Terry grabbed me by the arm and told me in no uncertain terms that this was just the beginning. Go to the police and I'll see what they're really capable of doing. And that threat stuck with me. Now, why do I think my story is important? Why have I spent the past hour humiliating myself again to you? Because I'm a no-one in the scheme of things. Yet they did what they did, and they had some really powerful clients who, I would guess, won't take lightly any form of bullying or intimidation from them. They'll do something about it. Maybe have the McGregors killed. Over to you Chief Inspector.'

Taken slightly by surprise with the sudden handover, Deacon spent a few seconds absorbing Jessie's story. He felt sorry for her. Interestingly, what Jessie said wasn't a million miles away from what the team had deduced regarding the McGregors. Danny's fascination with sex, their kindred protectionism, and a willingness to close ranks to support each other. As for the bullying, he hoped Karl would come up trumps back at Dudbridge Holdings, with more evidence of it happening. He'd had listened intently. What he'd heard made sense of what they knew already. Although what Jessie told him was explosive. However, there was still something niggling him.

'Why now?' he asked.

Jessie raised her eyebrows. 'Because they're dead. And now I can talk about it and feel safe doing so.'

Deacon stared into her eyes, which were a stunning green colour. 'Safe, really? You wouldn't give me your name when you called and when we met here initially. You didn't want to come to the station in case there was somebody watching. When you arrived at the car park, you were scanning the area, clearly looking for anyone suspicious who may have followed you. And you chose a location where we could and talk with a panoramic view, so there was no way anyone could creep up and surprise us. Hardly the actions of a carefree soul? So, why now?'

Deacon knew fully that Jessie had bared her soul and had found it stressful, but he needed to know the reason. If it's for pure revenge, he would have to tread carefully on what he accepted from the story and what he may consider being embellished.

It was now Jessie's turn to stare deep into Deacon's eyes. 'Because I need to get this monkey off of my back. The burden. The weight of that period of my life has seriously impeded my life since. I want it to disappear from my memory. And the only way I can see I can do it is to talk to you and hope that it helps with the investigation. Also, Chief Inspector, I'm married now. I have two lovely children. But it hasn't been easy since that time. Relationships have been difficult. The boyfriends I've lost who just couldn't cope with my paranoia and the need for me to lock all doors before I engage in any intimacy with them, not allowing them to be even slightly adventurous. Finally, I found someone who loves me for who I am, quirks and all, paranoia and all. Seriously, Chief Inspector, they nearly ruined my life. My confidence. But now? Yes, it's difficult for me sometimes, but I now have a family who I love and who love me back. I never thought that would ever happen. That's why. Those guys were dangerous. Believe me. If they wanted something, they'd get it.'

Deacon could see that she was holding back the tears. 'Did you ever speak to anyone else about what happened?'

She paused. 'There was one person who talked to me and would offer, you know, a shoulder to cry on. She believed me. She suggested at the time that I report them, but... after what they did and the threat from Terry. No way.'

'Did you keep in touch?' asked Deacon.

'Only for a short while after because I just wanted to put everything behind me. But you know what? I always had the feeling....'

'About what?'

'It doesn't matter. I was going to say something that was speculative, which doesn't help.'

'Try me, Jessie.'

She gave a sigh. 'I don't know. I just had the feeling that she'd also experienced a similar thing with them, which could have been even worse in her position.'

'Why, what position?' asked Deacon.

'Because she was Danny's sister,' said Jessie.

Deacon's heart was pounding. 'Libby?'

Jessie's eyes widened. 'You know her?' she said, surprised.

'I do indeed,' he replied.

Cara removed her headphones and placed them on the desk. She brushed her fingers through her hair to make it feel lighter and airier. As she slowly massaged her temples, she looked at the time on the monitor—7.48pm. Save for the odd bathroom break, she'd been gathering information for around nine hours straight! It had been a productive day. She'd created an electronic folder and filled it with the fruits of her labour based on the hit-and-run case of Alison McGregor in York, full of documents that she could download and notes official reports. The folder also included the case file relating to Alison's case and relevant police statements.

Following Deacon's instructions, she used the day to collate as much information as possible, rather than wasting time reviewing and analysing it. Tomorrow, with a clear head, she can analyse and contrast the information in detail and make assumptions and potential connections. Earlier, Cara had a phone conversation with DCI Phil Cooper, of the North Yorkshire Police force. It was his team that was assigned to Alison McGregor's accident. He was most helpful and remembered the case clearly. He also told Cara that all of her visits Alison made to the Royal York Hotel included a male friend that was apparently lovely and good fun. The staff had nothing bad to say about him. The staff assumed he was Alison's boyfriend, because they couldn't imagine her as a woman with "a bit on the side". However, on the day she was hit by the car, he didn't show up, even though she had booked a double room as always.

The Hotel's staff were able to give a description of Alison's companion, and all agreed that his name was Andrew. But they couldn't remember ever seeing proof of this, be it a debit or card. When he paid at the bar, he always paid cash. The investigation team had carried out the normal lines of enquiry to identify Andrew, but there was simply no trace. Nothing on Alison's mobile phone, no emails, when they checked her computer, no letters, nothing. The team even considered her having a second phone, used to contact him and arrange their clandestine meetings, but again, there was nothing. It was like he didn't exist. The investigating team still considered Andrew a person of interest but not necessarily involved in Alison's cause of death. This was mainly because he had not booked in at the Hotel or seen on that day. DCI Cooper promised to send the case file over to Cara asap as she thanked him for his time.

Following the call Cara tried to make sense of what she'd been told. The unidentified man was intriguing. Yet, there was a possibility that Andrew was the driver of the vehicle that killed Alison that day. Maybe they had an argument, although killing her would have been an over-reaction on any level. Of course, she and Andrew could have been found out. Could John McGregor had taken it upon himself to make his wife pay? All considerations, all possibilities, but not for now. But tomorrow, Cara would look at what she had, compare it to the case report and the statements and bring in whatever other information she had to triangulate and validate a sequence of events and the players.

Deacon was pleasantly surprised when he arrived home. Susan was busy boiling a pan of pasta whilst another pan had a red, meaty sauce simmering away.

'What's the occasion?' he asked.

'Firstly, I'm hungry and feel obliged to make you something before you moan that I'm selfish and only looking after my own wellbeing,' said, with her usual air of sarcasm.

'And I would.'

'I know, Dad. But more importantly, I thought that it would be useful to keep you well fed because, what's the saying, healthy food, healthy mind? As my birthday's coming up, I need your decision making regarding my present to be well considered.' They both laugh.

When they sat down to eat, Deacon opened a bottle of Pinot Noir for them to share. He really enjoyed sitting with her and chatting about, not just her mum, but the weather, politics and why the Beatles are better than the crap she listens to. Ok, maybe that was more of a mocking debate. It was good food, good company, good wine, and an ever-growing relationship developing between himself and his daughter. Following the meal, he offered to wash the dishes and so Susan finished the last of her wine, she only had the one, which was fine, it meant more for him. She then went up to her bedroom to chill out and have a read.

Once the kitchen was cleaned, Deacon picked up his glass and the wine bottle and walked into his study. And there was the second surprise of the evening. Claire was smiling at him from a new gilded frame. The broken fragments of glass nowhere to be seen. He leaned towards the photograph, stared into her eyes and smiled.

'Our beautiful daughter is turning into you, Claire,' he said, and kissed the picture. He spent another twenty minutes reflecting on the evening whist he finished off the wine. He decided to have an early night so retired to bed.

Deacon lay in bed, eyes closed but very much awake. He'd spent much of the day re-reading reports, interview transcripts and notes, and reviewing for the umpteenth time the evidence gathered thus far. Karl called earlier. After reading through statements taken from the Dudbridge staff previously, he felt there were a couple of people, if the statements are verbatim, who deserved a follow-up, away from the company offices, and especially away from the watchful eye of Margaret Wilson. Deacon had agreed that it was a good idea.

The meeting with Jessie had been really useful in giving a more rounded profile to the murdered men. It supported their profiling of the men. They certainly seemed to be ruthless in their business dealings. But what Deacon found particularly unsettling was their absolute commitment to each other; their willingness to cover each other's backs, no matter what the crime. Blood is certainly thicker than water. Jessie gave good examples of that in practice. And of course, her mention of Libby McGregor gave him more reason to take Libby more seriously.

He opened one eye and reached for his mobile to check the time. 1:23am. He really needed to get some sleep, but as he closed his eyes, his brain felt like it was fizzing. He assumed it was working in the background. The neurons exploring potential pathways. Searching for new doorways, looking for connections, solving puzzles and generating some kind of logic to his thoughts. He took long breaths, hoping it may relax his body more so he could doze off to sleep. But his brain was having none of it. So, he felt compelled to go with the flow.

The way the men died is significant. Why? He stills has to figure that out. Were the murderers, and he's sure there's more than one, sending out a statement? He believed so. What did the pathologist say? He said the deaths were creative. So, if there was a message, who's it for? After all, there's no point if no one understands the message. A lot of thought went into the killings, a lot of planning, premeditation. Deacon believed if he could decipher the message, he could identify the killers.

He tried again, slow, deep breaths to relax his body and

hopefully exchange his busy mind for sleep. This time, it seemed to work. He was feeling more relaxed. Lighter. The fizzing sensation in his brain was fading.

The computer had just finished the slow process of verifying numerous security codes that Cara had to confirm to load up the ever-increasing programmes installed by the police computer system. During which she ate and really enjoyed her breakfast bap, purchased from the shop around the corner and washed it down with her freshly made mug of tea. She was now finally able to get to work. With some anticipation, she opened the email sent by DCI Cooper of the North Yorkshire Police. He had simply typed FYI. The first was the report, which she would read it in more detail later, but for now just scanned through, mainly to see how much information there was. When she opened the second attachment, a photograph displayed on the monitor piqued her interest. The picture was of Alison, taken in a pub or hotel bar. Alison was smiling at the camera and was holding what looked like a glass of wine towards the camera. Cara was about to close the image when she noticed something.

On the wrist of the hand that held up the glass was a bracelet. It was quite an unusual piece of jewellery. It was a large, beaded bracelet made up of either stones or wood shaped like large Brazil nuts? Laid out in alternative colours of brown and cream. But in the middle was one small green round bead about the size of a pea, separating them. The green bead was distinctive but spoilt a nice piece of jewellery. Where had she seen that before?

CHAPTER TEN

Although Deacon had been awake half the night, he felt alert and refreshed following his shower. He stood in the kitchen, putting on his tie, waiting for the toast to eject from the far too powerfully sprung toaster. It didn't take long before it popped, and the two slices of hot toasted bread did their normal leap out of the machine and onto the worktop. He was about to grab the butter as his mobile rang. He picked up the device.

'Hello, Deacon,' he answered.

'Sir, it's Cara... Will you be in the station first thing?'

'I'll be there in about forty-five minutes. Why, what's wrong?' he asked.

There was a pause. 'Because I think I know who Alison McGregor's boyfriend is, whatever you want to call him. The man she used to meet in York,' she said, barely containing the excitement in her voice.

Now it was Deacon's turn to get excited. 'Who?'

'Steven Hawthorne.'

'Are you sure? What makes you think it's him?'

'I'll need to show you, sir. There are a few things.'

'I'll be there at around eight-thirty. Call Gill to see if she can meet us in my office. I'll contact Karl.'

'Ok, sir.'

Deacon picked up his toast, thinking of what Cara had said. He threw the toast into the bin, grabbed his coat and bag, and made his way to the station.

DC Karl Goodman was the last to arrive and joined the others, taking coffee from the make-do tray, which in reality was a cardboard lid from a box. After the initial greetings, Deacon got things moving.

'It's good to see everyone. We may have something here that influences our investigation. Let's listen to what Cara's discovered.'

'Thank you, sir. As you all know, I've been finding out what I could about Alison McGregor, particularly regarding the hit-and-run that took her life in York. I've gathered several documents I still need to analyse. However, yesterday, I spoke with DCI Cooper of the North Yorkshire Police, who was the investigating officer for the incident. During their enquiries, they discovered Alison went to York about once a month, and stayed at the same hotel called the Royal York. So, nothing too out of the ordinary there. But she always shared a room with a man. Now, this is where it gets interesting. The staff knew him as "Andrew", but couldn't confirm his full name, and none of the staff ever remembered seeing anything that would identify him as such. A credit or debit card, for example. He always paid cash at the bar, and Alison always settled the bill.'

'I suppose if he didn't want any trace of where he was, for example, if he was married, then cash is best, rather than an embarrassing transaction on a bank statement,' said Deacon.

'And "Andrew" may not be his name?' suggested Karl.

'That's true,' said Cara. 'And I'll come to that. Anyway, DCI Cooper sent the case file as promised, which is quite substantial, and again, because of time, I haven't been able to read it yet. But it was something else that gave me the connection to Steven Hawthorne. The file, as you'd expect, had a photograph of Alison McGregor.' Cara held up a print of the photograph and stuck it onto the office wall with sticking putty. 'It's a different photograph to the one we've been using and features something very distinctive—the bracelet. As soon as I saw it, I recognised it. It's quite a nice piece of jewellery but it's spoilt by the pairing of the two dark stones, or whatever they are, which disrupts the alternate pattern of the piece. And there's that little, horrible green stone in the middle, which doesn't seem to fit at all.'

Gill looked closely at the bracelet on the photograph.

'Do you recognise it, Gill?' Asked Cara.

'Not necessarily, *recognise*,' said Gill, 'but there is something familiar about it.'

'I'm intrigued,' said Deacon, getting a little impatient with the Agatha Christie type of reveal, but appreciating that if what Cara's discovery is significant, it could be the break they've been looking for. 'Please, put us out of our misery.'

'Sorry, sir. Now we know Steven Hawthorne would go away some weekends to draw, which was a passion of his. It's mainly buildings or street scenes. Gill and I looked through tons of his stuff, which is high quality. He was quite a talented artist. But, among the piles of drawings was a couple of sketches sketch of a woman, which is beautifully drawn and very detailed—even down to the bracelet.' Cara held up another sheet of paper which had a print of the drawing in question. She stuck it on the wall next to the picture of Alison. 'This is where I'd seen the bracelet before,' she said, pointing at the pictures.

Everyone stared at the two pictures, and Deacon had to admit that the similarity of the bracelet was uncanny. But is it enough to make such a connection?

'I see what you mean, but it could be coincidence,' said Deacon. 'We need more.'

'And I have more,' said Cara. 'When Gill and I saw the sketches originally, we commented on what a great piece of work they were, but how he wasn't that good at faces because it looked nothing like his wife. I think that's because it isn't his wife. It's Alison.'

Deacon looked at the faces of the two images and couldn't help but see the resemblance. It was striking. The shape of the mouth, the nose, the shape of the eyebrows, the way she brushed her hair behind her ear. Now, he was getting excited, and believed Cara was really onto something.

'And finally,' said Cara, eyes widening, 'I quickly put together a bit of a table with the descriptions given by the staff at the Hotel of their man "Andrew". I compared them with those supplied in the pathology report, and from my own recollections. I've highlighted the similarities in yellow.' Cara handed each of the team a sheet with a table printed on it with several bright yellow sections. 'As you can see, it strongly suggests that Steven Hawthorne and Andrew are the same person.'

'That is impressive work, Cara. Thank you and well done,' said Deacon before turning to the rest of the team. 'I suggest we take an hour to digest that we've learnt and get together again at eleven o'clock?'

When Gill, Karl and Cara had left the office, Deacon swigged the last of his coffee, wincing - he hated cold coffee. He studied the two pictures for a while. The more he looked, the more convinced he became Cara had got it absolutely right. And the descriptions given by the staff in York, and their similarity to Steven Hawthorne's profile, cemented his opinion further. He has two people, part of two separate investigations that are romantically linked. That was too coincidental for his liking. Either their relationship influenced one of the cases in some way or both.

The food arrived via bicycle by an overly fit delivery man with minutes to spare. The smell from the pizzas began absorbing every inch of Deacon's office. On cue, Gill, Cara, and Karl suddenly reappeared.

'Take note,' said Gill, 'the boss has finally treated the team.' Everyone laughed.

'Mock as much as you like, Gill. It may be the last time if you continue roasting me,' he said, with a smile. 'Have as much as you want, everyone.'

They all grabbed some slices and put them onto the odd assortment of plates that Deacon had found in the canteen/kitchen area. They sat at a makeshift table at the side of the room that Deacon had hastily put together. As they were settling down for their meeting, Pau walked into the room.

'Good morning, everyone.'

'Morning, ma'am,' replied Gill, along with nods and smiled from the others.

'Do you mind if I have a slice of pizza? The smell's driving me mad.'

Pau grabbed a pizza slice and walked closer to Deacon.

'I was at a strategy meeting this morning with our colleagues from the SOCO unit. Oh, Trevor Jardine sends his love.' Deacon smirked at the comment. Pau continued, 'and the forensic and pathology labs. And guess who I met? The elusive Dr David Freestone. A charming man and hilarious.'

That could have gone the other way had Freestone been in one of his dark humour moods, thought Deacon.

'Anyway, he said that he'd completed the postmortem on

the third victim and can confirm that it's Danny McGregor. Right down to, I quote, "the clap he seems to have caught along the way".' Pau smiled and shook her head. 'Only he has the charm to get away with saying such things. He assured me he'd send over his initial findings.'

'I thought so. When does he think he died?'

'He estimates around forty-eight hours before you found him. So, the murderer seems to have kept him alive longer than the others, which matches with Dr Freestone's other findings of dehydration and an empty stomach.'

Deacon was quickly trying to compute what he had just learned. 'Thank you. At least we know for sure who we have and a timeframe.'

'Pleasure.' Pau placed the last piece of the pizza slice into her mouth and made her way towards the door, grabbing another slice as she passed the table.

Deacon shook his head and smiled. 'Ok, throw in any thoughts or ideas as you see fit. So, do we all agree Alison was meeting a friend during her weekend jaunts, and strongly believe that person to be Steven Hawthorne?'

Everyone did.

'A Question. Does anyone here think there's a connection between Alison McGregor and Steven Hawthorne's deaths?'

'The three of us were discussing this earlier,' said Gill. 'A car killed one of them and the other was a suicide. So, from that perspective, it's difficult to make a connection. Although Cara has a thought on this.' Gill looked at Cara.

'I have two thoughts, sir. What if Steven was responsible for her death? After all, he never actually arrived at the hotel as normal. Maybe the guilt got too much, hence his suicide. Or, without meaning to sound romantic, Alison's death may have been too much for him to deal with. It broke his heart, and he couldn't take her loss any longer.'

'You never know, Cara. The human mind and emotions are a complex and fickle combination,' said Deacon.

'There's another possibility,' said Karl. 'What if Steven witnessed the hit and run and the driver saw him and threatened him to keep quiet? Eventually it became too much.'

'It's possible,' said Deacon. 'That could also explain why he didn't turn up at the hotel. He ran away and hid. Of course, it's also possible that Alison's death was no accident. Someone targeted her. Therefore, if they knew where she was and where she stayed, surely they'd know about Steven Hawthorne?'

Deacon closed his eyes for a moment and massaged his temples. He looked at the detectives sitting at the table.

'I think the link between Steven Hawthorne and Alison McGregor is too strong a connection to be a coincidence. So, what if John McGregor had found out?'

'Do you think he could have killed her, sir?' said Cara.

'It's a possibility. From what we know, he was very vindictive.'

'Actually, guv, I hope I'm not speaking out of turn,' said Karl. 'I'll be able to add more strength to that thought from what I discovered with the follow-ups at Dudbridge Holdings.'

'In which case, I think now would be a good time.'

Karl opened his notebooks. 'As requested, I read through all the previous statements to see if anything particularly stood out. I felt they were pretty tight. That said, there were a couple that mentioned something that suggested there could be more to say. So, I followed them up and spoken with each of them again. This time away from the business in the hope they'd feel freer to speak more openly, without constantly looking over their shoulders and, of course, away from the glaring eyes of Margaret Wilson. Now, just to put everything in context, one lady still works for the business, and the other left a year ago but got mentioned by another current employee in a statement.'

'And they were happy to talk to you?' asked Deacon.

'Yes, guv. They were more than happy.'

Deacon raised his eyebrows. 'Tell me more.'

'Amanda, who's currently employed in Dudbridge, has never had a problem with the McGregors as such. She said that they left her alone, probably because she wasn't thin or that attractive, so she wouldn't have been on their shag list.'

'Did she honestly say that?' asked Gill.

'Yes. And I felt for her, although she doesn't seem bothered—outwardly, anyway. However, the person she has an issue with is Margaret Wilson. She explained that her job at the company is to be the interface with the clients, those using the company to sell land or properties and those who use the company to gain land, etc. Now, she knew that there was conflict and fights with some of their clients, because a few had told her—she guessed those were the ones who had got the better of her bosses. But there were about half a dozen occasions in the three and a half years that she's been working there when clients, businesses and individuals, have been using Dudbridge to deal with a purchase or sale, where they have telephoned her, often in a rage, accusing the business of ripping them off. And these people would get quite abusive and threaten with legal action. In which case, she would have to pass them onto Margaret Wilson, and that's the last that was heard about it. And she says that to her knowledge, there was never any legal consequence.'

'But it's possible there wasn't anything wrong with what they were doing?' said Deacon.

'They probably didn't read the small print. You know how dodgy that can be,' suggested Gill.

'Absolutely. But here's the interesting thing she said. Three of the sales that she'd received complaints about a month or two later ended up on the Dudbridge Holdings "acquired land and properties" list. She just found that to be odd. If you were brokering deals, why purchase the properties yourself? She'd asked Margaret Wilson about them but was told her to mind her own business and do the job she's paid for.'

'Some strong-armed tactics, maybe?' said Cara.

'Bullying. Intimidation?' said Deacon. 'If you remember, a similar thing happened to Jessie, with the house her parents were renting. I mean, this is maybe something or nothing, but there definitely seems to be a sniff of something, if not illegal, not in the spirit of good business practice.'

'What about the other lady?' said Deacon.

'Jackie. She said she'd seen firsthand what they can do and how they do it. According to her, there were clients Margaret Wilson and the McGregors would keep happy. The important ones to ensure their reputation keeps good. But there was a darker side to them as well. They exploit people's vulnerabilities and take advantage. Jackie said that there was a "trick" as she called it, that she saw done on more than one occasion. This involves people who want to sell on land. Often old or desperate people. Rumour has it, they kept a portfolio on such people. The McGregors would go in and act as the broker, and say they've got a buyer, which is not true. The seller, the fictitious buyer and the McGregor's dodgy solicitors would sign a fake contract. They would take their commission for facilitating the deal, which was quite a high cut that had to be made before the sale. The fake buyer would drop out. The commission is non-refundable, and of course, the seller is a few thousand pounds down with land they are desperate to get rid of. Dudbridge would step like the good Samaritans they are, and offer to buy the land at an extortionately low price, and sell it on at a more inflated price later.'

'Absolute scumbags,' said Gill.

'And they carefully target who they do this with,' said Deacon.

'Both ladies corroborated each other with similar stories, guv,' said Karl.

'And, again, it seems Margaret Wilson is very much involved,' said Deacon.

'She is. I'll tell you what I've found out when Karl has finished,' said Gill.

'Jackie also told me about one particular incident that occurred which was the final straw, causing her to walk out of the job.'

'Go on, Karl,' said Deacon.

'Jackie seemed to think it happened about eight years ago. One of the county farms had about thirty acres of pastureland that they never used, and they couldn't attract other farmers to rent as land for their livestock. So, desperate to sell, they contacted Dudbridge to broker a sale. She couldn't remember the figures that were discussed but, it was around the two hundred thousand to a quarter of a million-pound mark and worth about sixteen thousand pounds plus in commission. Anyway, with an assurance there was a buyer in place, they paid their commission and the deal fell through - surprise, surprise. Obviously out-of-pocket Dudbridge, or shall I say the McGregors, offered them a piss poor offer which they had to take. Anyway, one of the family waited for Terry McGregor to arrive at the carpark and the two got into an almighty altercation, resulting in Terry being punched in the face, and while on the floor, covered in blood, the man tried to strangle him. All the girls in the office saw it. John McGregor went running out and pulled the man from Terry. They obviously couldn't hear what they said, but eventually the man got in his car and drove away.'

'And so, another enemy was born,' said Deacon.

'Well, the office girls got sent to their desks by Margaret Wilson, to do what they're paid for. Anyway, Terry gets cleaned up, but there is a lot of what she describes as hushed, frantic activity with Margaret and Danny. A couple of hours later, the McGregors all got into their cars and drove away together.

After work, Jackie went to pick her sister up from the Royal Infirmary, who is a nurse there. She was waiting outside A and E, having a cigarette, when an ambulance raced up the drive and rushed their patient from the vehicle, past Jackie into the hospital. She didn't know how, considering the state he was in, but she recognised him as the person who attacked Terry McGregor. He looked like a bus hit him. He had dried blood and dirt all over him. She heard later on local radio about a man found in a ditch by the side of the road just outside the village of Queniborough. He had severe injuries, which Jackie's sister was to find out later included a broken arm, two broken ribs, a broken nose, missing teeth, and severe bruising all over the body. The police assumed it to result of being hit by a vehicle. Jackie's convinced the McGregors inflicted the injuries. She resigned from the company the next day, telling Margaret Wilson it was because of a family emergency, scared of a reprisal.'

Everyone sat in silence for a while. Cara who spoke first.

'There's something really wrong with that business.'

'We're learning more each day,' said Deacon. 'Great work, Karl. We'll need an official statement from both women.'

'Already done, guv,' said Karl.

'This investigation is framing itself, don't you think?' Deacon nodded towards Gill. 'What can you tell us about Margaret Wilson that we don't already know?'

'Ok, let's start with whom she is. During the conversations I've had with several associates of different shapes and form, most assumed that she and John were an "item". Interestingly, there's no photographic evidence or posting of them together anywhere. She has a lovely property in Oakham, which is mortgage free, fully paid for by her, over a three-year period. Interestingly, when we followed the money trail more closely, she received payments into her personal account by either Dudbridge Holdings, in lieu of bonuses—although what qualifies as bonuses? Or subsidiaries of the company, which we couldn't find, but apparently, technically legal. All such payments coincidentally match the value of her property, so make of that what you like?'

'And it's a nice place,' said Karl.

'I'm sure it is, Karl. Which brings neatly to the next point. Does she have any ownership or investment in Dudbridge Holdings? And the answer is, yes. She's a partner.'

The others around the table stared at each other.

'I've always thought Ms Wilson has too much involvement in the running and decision making of the business to be just an average employee on the payroll,' said Deacon. He paused before continued. 'Knowing this for sure very much brings her into the equation. She could be complicit in any actions taken, legal or not.'

'I've more,' said Gill. 'The dates don't really matter at this stage, but David and Alison Dudbridge originally registered Dudbridge Holdings Ltd in nineteen seventy-eight. And at the millennium's turn, they added their eighteen-year-old daughter, Libby, as a future partner and heir to their business, which was growing. Two thousand and eight had the addition of John McGregor, following David's death two years earlier. And eighteen months later, Terry and Danny replaced Alison. Clearly, she had to give permission both formally and legally, which she did through Wrights Solicitors, and she left Libby as a partner.'

'I got the impression Libby doesn't even know she's a partner in the business,' said Deacon.

'Really? That's interesting,' said Gill. 'Anyway, Margaret Wilson became a partner ten months later.'

'Don't you need agreement from all current partners for additions?' asked Deacon.

'Generally. But it depends on the contract. The contract may be that, for example, three of the four partners need to sign, to prevent any fraudulent activity. But let's be honest, from what we know of the McGregors, they would have got the numbers.'

'True. Is there anything else of interest?' said Deacon.

'Oh yes. She had an abortion in two thousand and eleven. Went private, of course, and paid for by John McGregor himself.'

'No!' Deacon was definitely not expecting that news.

'And that's everything from me.'

Deacon shook his head. 'Bloody hell! Thank you, Gill. You guys and girls have absolutely nailed it. Let's have a break to stretch our legs, have a coffee. Let's come back at three thirty?'

Gill, Cara, and Karl were sitting around the table chatting amongst themselves as Deacon entered his office.

'Any thoughts?' he asked.

'Margaret Wilson needs bringing in for an interview under caution,' said Gill.

'I couldn't agree more,' said Deacon. 'Karl, try to get more specific dates, or as close as possible, to when everyone witnessed what they did. Also, contact Jessie Ryan, known as Jessie Bateman, back then, to get a more defined timeframe of her ordeal.'

'No problem, guv,' said Karl.

'Now, Cara. Find out if James knew anything about this

relationship his brother was having with Alison. A part of me thinks he did, and it was part of the reason Steven perched himself on a branch.'

'Ok, sir.'

'This leaves us with Libby McGregor. We'll need to have another chat with her. I don't think she's involved with the murders, but think that she knows something that may help us. I'm also interested in confronting her with the name "Jessie Bateman", and see the reaction. You never know, it may jog her memory. Is everyone Ok with that?'

The team nodded.

'We're getting close. I can feel it.'

———

The silence in the office allowed Deacon to focus on the mind-map that he had developed earlier, as the meeting had progressed. The connections were there, the new information strategically placed giving a good picture of where they were at this point in time, and the areas when they needed to focus their investigation. He felt pleased with himself. He often conducted brainstorming sessions during investigations. It was a wonderful tool for highlighting known facts and, more importantly, what they don't yet know.

Deacon believed that he and the team were getting closer to that faint light at the end of a very dark tunnel. They were making the right moves. He knew what he now needed to do. Scrolling through the list of names on his mobile, he selected the number.

'Good afternoon. Petals Garden Centre.'

'Is Libby there, please.'

'Speaking. Who am I talking to?'

'Chief Inspector Deacon.' There followed a long pause.

'Hello, Chief Inspector. I would say it's a surprise hearing from you, but I thought you'd be in touch.'

'Really. Why?' A shorter pause and an awkward sound response.

'I don't know. Look, I'm really busy at the moment, but if you want to come over to the centre, in the morning, I suppose...'

'No, Libby,' interrupts Deacon. 'I not prepared to fit around you anymore. We need to talk. Properly. About your mother, your stepfather, brothers, oh, and Jessie Bateman. I don't have the time to keep chasing shadows. So, we arrange a couple of hours or you force my hand and I'll arrest you and we'll go to the station.'

'Sorry? Arrest me for what?' asked Libby, in a raised voice.

'Withholding information? Obstructing the course of justice? Don't put me in that position.' A long pause followed. 'Libby? Are you still there?' he asked.

'Yes, yes. I'm here. How about tonight at my house?'

Libby gave her address and suggested he arrived for seven-thirty. He would need someone with him to take notes. Ideally, a female officer to avoid him being accused of doing something inappropriate. Not the first time a police officer has faced such an accusation and, true or not, shit sticks. He called Cara, who said she was happy to help.

———

Gill took a bite of the Bakewell tart slice she bought half price in the local shop. She closed her eyes as she chewed. The short crust pastry, almond sponge and strawberry jam complimented each other perfectly. Absolutely delicious. She had forgotten how nice it tasted. It brought back memories of visits to her grandmother when she was a child. As she dialled a number on her phone, she smiled. It rang for a few rings before being answered.

'Hello. Margaret Wilson. Who am I speaking to?'

'I'm DI Foster of the Leicestershire Police. We met a few weeks ago with DCI Deacon, regarding the deaths of John, Terry and Danny McGregor?'

'Oh, yes. Hello.'

'Thank you for helping us with our enquiries. They are progressing really well. We're at the point where we need to narrow our focus and begin closing in towards a conclusion to the case. Therefore, we would like to invite you to the station in an official capacity to enable us to conduct a formal interview under caution.'

'Are you accusing me of something, DI Foster?' asked Wilson.

'No. We simply believe it would be pragmatic to conduct the interview under legal conditions, on the record, so to speak.'

Gill was enjoying herself. Margaret Wilson seemed a little rattled and, in truth, she wanted her to be. Both Gill and Cara felt she was holding back on information to protect the McGregors.

'Do I need legal representation?' asked Wilson.

'That's up to you,' said Gill. 'My normal advice is, if you are guilty, then yes, it would be a good idea. If not, no.' Gill was enjoying the exchange and trying hard not to laughed. 'Anyway, I was thinking tomorrow morning at ten-thirty?'

'I have a business to run. I can't just drop everything at a drop of the hat.'

'Ok, let's make it twelve-thirty. It should give you time to make alternative arrangements.'

'This is outrageous! How dare you.'

Ignoring her response. Gill countered. 'If you could ensure

that you are at reception ten minutes before, we would appreciate it. It gives us the chance to sign you in.'

'And what if I'm not prepared to bow to your demands?' said Wilson.

'We'll arrest you. I look forward to seeing you tomorrow. Goodbye.' Gill hung up with a big smile and put a piece of Bakewell tart into her mouth.

Deacon parked his Audi outside a very picturesque cottage in the village of Gretton. The roof of the cottage, mostly thatched, appeared to have had an extension in its life, which oddly had a tiled roof, adding to the quirky charm of the place. There were six black panelled windows that faced the front garden in stark contrast to the whitewashed walls of the building itself. Four black framed windows overlooked the road along with a small, black oak door. Next to it was a black plaque with 'The Sanctuary' tastefully painted on it. Is that really what this place is to Libby? thought Deacon.

A curved trellis covered in flowers gave the impression that you were entering a special haven as Deacon and Cara entered the garden, offering an explosion of colour and scents from a vast array of plants and flowers. As he reached for the forged metal knocker, the door opened, and Libby stood in the warmly lit house.

She invited her guests through to the kitchen that overlooked the rear garden, which showed a perfectly manicured lawn surrounded by a sea of colourful flowers. The three of them sat at an old-looking oak table. Deacon noticed the difference in Libby's demeanour as soon as she opened the door. She seemed more welcoming, less guarded. Gone were the practical, casual jeans and tee-shirt that she favours at the Garden Centre. Today she was in a bright floral print short sleeved dress with her straight brown hair allowed to hang freely at its full shoulder length. She wore black leather flip-flop sandals that partially covered a tattoo of what looked like a dove on the top of her right foot.

The cottage was as beautiful inside as out, with the old cottage theme kept throughout. And pride of place at the end of the kitchen was a must have for a cottage such as this - a cream coloured Aga Cooker.

'I've sorted your coffee, Chief Inspector,' said Libby, placing a mug onto a coaster. She turned to Cara. 'I'm sorry, I don't think we've met?'

'I'm DS Matthews.'

'Pleased to meet you,' said Libby. 'Can I get you a drink of some sort?'

'No, I'm fine, thank you, Miss McGregor,' said Cara.

'Please, call me Libby, like your boss man here.'

'It's a delightful place you have,' said Deacon, trying to break things in slowly.

'Yes, it is,' said Libby. Over the last couple of years, I've added several sustainable features. My goal is to make this place a zero-carbon home, which has its challenges because of its age and the materials it's made from. But I enjoy trying to solve those problems. So, don't be fooled. As nice and traditional as I like it to look, there is a lot of twenty-first century technology hidden away to make it self-sufficient. I rarely invite anyone here. It's my...' she tried to find the word.

'Sanctuary?' said Deacon.

Libby smiled. 'Yes, my sanctuary. But of course, I had to break protocol and invite you here after you threatened me with arrest.'

Deacon saw Cara pass a glance at him. He realised she hadn't been privy to his conversation earlier.

'Not a threat. Reality,' said Deacon, calmly. 'You were forcing my hand. Look, we *really* need to know everything you can tell us. We have a number of gaps in what we know, so we're here to find out if you can help us fill in the gaps.'

Libby gave a wry smile and gave a slight nod of the head. 'I would like to clarify something before we get into this. What I told you about those bastards of a stepfamily is absolutely true.'

'I've never denied that. But I also think there's more you could have told us. Now, whether it's intentional is partly why we're here this evening. We want to put this case to bed. Find the guilty people and lock them up so they can't do anything like this again.' Libby went to speak. Deacon held up his hand. 'Let me finish. I know your thoughts on the family, and you have every right to your opinions. After all, you've experienced them firsthand. But believe me, the people who murdered them, and certainly the way they were killed—and I can't give you the details, must be taken out of society.'

'That's fine,' said Libby in between sips of her coffee.

'Some of the questioning may seem somewhat random, but like I said, we're here to bridge the gaps in our knowledge. So, let's get started. First, did you know that Margaret Wilson was a partner at Dudbridge Holdings?'

'I think I told you before. It wouldn't surprise me if she was,' said Libby. 'But no, I didn't know for sure.'

'Did you know you became a partner in the business when you were eighteen?' asked Deacon.

'Yes. Mum and dad told me. But to be honest, I wasn't that interested—then, anyway.'

'Does that mean you would be now?' asked Deacon.

Libby thought before answering. 'I don't know. In a small way, I think I should have kept their legacy going, although that got ruined long ago. Anyway, I would imagine they couldn't get my name removed, quick enough.'

'By "they", I assume you mean the McGregors?'

'Obviously,' Libby replied.

'Obvious to you, but we need to be clear what and who you mean. Anyway, I have some news. You're still a partner in the business. It seems your mother was cunning enough to keep you registered.'

Libby looked up at Deacon. 'No! The sly bugger,' she said, with a smile.

'I know I've asked you before, but I need absolute honesty, Libby. Did either John, Terry or Danny McGregor ever attack you, either physically or sexually?'

'No,' said Libby, abruptly.

'Are you sure?' Pressed Deacon.

'I said *nothing happened*,' replied Libby, raising her voice.

Deacon stared at Libby. They both held each other's gaze momentarily. He still wondered if she was hiding something. He appreciated that reliving some memories could be painful. But he needed to know. He changed tack.

'Tell me about Jessie Bateman,' he asked. Deacon had purposely mentioned Jessie's name to Libby earlier when he called, to give her time to recollect any memories.

'She worked at Dudbridge a few years back,' said Libby.

'And?'

'And, what? She worked at Dudbridge.'

Deacon waited for Libby to elaborate, but she was offering nothing.

'You see,' said Deacon. 'This is why I'm never fully convinced you tell us everything. Jessie and I met at Bradgate park for a chat. Why there? She chose the location so she could see if anyone linked to the McGregors, were watching. After all this time, Jessie still feels scared. And she told me her story. The relationship with Danny. The ordeal. The embarrassment. What happened to her - and you.' Libby's face seemed to drain of blood and she became pale. 'So, I ask again,' said Deacon. 'Tell me about Jessie Bateman, and then we'll revisit the question I asked prior to that.'

Libby gave Deacon a piercing stare before averting her eyes temporarily towards the table. She looked back at him.

'I genuinely didn't know who Jessie was until she started dating Danny and he brought her to the house. Someone, and no, I can't remember who, told me she worked at Dudbridge. I wouldn't have known because I stopped going there when John took over the business. Anyway, we'd exchange pleasantries if we saw each other in the house, and that was about it. To be honest, I felt sorry for her because she seemed a really nice person, but she was one of many girls he was screwing. I remember I wanted to tell her what he was up to, but guessed that she wouldn't believe me. True love and all that. Anyway, as things progressed, there were a couple of occasions when I saw them leave the house, because Danny would take her out somewhere or home, where she looked in a bit of a state, you know, messy. And each of those times there seemed to be some friction between them. So, I was wondering if things weren't going so well between the pair.'

One day, I heard them shouting. In fact, she was absolutely screaming at him at one point, and I was going to find out what was going on. But as I opened the living room door, I could hear I think it was Danny and Terry laughing at something at the top of the stairs. I assumed they were playing a joke, because together they could be a right pair of childish dickheads. Later, after more shouting, I heard the front door slam. I looked out of the window and saw Jessie marching away from the house on her own along the driveway, so I guessed something serious had happened. I was going to follow her in my car and give her a lift because we weren't exactly local to anywhere. But. I don't know why; I decided not to because I didn't want Danny or Terry to see me leave, because as thick as they were, I didn't want them to put one and one together and figure I was going to help her.' Libby sat silently for a few moments, eyes wide, like she replayed that day in her head. 'Like I said, I don't know why that stopped me because I didn't give a shit what they thought. Maybe I was worried they'd take it out of Jessie.

Through the open door, I could hear bits of a conversation between Danny and Terry. From what I could make out, Danny, as usual, was happily recalling his sexual exploits, and the bits I thought I heard were bad if true. In fact, I would liken it to rape. Terry kept asking him questions about it because, well, he was just a weirdo. A pervert. Thinking about it, I can't ever recall him having a girlfriend. He just seemed to get off by listening to what his brother had done. They were clearly finding the whole thing funny, and I was feeling bad for Jessie. So, I thought, fuck it, I'll help her. I left the room and grabbed my car keys from the shelf in the hallway. Just as I was about to leave when John said something like, "how nice, your little sister is going to help the crying little tart?" And hearing that said from their dad, for fuck's sake, absolutely shot through me like a bolt of lightning. And do you know why?' Tears were rolling down Libby's cheeks. 'Because that was the point when I realised how dangerous they were. I mean, their dad, for Christ's sake, going along with it all. And that suddenly made me scared of them. I've said this to you before. They're scum and will cover each other's backs through thick and thin. They're like a twisted version of the three wise monkeys. See no evil, hear no evil, speak no evil. That's the McGregors to a tee. Excuse me a moment.'

She got herself a tissue from the windowsill and dried her eyes. Libby grabbed the jug of coffee from the machine and topped up her and Deacon's drinks and grabbed a mug and poured Cara one. She settled down again at the table.

'You, Ok?' asked Deacon. Libby ignored him.

'I drove around but couldn't find her, so I guessed Jessie had caught a bus or got a lift. A few days later I got her mobile number, mum asked someone from Dudbridge to get it. We met about half a dozen times after that. The second time we met at a coffee shop, which is when she told me what happened with Danny. It confirmed my suspicions to a degree, listening to the details was more horrific. I tried to convince her to report it to the police, but she wouldn't. So, it just seemed pointless, because that's what I wanted, I think. Them to be held accountable.'

'Did you ever approach Danny McGregor about what you suspected?' asked Deacon.

'You bet I did, but he dared me to "dob him in", to use his turn of phrase. Listen, as far as they're concerned, they were untouchable.' Libby took a large swig of her coffee. 'So, there's your answer regarding Jessie Bateman.'

'Thank you, Libby.' He gave a reassured smile. 'Now, I'll ask a question again, and no matter how difficult it is, I want an honest answer. Did any of the McGregors ever attack you, either physically or sexually?'

'No. Danny tried it on once, grabbed one of my tits, but a perfectly placed kick in the bollocks and a knee in the face put paid to that.'

'Why do you think the empathy and support you gave Jessie made her think you'd experienced the same as her?'

Libby's eyes filled with tears once more. 'I caught John raping my mum.' She slowly broke down into floods of tears.

Cara stood up and took hold of Libby's hand.

Fifteen minutes passed, during which Libby went to the bathroom to wash her face and calm down. She walked back into the kitchen looking more refreshed and composed and sat at the table. She gave a smile to her guests.

'I'm sorry. It's been a long time since I've allowed myself to think about that day.'

'And I'm sorry to have to put you through this, Libby, but we need to know what happened.'

Deacon had a hunch, and after some thought, rolled with it. 'When did you and your mother meet Steven Hawthorne?'

Cara turned to him in surprise. Libby's eyes widened as she raised her eyebrows. She smiled and slowly shook her head.

'When did you find out?'

'Just now when you answered my question,' said Deacon. 'Tell me more.'

Libby gave a long sigh. 'Mum met him at a restaurant in Leicester. It was at a mutual friend's birthday celebration. They got talking, met up a few times afterwards for drinks and fell in love. He's a farmer but also a talented artist, you know sketches, that kind of thing. However, he, like mum, was married, and like mum, not happily. So, they would meet up secretly, and the easiest way was to go away for odd weekends. But the fact you've said his name means you probably already know that?' said Libby.

'Most. I take it you were the go between, so as not to risk John finding out?'

'Yes. I'd call Steven or he'll call me and arrange dates and trips. Occasionally we used email.'

'He didn't arrive at the hotel on the day of the tragedy? Do you know why?'

She sighed. 'Steven *was* in York. He arrived early so went into town to do some drawing while he waited for mum to arrive. I received a call from him to let mum know, which I did.' Libby paused and swallowed. 'He called me the next day, after the police let us know. He was in bits and very apologetic, but wanted them to tell me first. That way I'd react the way they would expect. In York, he said he was walking towards the hotel when he saw mum crossing the road. Before he could call her name, there was a screech of tyres and out of nowhere a black Mercedes drove at full speed towards her. And within a couple of seconds, it hit her, and she flew into the air over the car as it sped away.' She paused for breath. She continued, now sounding like her throat had swollen. 'Steven said the car was gone before she landed on the road. He immediately ran over to her, but she was dead. He rang the police and reported it and ran away in a panic in case someone got his name and John found out she was meeting him. That about sums him up. He cared about mum right at the end. I think he said that he slept in his car in a layby. He couldn't go home early, otherwise his wife would wonder why.'

Deacon listened intently. He believed her and also thought about Steven Hawthorne. He certainly seemed to care about Alison and Libby. It was a good thing that Steven didn't go home early. The last thing he needed in his state was to find his brother sharing the bed with his wife. Or did he know?

'Did you keep in touch with Steven?' asked Cara.

'We do occasionally text each other. He's come over to Petals a couple of times for a coffee. He's a lovely man.'

Cara looked at Deacon before asked the next question.

'When was the last time you heard from him?'

Libby tapped on the screen of her mobile. She showed it to Cara. 'About three weeks ago. It was a bit of a weird message. He seems to have his moments when he's sad and reminisces about mum.'

'What does it say?' asked Cara.

Cara read out the message. 'I hope you are good. Your mum must be looking down from heaven, very proud of you. I miss her like mad. I look forward to the day I meet with her again.'

Cara turned to Deacon; eyebrows raised. He knew what she was asking him. But he gave a small shake of the head. Now wasn't the right time. He turned to Libby.

'He clearly cares deeply about your mum. And that's

something that hopefully brings you comfort. Thank you for opening up today, Libby. I know it's been painful, and you've revisited memories you'd rather forget. But from experience, there will come a time when you'll be able to face the past and hopefully make peace.' Libby stared down at her drink and nodded. 'Is there anything you want to ask us?'

'No,' she answered in a whisper, but looked at Deacon and said more assertively, 'Sorry, one thing. When you find out who killed them, will I be told?'

'Not necessarily. It depends on a number of factors. But judging by your relationship with these people, you'll find out more than most.'

Libby gave a shrug. Deacon and Cara stood up and said goodbye and left Libby in her sanctuary.

———

Nothing seemed to help. The drink wasn't doing what it usually does. The cigarettes are not calming her down the way they normally do. She still had this heavy pressure on her chest. A horrible tingling feeling of anxiety. She's had nothing like this before, never felt anxiety at such a level. But since that call, she's felt nothing else. Margaret Wilson opened her second bottle of wine in thirty-five minutes and poured some contents into the mug in front of her. She took a large gulp, closing her eyes as a liquid went down her throat and slowly penetrated her body. Yet still, this tension she felt remained. With the anxiety level creeping up another notch, her hands shook. Ash dropped from the smouldering cigarette onto the table. The remains had burned down into the tip. She stubbed it out in the existing pile of butts that threatened to fall out of the ashtray. Looking through the mist of blue smoke slowly circulating the room, Margaret opened the living room window to allow it to escape. She lit another. She watched intently as the match flared into life before quickly transforming into a quiet, relaxing flame. The cigarette smouldered and glowed as she brought the match to it and sucked on the tip. She remembered reading somewhere that alcohol slows the heart rate down, but cigarettes sped it up. Is that true? She wondered. If so, she must be playing hell with her heart.

Her body felt hot and clammy. She thought back to the phone call. The rude detective telling her to go to the station to be questioned regarding the disappearance of the John and the boys. What was she trying to insinuate? The police think they know things - but know nothing. Not what she knows, and one thing's for sure, she'll never tell. Whatever's happened to them, and God knows what, has nothing to do with her. But to keep the business and their legacy alive and give her the chance to really prosper now, she's the sole owner, is what she needs to focus on.

So why was that bitch like that when she called? Her heart felt like it was banging against her chest at high speed. Was it getting faster, or was she imagining it? She was getting worried, which made it worse. At what point do you have a heart attack? What are the signs? At this moment, she has no control over her body. She felt more anxious and worried. What if she doesn't go to the station tomorrow? What are the police going to do? They're hardly going to come and fetch her. It's all false threats from the bitch on the phone. So, you know what? They can shove it. She picked up the mug with a shaky hand, downed its contents, and topped it up again. She'll go into the office instead. But it still didn't make her feel any better. Most likely because she's trapped in something that she can't escape from and probably suspected of something that she hasn't done. But what was worrying Margaret was the knowledge she knows stuff that others didn't. And the consequence of what she knows scared her.

'Dad! Dad, wake up,' beckoned Susan, breaking Deacon from a deep sleep. His heart racing at the sudden shock.

Opening his eyes slowly, he tried to get his bearings. He wasn't in bed, but in his study, where his wife's photograph looked down on him and his daughter stood holding out a hot mug of tea. After rubbing his eyes, he took the drink from her. He couldn't remember coming into the room after returning from his interview with Libby last night. There was a glass of red wine on the desk that seemed mainly untouched — very unlike him. Susan was wearing his dressing gown, with the Who maximum R&B logo on the back, that she borrowed, stole, recycled, whatever she wanted to call it, for her own use. Ironic because she hated the band.

'I must have nodded off in here.'

'Considering you're still in here in the morning, I would imagine that's true,' jokes Susan. 'I thought I'd cook us a breakfast. What do you think?'

'You know what? That would be perfect,' he said with a smile.

'Egg, bacon and tomatoes Ok?'

'Just what the doctor ordered.'

'Talking of doctors, if I was reliant on you feeding me, I'd have malnutrition.'

With that, Susan disappeared into the kitchen and Deacon forced himself out of his chair and upstairs for a shower.

The breakfast tasted wonderful as he sat with Susan in the kitchen. He'd noticed quite a change in her in recent days. She seemed to deal with her mother's passing much better now. And dare he say it, they were enjoying each other's company.

'So, what kept you last night, Dad? Did something happen?'

'I had to interview someone.'

'Oh, Ok. I came downstairs at about three o'clock last night for a bottle of water and noticed the light on in your study. I was going to wake you, but you looked so peaceful there in your chair facing mum.'

Deacon wasn't sure if he blushed, but he certainly felt embarrassed by what she said.

'I honestly believe mum's watching over you,' said Susan. 'So be careful what you say to her. She'll probably have her fingers in her ears like this,' she put her two index fingers in her ears, 'and says la, la, la, la la, to herself so she doesn't hear what you are saying.'

Deacon smiled, but watching Susan with her fingers in her ears triggered something. Danny McGregor with a drill through his head. Deacon's brain was now making connections. Terry McGregor with a hook through the eyes, and John McGregor with his mouth burnt away. What did Libby say last night? See no evil, hear no evil, speak no evil. Hook through the eyes—see no evil; drill through the head—hear no evil; mouth burnt out—speak no evil. That was it! The effort. The imagination. The sheer inventiveness. It was as he thought - a statement. It was a punishment to make a point and send out a message. But to who?

'Why have you stopped eating, Dad? There's nothing wrong with it, is there?' asked Susan, interrupted his thoughts.

'No, not at all,' said Deacon, feeling very excited and energised. 'I think I've solved part of the puzzle.'

She did not know or any interest in what he meant, but that was fine. He never wants her to know what he deals with daily. It wouldn't help her healing regarding Claire's death. He was now keen to eat up and get to the station.

'My God!' said Gill. 'It's there in plain sight.'

'This just seems too Hollywood. Why would anyone go to so much trouble? It's not like we found the bodies in the right order to make the connection. It's got to be coincidence, sir,' said Cara.

'As I've said in the past, Cara. I don't believe in coincidence,' said Deacon.

'And all three deaths fit perfectly with the proverb. That can't be accidental,' argued Karl. 'There's probably a ten million to one chance of having such a correlation.'

'Come on, Cara. Think about it,' said Gill, arms stretched.

'I get it, and it makes absolute sense,' said Cara, 'but I really can't comprehend that anyone would go to such trouble to kill people in such an outrageous way. The McGregors must have done something terrible.'

'And that's the point,' said Deacon. 'I said before that they're like statement killings. Let's hypothesise for a moment. Assume that John McGregor does something bad, and I mean *really* bad. And whoever's on the receiving end expected John's two sons to acknowledge it. But they don't. Instead, they stand by their dad, no matter how much damage it does to the person. So, the person seeks revenge and to make a point. So, he or she kills the McGregors in a way that states what they were.'

'And the killer probably feels better for killing them in that way,' said Gill. 'But why would you put the bodies in places where they'll be found? You've appeased yourself by murdering them in a way they deserve to go. So, why not hide the bodies? Bury them?'

'And that's my point,' said Deacon. 'Whoever's responsible wants the bodies to be found. Ok, they haven't made it easy, but I think that is partly because of access to the places, time to move the bodies into position without being seen. They needed the bodies to be found to get the message out. And there is someone out there who knows exactly what this means and, possibly, who's behind it. However, where it's gone wrong for the perpetrators is, we haven't released the details into the public domain. So, their hard and creative work goes to waste.'

'This is fascinating,' said a voice from the back of the room.

Deacon turned to Pau as she walked into the room.

'I appreciate it seems far-fetched, but this entire case has been about extremes.'

'I couldn't agree more,' said Pau. 'I think you're onto something. Never be afraid to think outside of the box. This case hasn't been straightforward by any stretch of the imagination, but you have persevered and picked up the pieces of the jigsaw along the way. I genuinely think you're getting close to solving this. I absolutely appreciate everything you are all doing and the time you've put into this. So, if you are correct in your thinking about the discovery of the bodies and the cause of death being a message—who's it directed at? I'll leave you with that thought.'

Pau glanced at her watch and left the room.

'Margaret Wilson is an obvious target,' said Gill.

'Agreed. She's at the centre of everything,' replied Deacon.

'It could be an angry client who we haven't discovered yet,' suggested Goodman. 'I'm still following up the two lines of enquiry, which may highlight someone.'

'I agree. If you can push on with those, Karl, we'll know what we have.'

'As soon as we're finished here, guv,' said Karl.

'Thank you. Cara?'

'I'm wondering if Alison's hit and run has more significance to the McGregors' deaths? I know we have the relationship with Alison and Steven Hawthorne. But everyone I've spoken to who knew him comments how gentle he was and it seems unlikely he could be involved in this. And reading through the report on Alison's death, the North Yorkshire police were very thorough, and all the McGregors had solid alibis.'

Deacon pondered a moment.

'I think you're right. It has to be on the table until we can definitely dismiss it. Thanks for that, Cara. And of course, it could be a combination of everyone?' said Deacon. 'We haven't established such links yet, but nothing's out of the question. So, what do we have on today? You've told us what you're doing, Karl. How about you, Gill?'

'I've Margaret Wilson coming over to the station for a cosy chat,' said Gill, smiles.

'That'll be interesting. Was she keen when you asked?'

'Not really. And to be honest, I didn't exactly ask.'

Everyone laughed. They had all experienced Foster's 'persuasive' approach with suspects.

'Would you like me to join you at some point?' asked Deacon.

'Why not?'

Deacon turned to Cara.

'I'm speaking with Rosemary Hawthorne this afternoon. I sent a request to speak with James Hawthorne, but I'm waiting for a response. Straight after this meeting, I'll follow that up.'

'Excellent,' said Deacon. He felt really positive about today. 'We all know what we need to do. In the back of your minds, consider who is the message for? As always, you're doing a fantastic job. Keep in touch. We'll meet tomorrow afternoon for a catch-up.'

Margaret Wilson walked into the police station with a strong smell of tobacco and the faintest hint of wine. Clearly annoyed at being summoned for a formal interview, she responded by not turning up—initially. As a result, the appearance of a couple of uniformed police officers who duly arrested her made her mood worse. That happened as she entered the carpark of Dudbridge Holdings, in view of the staff who watched from their offices.

Dressed in a blue business suit, white blouse and mid-height black stilettos. She scowled as Gill greeted her in interview room two. Gill noted that Margaret's makeup looked pasted on her face far too thick, making her look like the old woman she was trying to disguise her aging skin. She sat at the table as directed by Gill, with arms folded and a face like thunder. It was what Gill's mum would have referred to as a 'strop.' The east facing sunshine of the morning shone brightly through the two narrow windows positioned near the ceiling, that seemed to light up the entire room. Although there was no need for artificial light, Gill switched on the room lights, anyway.

'My lawyer has just arrived, so I'm not prepared to say anything until she is in here with me, said Margaret.'

'But you just have,' mocked Gill.

'Good morning, guv,' said Karl, as he knocked on the open door of the office.

Deacon looked up from his computer. 'Hi Karl. Please, come in.'

Karl entered the room and sat opposite Deacon. 'I've been going through the books at Dudbridge with our accounts specialist and he's found several anomalies, or "creative" accounting, as he calls it. But what really caught my eye was a business transaction "creative account" which involved none other than Hawthorne Farm.'

Deacon felt a rush of excitement shoot from the base of his spine through his whole body. 'When was this, and with who?'

'Twenty-sixteen. I'm working my way through the file but haven't found a name yet. But it shouldn't take long.'

Deacon thought for a moment regarding this new revelation. 'If it's Steven Hawthorne, his name's cropping up too much. You say there was something wrong with the accounts? In what way?'

Karl frowned, rubbing his brow. 'From what we can figure out, from a money perspective, at least, it was for a large area of land, two-hundred and eighty hectors, I believe. Hawthorne Farm paid Dudbridge to find a buyer, which is standard procedure. Dudbridge found a developer who was very interested in the land and paid a substantial amount of money into Dudbridge Holding's account—again, which is perfectly normal. What happens next is that Dudbridge take their commission and transfer the remaining money from the sale to the seller.'

'Of course,' said Deacon. 'So, what's wrong with that?'

'The money got released—except it didn't go to the Hawthorne Farm.'

'So where did it go?'

'It went to a business account that, from what we can find so far, doesn't exist.'

'A ghost account?' asked Deacon.

'Pretty much,' said Karl. 'It's kind of there, but no.'

Deacon's mind was buzzing, processing what Karl had told him so far. 'Does this tie in with any of the statements that you got from the two employees?'

Karl nodded his head. 'Yes. Do you remember the story about the man who threatened Terry McGregor, who, as a result, had seven bells kicked out of him and ended up in hospital?'

'Yes, seen by the lady whose sister was a nurse?'

'That's the one. I went back to speak with her and her sister. But neither of them remember his name. However, the timelines are about right.'

Deacon felt they were closing in on whoever was responsible for the murders.

'Ok, Karl. Pull someone from next door to work on the files. See if you can find out where this land is and if we can get access to it. We can go for a drive and see what's there. I'll update Cara. She can raise this when she visits the Hawthorne's and maybe get some clarity on what they had and what happened during the transaction.'

As Karl left the office, Deacon looked at his watch. Time to see what's going on in the interview room with Margaret Wilson.

———

'Ok, Margaret. So, just to clarify while you are here. We want to speak to you in relation to the deaths of John, Terry, and Danny McGregor. During our investigation, we have learnt your relationship with the family was very close. Do you agree?'

'You know that. I've told you before,' said Wilson.

'You've told us bits, Margaret, bits. In fact, I would put it to you that you've told us what we needed to know—just enough.'

Pleasantly surprised Margaret's solicitor didn't harp up, as they often do at the insinuation, she continued.

'For example, you told us you were just an employee at Dudbridge Holdings, yet we find out that you've been a partner in the business since 2011! So, that begs the question, why were you lying? What were you hiding?'

'Nothing,' replied Margaret. 'John thought it would be best to keep it quiet, to prevent any jealousy from the other girls at the office.'

'But we're not the girl from the office. We're a police force trying to solve a multiple murder. And all you're worried about is what people might think of you? As far as the girls in the office go, why would they care? You were clearly in the McGregors' pockets; they've all said as much?'

Margaret was about to speak, but her solicitor, Mary Wells, stepped in. 'That's hearsay. Please change your line of questioning.'

Gill rolled her eyes. 'You said in a previous interview that the McGregors were hard but fair businessmen. Yet we have evidence of intimidation, bullying, *violence, fraud*. I can go on. Is that what you mean by hard and fair? Because you're a partner in the business, so you must know?'

Margaret turned to her solicitor wide eyed for an interjection, but Mary Wells gave a slight shake of the head and a nod for Margaret to answered the question.

'I don't know what liars you've been talking to, but no such thing has ever happened. They were not like that. And I would know because I worked closely with them,' said Margaret calmly.

'*I would know*? No, Margaret. You *knew*. Because you're as heavily involved in the business dealings as your partners.'

'Speculation,' said her solicitor.

Gill looked at her and gave a wry smile. 'Speculation?' She returned her gaze to Margaret. 'What can you tell me about Jessie Bateman?'

'I don't know the name.'

'Let me remind you. She sat next to you in the office,

overseeing the accounts or caseloads, as you may call them. You know, the one you and your partners stitched up?'

'I don't like this line of questioning,' intervened the solicitor.

'What do you expect? It's an interview,' responded Gill, sharply. 'Ok, Margaret, I ask again. What can you tell me about Jessie Bateman?'

Margaret paused before answered. 'If it's who I think it is, she worked with us for a while and seemed very nice. But she stole from us, so we dismissed her.'

'Oh, that's very nice and tidy, isn't it? What happened before that?'

Margaret seemed surprised by the question. 'Nothing. I don't understand what you're asking?'

'Her relationship with Danny McGregor?'

'I know nothing about a relationship with Danny.'

'That's odd, Margaret, because she said that you would conveniently disappear when Danny was in the room, so that he could sit next to her and be a pest.'

'Rubbish. No such thing happened. She worked for us and stole money, so we dismissed her as any good business would do,' replies Wilson, very calm and measured in her response.

'Tell be about the many complaints the company received from clients, customers, whatever you call them, who felt cheated by Dudbridge. The ones that get passed on to you to deal with. And again, judging by the information we've received from employees and ex-employees, there are plenty.'

'No matter how good your business is, there will always be some who feel disgruntled, so I would engage with them and calm them down and find a solution.'

'You were obviously very good because, most times, they simply disappeared without a trace. And interestingly, you often had their property and land on your books at an obscenely low price afterwards,' said Gill, trying her hardest to get under Wilson's skin.

'Everything we did was legal. We're a high standing and respectable business. And the last thing I need is some trumped up policewoman trying to be intelligent and say otherwise about something she doesn't understand,' shouted Margaret, standing and banging her fist on the table.

Mary Wells tapped Margaret's arm and told her to sit down and be calm.

Gill liked the outburst. She was riling Wilson, and her solicitor knew it. When their clients get annoyed and go into a rant, they risk letting their guard down and saying something they would later regret.

'In answer to the point you made, I don't fully understand the workings of a business. That's why the fraud squad, who understands these things, is going through the books at Dudbridge as we speak,' said Gill, giving a big smile.

Did she see Margaret Wilson's face go a shade paler at her comment? She hoped so.

'Talking of disgruntled customers, tell me about the incident in the carpark when an angry client confronted Terry McGregor? When there was some kind of fight?'

Wilson was clearly thinking hard of the best way to answered the question.

'I vaguely remember it. I don't think it was a client. I believe they were ex-friends who had an argument. It's that alpha male thing. That's how they need to deal with things. It was just a disagreement between two people.'

'A disagreement between two people? That's interesting, because witness testimonies suggest that after Terry McGregor got cleaned up, by you, John and Danny, the three of them got into their respective cars and went somewhere with some urgency.'

Wilson smiles. 'That means nothing. They were businessmen. They obviously had appointments. You are reading too much into these things to make them seem like criminals.'

'I'll continue. Later that day, the man who had the altercation with Terry ended up in a ditch badly beaten. And guess what? One of your employees who witnessed the incident in the carpark, saw him arrive at A and E as she waited for her sister to finish her shift.'

'I know nothing about that, and you can't pin that on the boys,' replies Margaret.

'*The boys*? Is it some kind of firm? A bunch of heavies?'

'That's not what I meant,' said Wilson sharply.

'Let me tell you what I think. You either know what happened or you're very naïve, ignorant or stupid....'

'I object to you insulting my client in such a way,' intervened the solicitor. Gill held up her palm to shut her up.

'However, Margaret. I don't think you are any of those things. And do you know why? It's not because you're clever, because I don't think you are. But because you are complicit. You are involved. You are as guilty of anything they have ever done. You aided and supported them. And you and your legal beagle here can complain as much as you like, because, Madame, you are in trouble and deep.'

'That's it! Enough,' said the solicitor, red faced. 'My client is not here to be abused and accused of anything that comes into your head. I'm demanding that you stop this interview now and I want to speak with your superior officer. Do I make myself clear?'

So, the lady has balls, thought Gill. She may choke on them in the not-too-distant future, but it was good, and slightly amusing, to see the young lady make a stand. Although in truth, Gill didn't give a shit, because she knew who would watch proceedings via the CCTV camera throughout the interview. She turned towards the recorder.

'Interview with Margaret Wilson paused by request of her

legal representative, Mary Wells.' Gill paused the recording and smiled at the two ladies in front of her. 'As requested, I'll call my superior officer.'

Gill left the interview room and met with Deacon and Pau.

'Good work, Gill. I get the impression she's unsettled. Panicky,' said Deacon.

'Yes, well done, DI Foster. I agree with DCI Deacon in principle. However, there are lines we mustn't cross, and I felt you were trying to redraw them. Be careful when you're in these situations, or they'll have grounds to cry foul. Do I make myself clear?'

Gill's heart dropped. Had she gone too far? Arguing the point would make things worse, so she thanked her for the advice. If Pau heard the apology, she chose not to acknowledge it.

Deacon walked into the interview room and listened intently to Mary Wells' issues with Gill. After convincing her he would look into Gill's behaviour, he suggested he continued with the questioning. He got the impression, looking at Wilson, that she was happier to have him in the interview room. She was smiling and trying her hardest to make eye contact, and was she trying to flirt? Whatever she was expecting, she would find disappointing.

'Ms Wilson, why did you deal with certain accounts that Jessie Bateman could not deal with?'

'My caseload comprised the more, let's say, *sensitive* accounts.'

'In what way?' asked Deacon.

'Well. They could be high-profile names, or people and organisations that wish to remain anonymous.'

'Why? It seems a little convenient. Are they criminals? Is there activity that you're covering up?'

'As you can appreciate, Chief Inspector, I cannot reveal who they are. It's confidential. And no, we would not get involved with any such criminal activity, let alone cover it up,' said Wilson calmly.

'What about some of the more deceptive dealings by the McGregors? Or should I say the McGregors' and yourself?'

Mary Wells stood. 'I'm not accepting this line of questioning on....'

'Really?' Raising his voice and staring deep into the solicitor's eyes. He turned to Margaret Wilson. 'Tell me about the purchase of the cottage of Jesse Bateman's parents.'

'Not that Trollope again.'

'Trollope? You refer to her as a Trollope, Margaret. Why?'

'Because..'

'Because what? According to you, she was just an office thief. According to you, you knew nothing about any relationship with Danny McGregor. Yet, according to you, she's a Trollope? Why would you use that term? I think I know why. Because you knew that Danny and Jesse were in a relationship—which you denied earlier with my colleague. And, by the way, I was watching the whole thing via that camera up there. Now, I ask you again. Did you know they were in a relationship?' Deacon couldn't understand why he was so annoyed, but the denial was eating away at him.

'Yes,' replied Margaret in a whisper.

'I'm sorry? Louder, please for the recording.'

'Yes, I knew. And he would ask me to lose myself while he spent time with her.'

'Spent time?' Deacon realised he was becoming animated, with his arms outstretched. 'He was harassing her; he was touching her up, he was bullying her.'

'I didn't know he did that,' replied Wilson.

'I don't believe you!' responded Deacon. 'Margaret, we have evidence that he raped her, and you let him!'

'How dare you!' shouted Wilson.

'Quiet.' Deacon was now bordering on angry and was trying to calm himself down and control his emotions. 'You know about the purchase of Jessies parent's cottage, because it was in your case file that Jessie Bateman confronted you about.'

'I don't remember that.'

'The purchase of the cottage or the confrontation with Jessie over it? Because, believe me, we have evidence of the transaction, and yes, it was above board, but why would you purchase such a property? It isn't the thing you normally deal with. And why would it go to your case file? They're not rich or have any fame. They certainly had no criminal record. In fact, the church extolled the voluntary work they did for them. I'll tell you why you bought it and why you had it under your remit. To spite Jessie for dumping Danny and threatening to go to the police about his behaviour and rape. And yes, I said rape. You knew exactly why Dudbridge purchased the cottage. Yet you did nothing. That makes you as complicit and guilty as your partners.'

'You're just making this up, Inspector. I thought you were better than this, but you're as bad as your detective that was in here earlier,' said Wilson, now visibly sweating and shaking.

'So, you deny it?' asked Deacon.

'I don't deny we purchased the property, but the reasons, yes.'

'So why did you buy it?' replied Deacon.

'I can't remember.'

'I can't remember. How convenient. Tell me about your abortion?'

The question hit Margaret like a knockout punch to the chin. Her eyes widened, and her jaw dropped. She stared at

Deacon wide-mouthed for a good ten seconds. 'You bastard,' she said, with piercing eyes.

'Who was the father? Was it John, Terry or Danny?'

'You complete and utter bastard!' Wilson remained, staring wide-eyed at Deacon. Tears rolling down her face.

Deacon continued. 'We know John McGregor paid, but as we now know, they were always in it together and took collective responsibility, so it's very difficult sometimes to separate one.'

'Fuck you, Chief Inspector.'

'No problem. The data base is being scanned as we speak, so the labs will give us the answer in good time. I'm afraid, Margaret, following our investigation and the evidence we have so far, you are so deeply ingrained in the case, you are likely to stand trial for all the bad things your partners did, because you're the only one alive. And you have put your loyalty with them and not offered to help reveal what really happed in your company, and go some way in healing those hurt by your actions. Do you have anything to say, Margaret? This is your chance.'

Margaret Wilson sat rigid, staring at the wall in front of her. Eyes red and tearful.

'People have likened your business partners, as a corrupt version of the three musketeers—All for one and one for all! Others have them as a twisted version of the three wise monkeys—see no evil, hear no evil, speak no evil. Now here's something you won't know, but while you're here, I'll let you in on a secret. There was a theme to the killing of John and the boys, as you like to say. It seems to be based on the on the three monkeys. And you know what, Margaret? Those responsible for the deaths of John, Terry and Danny were clearly paying them back - paying you all back for some wrong you'd committed. They died a slow death. And they died in agony.' Tears were rolling down Margaret's cheeks.

Deacon continued. 'They were clearly sending a message out to someone. And do you know who I think that is, Margaret? It's the fourth monkey. Now, many people don't know there is a fourth, and the moniker is "do no evil". Or in your case, pretend you did no evil. I believe the message was for you. The problem is, we never made the causes of death public, so you wouldn't be able to make the connection. However, if anyone who can commit such barbaric crimes feels strongly enough to target *you* with such a message, means you must've been involved somewhere along the line. Margaret Wilson, I am arresting you in connection with fraud, withholding information and obstructing a murder enquiry.'

Margaret sat motionless in her chair, staring at the wall.

Deacon turned to Mary Wells. 'We will keep her in the cells overnight for further questioning tomorrow, and for her own safety, as we strongly believe her life could be in danger.'

Mary initially tried to argue for Margaret's release but realised it was probably for the best, considering the potential consequences to her client's life if not protected.

Deacon was deep in thought. He'd received an email from Katie from the incident room. Apparently, Mrs Timmins of Bakewell Farm had called and wanted to speak with him. Something had triggered a memory of the night when she heard the vehicle driving near their farm the night before they discovered Terry McGregor hooked up to her husband's tractor. Deacon had returned her call immediately. What she said was interesting.

While waiting for a bus to take her into Uppingham, she heard a sound that immediately reminded her of the night in question. She said she always felt there was something else, but be it old age or whatever, she couldn't remember it. But in a nearby field a farmer was driving with a livestock trailer that they used to move sheep and such like about. It was the rattling and squeaking which she now remembers vividly was the same as what she heard that night. Deacon had thanked her for the update in between several apologies from Mrs Timmins for being so forgetful.

By taking the bodies to the locations using such a trailer, prevented contamination in an actual vehicle. The cleaning of the trailer could remove any residue, or even filled with livestock again, contaminating existing traces. Which begged the question: was the murder of Terry, John and Danny McGregor done elsewhere? It would certainly make sense to sedate them, to prevent any agonising screams, reasoned Deacon. Witnesses close to the locations where the bodies appeared did not hear any shouting or screaming.

And this has always been a niggle in Deacon's head regarding the deaths. They always appeared to be in the same position in which they met their death, as confirmed by the pathologist. Therefore, if the murder took place elsewhere, the relocation and positioning of the bodies took considerable care; stage managed almost. Therefore, a suitable mode of transport would need to be used, which could be a livestock trailer, which has space and wouldn't raise any suspicions. And such a place would need to be remote. He'd need to speak with Dr Freestone to run the feasibility of his theory by him so quickly sent him an email marked 'Urgent' with his general thoughts.

'My talk with Rosemary Hawthorne was really quite revealing,' said Cara, when she returned to the station. 'She was pleasant and, I won't say, happy to see me, but willing to talk. It was Steven's funeral on Monday, so I suppose there was closure.'

Deacon thought back to his wife's funeral. 'It has the strange effect of focusing your mind on the next chapter without them.'

'First, sir, I have to say that the guy's next door did a lot of the legwork. It was a genuine team effort.'

Deacon nodded in acknowledgement. Cara handed Deacon a copy of her typed notes and read through them.

'After leaving school in nineteen ninety-six, James Hawthorne joined the army rather than the family business on the farm. According to Rosemary, it disappointed his parents, but they gave their blessing. He became part of the ground force that moved into Iraq at the start of the gulf war. He remained there until two-thousand and four when an IED exploded near him during house-to-house searches.'

'An IED? Is that an Improvised Explosive Device?'

'Yes, sir. He spent two months in a military hospital with injuries to his leg. As a result, the army retired him on medical grounds following his recovery. He returned to the farm for a few months, but then did a business course in Birmingham, which was funded by the military transition programme. After completing his diploma, which I believe took two years, he started up his own business as a broker for farm vehicles and equipment. He sold the business in two-thousand and eleven and went into the property business. He has several residential properties in and around Leicester, Birmingham and Nottingham, university cities, where he mainly rents as student accommodation. And that brings us to the point when he returns to the fold, so to speak.'

Deacon listened intently to the information Cara presented. He was staring at the notes she gave him but not following them as such. He could concentrate and think much more when listening, and especially when listening to someone who presents the information so clearly. Cara continued.

'Hawthorne farm was doing Ok, but not as good as it could be, so their father suggested it would be a good idea for James to get more involved and help develop it from a business perspective and modernise some practices. According to Rosemary, he was initially reluctant to do this because her father-in-law had sold off land for next to nothing, which James felt was an unfair deal. He recognised the need for funds and land for expansion and bring the farm up-to-date and more profitable. So, for the sake of his family, became involved with the farm again.'

'Did Rosemary say what Steven thought about this?' asked Deacon.

'She said that he wasn't keen at all. As far as he was concerned, James had abandoned the family business and Steven and his dad had put all the hard work in between them. She thinks he was also reluctant to any form of modernisation. He felt it was commercialising the farm, and he wanted it to remain more traditional in its practices. But his dad was onboard with James' vision, so it was a case of put up or shut up.'

'Interesting,' said Deacon.

'Their father stepped back from the day-to-day work because of his age and left that side of it to Steven. But he would occasionally go out to meetings with James on farm business. It was following one of these that their father collapsed at home and suffered a fatal heart attack. That devastated the whole family. And two months later, they lost their mother. She'd died of natural causes. So, the farm now belonged to Steven and James, and, according to Rosemary, although there was often tension between them, they'd learned to work with each other over the years. And that's what I discovered about James Hawthorne and the relationship with his brother.'

'Great work, Cara. I take it you didn't see James?'

'No, sir. He's away on business, but Rosemary tells me she's expecting a "visit"—she used her fingers to emphasise quotation marks—within the next week.'

Deacon smiled. 'Have you tried to contact him?'

'Yes, sir. No answer, so I've left a message for him to call.'

'Excellent. You said that the father had a heart attack following a meeting that he went to with James. Do you know who the meeting was with?'

'I asked Rosemary, but she didn't know. It's a question I want to ask James.'

'You've done well. I always like to have a background. There's probably nothing we've discovered that affects the investigation, but you never know. I think you deserve a coffee. Come on, I'll treat you.'

It was close to six o'clock when Deacon's mobile rang and lit up with Dr Freestone's name.

'Hi Dave. Thanks for getting back to me.'

'Yes, I'm very well, thank you. Thanks for asking. Oh, wait a minute, you didn't.'

'Sorry, Dave. Too much going on for pleasantries. Any thoughts on my theory?'

'I must say, Alex, you have a rather overactive mind. Still, here are my thoughts. They might have taken Victim one to the location at the farm after killing him. It was in such a state from being towed up the track. It would be hard to tell. And the SOCOs didn't find any trace of blood, so possible. The second body, our fire eater, definitely not. That happened there, of that I am absolutely certain. With the drying of the flesh and body tissue, there would have been telltale signs if anyone moved him. Maybe cracking of the body around the scorched area and neck. In truth, if he had cloth shoved in his mouth, he won't make a great deal of noise. And when in the building, the perpetrator or perpetrators can add accelerant to it. As I think I mentioned at the time, the fumes most likely rendered the chap unconscious. So other than smoke coming from the outbuilding, which no one would notice because of its remote location, especially with the deed committed in the early hours. Now, with our chap with the drill through his head. By the way, did you receive the preliminary report?'

'I did, yes, thank you.'

'Good. What was noticeable, but not necessarily unusual was the lack of blood around the body. Yes, there was residue on the shoulder of the victim, but I would have thought there would have been body tissue on the floor when you consider the drills spinning. However, that could depend on the speed that the drill was revolving, and the pressure exerted to drill through the brain and the skull. Again, the SOCOs found little trace.'

'So, you think someone placed the body in the conference room later?'

'Patience, Alex. What I am saying is that the evidence suggests he was alive when the deed was done, and again would have been in complete agony. He wouldn't have been quiet for the first few seconds, that's for sure, but that's your side of things, not mine. In answer to your question, could someone have moved the body and placed it in the room after the murder had taken place? Yes, is the answer. Although, care would have needed to be taken, because any stresses on the body during transportation would have shown up during my autopsy.'

'Possible, then?' asked Deacon.

Freeman paused before answering. 'As you know, I don't do conjecture. But I will say this. Someone tied the victim to the chair. He was in an upright position and rigor mortis had set in. Of the three, this would be a relatively simple body to move. However, I stress again, it would need to be done with care.'

'But it's not beyond the realm of possibility?'

'No,' came the quick answer.

'Ok. Thanks for your help, Dave. I really appreciate your time on this.'

'A pleasure. I thought you'd retired. That nice supply of patients you've been giving me seems to have dried up. I assume you're getting close?'

'I think so.'

'Good luck,' replied Freestone before ending the call.

No sooner had Deacon put the mobile on his desk, it rang again. This time Karl Goodman.

'Yes, Karl?'

'I've got the address of the property that the Hawthorne's lost. Guess who to?'

'Dudbridge?'

'Got it in one, guv,'

'Good work, Karl.'

'It was hidden in plain sight, so to speak. I was thinking of going over to have a "goosy".'

'Hold on.' Deacon checked his watch. 'I'll tell you what. Leave it for tonight and we'll both go in the morning. Shall we meet at the station about eight and drive over in your car?'

'Sounds good to me, guv. Bye.'

Deacon wished him a good evening and hung up. He's become more impressed with Karl's attitude and approach to his assignments. He'd still like Karl to be a bit more outgoing and mix with Gill and Cara more, but hey, small steps are being made. Maybe it's not in his makeup to be like that, but

Deacon needs that attribute for his team to fully gel. It would certainly be something they would talk about on his next appraisal. But now and for this investigation, he'd done very well and contributed as an equal to the rest of the team. Deacon was excited about tomorrow. It would go two ways. Either there would be bugger all to see, or they would find something of genuine interest. And he strongly believed it would be the latter.

CHAPTER ELEVEN

THE HEAVY RAIN lashing against the windscreen was too much for the wipers to deal with, even in their fastest setting. DC Karl Goodman slowed the car more to aid his vision, but their view of the outside world still seemed pixelated. But now they could see the Kerb stones that lined the road and the turnoff to their destination. A large aluminium gate blocked the entrance to the field. Deacon got out of the car and opened it to let Karl through. He jumped back into the vehicle, soaked. He dried his face with his handkerchief as Karl slowly drove them along a gravel track which seemed a good mile long. As they got closer to the green blurry looking building in the distance, it took a more defined shape.

They parked beside the large prefab structure. It was about ten metres wide and probably eight meters to the apex of the roof. The length of the place looked maybe fifteen metres long. The green coating still looked good, although the sun seemed to have slightly faded the south facing side. Like the fields that led up to it, overgrown grass and weeds surrounded the base. The front had a concreted area leading to a large shutter door. Deacon tried to lift the shutter, but it wouldn't budge.

'Guv?' Karl had opened a door to the side of the building.

'It would be rude to not go in,' joked Deacon.

Six skylights let sufficient light inside for the two of them to see. The sound of the rain resonating on the steel shell sounded like millions of marbles were being poured onto it from the heavens. The inside was tidy, and the walls were clear and uncluttered. It was, save for the odd spider webs, surprisingly clean. In the far corner was a rectangular shape covered in a large canvas sheet. Halfway along the same wall was a yellow portable jet washer with its cable neatly coiled up and a long black hose leading to the spray nozzle which was propped up against the wall.

The two men walked around the room, looking in more detail at what was there. After a while, Deacon stopped and scanned the room again. 'Have you noticed how clean the floor is, Karl?'

'Yes, guv.' Karl looked up at the ceiling and down to the damp patches on the floor. 'I'm trying to see if the roof's leaking, and I honestly don't think it is. Yet it's pelting down out there.'

Deacon nodded towards the jet washer.

'It must be, but why? I don't pretend to know anything about farming, but I've always thought of barns as places covered in crap.'

Deacon thought the same. He knelt down and rubbed his fingertips across the floor. A layer of sealant covered the concrete, judging by how shiny it was. It seemed a lot of effort and extra cost for what is essentially a storage unit.

Karl walked over to the far corner and lifted the canvas sheet, revealing two wheels and part of a silver trailer. He turned to Deacon and raised his eyebrows. He pulled the sheet back further. Deacon smiled and thought of Mrs Timmins whilst staring at the livestock trailer. He'd need to get the forensic team in to see if there was any trace of one of the McGregors having contact with it. But first, what else was here? Standing next to the shutter doors were two wide roles of thick polythene sheeting; one of which three-quarters used. Eventually, they both ended up back at the door. Karl flicked a switch on the wall, lighting five of the six tube lights that hung by chains from the roof.

'Why would there be power if it's not used?'

'Good question.' Deacon looked around the room again and noticed four double plug sockets on the wall too. 'And who's paying for it? We need to get the place powdered. Call forensics.'

'Will do, guv.' Karl brought up the number on his phone and placed against his ear. He looked down at his phone again. 'No signal. I'll make the call from the car.' He rushed out of the building.

Deacon stood quietly, still. His brain was tingling as he forced himself to process all the information he had. He was certain this was where the murderers held and probably killed the McGregors. It's isolated, so there's no way anyone would hear their screams while hammering a hook into Terry's eyes and shoving a petrol-soaked rag into the mouth of John. Danny probably witnessed their deaths and remained on his own for a few days before being tied to a chair and drilled through the head from ear to ear.

The jet washer can clean away any contaminated areas, such as the floor or the trailer, in fact, anything. And the polythene? Yes, of course, they would lay the polythene on the floor first. That's why there were never traces of the bodies being anywhere else. It gave the impression the victims were murdered in situ. Their deaths were a message that said, you're all in it together, and you're next. And Margaret Wilson is the target, he was certain. Now it made sense, and he doesn't know why they did it, but he knows who the murders are. Because there had to be more than one. He heard footsteps return to the building.

'Did you get through to ...'

The piercing pain he felt as he received a blow to the back of the head was excruciating. Within a second, the blood and energy drained from his body at the speed of an express train in contrast to the slow shutdown of his body. Then he was in darkness.

Gill and Cara had become increasingly concerned when they couldn't contact Deacon or Karl Goodman. Deacon's phone would ring, but there'd be no answer. It could be on silent, but generally, Deacon didn't bother. Only occasionally, if he was in a meeting with the top brass or interviewing suspects, would he set it to vibrate to ensure that he received every notification and missed nothing important? Karl's phone was just dead, probably switched off, or the battery was flat. Then again, has something happened to them?

They knew Karl was following up some leads on the case, and that Deacon had gone out somewhere with him, because he left a post-it on his desk saying so; but not where? It was Cara's comment, wishing Deacon was more anal with the detail in his notes like Karl, that prompted them to rush to the computer and access Karl's calendar, and there it was, post-code and all.

The first sense Deacon felt was the sharp, throbbing pain at the back of his neck. It felt like pulses of electricity were being shot into his head. The second sense was the hard surface against his left cheek. After a while, he reasoned, he must be chest down on a hard floor with his neck twisted to his right, which made it things even more painful. He was still in darkness. He tried to open his eyes without success. They seemed glued together. As his senses were slowly returning, he noticed the sound. It was a constant drone, a kind of bubbling sound, he thought, even with the occasional flutter. He recognised it but couldn't think from where. His mind was foggy, and he was feeling nauseous. He had a horrible taste in his mouth and coughed, which hurt the side of his neck and caused his head to lift slightly from the floor before landing again with an agonising thud. There was the smell, too. The intoxicating smell that he knew, but again he couldn't remember from where. He eventually opened his eyes. The exhaust pipe was close to his face, pumping out fumes, making his eyes sting.

Sleepy and fatigued, he knew he had to move. He was in pain and his arms at the side of his body, which for a while he couldn't get to move. He mustered up every piece of energy in his body to get himself away from the vehicle by snaking backwards along the floor until his feet hit something solid. A wall, maybe? It took a while, but fought the fatigue and turned around on the floor using his arms, even forcing himself to lift his head slightly to save it by scraping along the surface, although it was agony on his neck muscles. He could see the exit door. He slowly inched his way higher until he could grab the door handle with his right hand and pull down. But the door didn't budge. Locked?

Deacon slumped to the floor. He was panicking. And even in his confused and foggy state of mind, could reason that he needed to find a way out. His eyesight was sharpening. There was the large shutter door. That would be his only option. He could move a little more freely, making his way using his arms, elbows, and legs. When he reached it, his heart sank. Seeing the large padlock made him want to cry. He felt helpless. Trapped. But he had an idea that would either enable him to escape or kill him. He was feeling sick. He was feeling sleepy. His body ached all over and his head was pounding like a drum.

Gritting his teeth, he moved towards the car that was still humming away. He propped himself up against its side, grabbed the door handle and pulled as hard as he could. The door clicked open. After pushing the door wider, he somehow got himself into the car, slumping into the driver's seat. He spent some time trying to gather his thoughts and clear his head the best he could. He needed to be certain what he did was right, as far as he could remember, anyway. The keys were in the ignition; the car was still running. He thought he recognised the car but didn't know from where, but was reasonably clear in his mind how to operate it. Sitting rigid, he stared through the windscreen and clenched the steering wheel. His knuckles had gone white. He stood on the clutch pedal and put the gear lever into first gear with his shaking left hand. After releasing the handbrake, he closed his eyes and lifted his foot from the clutch whilst stamping down on the accelerator as hard as he could. The car screeched forwards at speed. Deacon felt the impact when he smashed into the shutter door, causing the engine to stall, along with the sound of glass shattering.

He didn't know how long it was before he conjured up the courage to open his eyes. He seemed to be in one piece but covered in safety glass. The jammed car was halfway out of the shutter door, but at least it had forced an opening at the bottom where the natural daylight from outside shone through. The driver's door was still open, so Deacon managed, with some effort, to get his legs outside the car and drop to the ground. He scrambled through the gap and out of the building.

He sat for a while, sitting on the wet concrete, breathing

in the cool, fresh air. Although the rain was soaking him, it felt good against his face. Cleansing him. Helping clear his mind and gather his thoughts. His head was pounding, but he was remembering where he was, and fragments of what had happened. He looked back at the crumpled car. Probably beyond repair. He was with Karl Goodman; he remembered. The car is Karl Goodman's car. Deacon vaguely recalled Karl going outside the building to make a phone call and he thought he heard him come back. But he doesn't remember much more after that. That's when it all went black. He scanned the surrounding fields. There was no one about. Where was Karl? He tried to call his name, but his throat was dry and felt like tree bark. All he managed was a whisper.

Cara was showcasing her driving skills to full effect as she snaked through the busy traffic in their white unmarked Skoda Octavia. The blue lights flashing through the front grill and the rear window having the desired effect, opening up the road like Moses parting the red sea, thought Gill. Cara's controlled and calculated skills behind the wheel were always impressive, but she noticed that today her partner was taking slightly more risks, driving through narrower gaps than usual. The lashing rain made the experience more uncomfortable for her, but she said nothing and allowed Cara to drive using her own discretion in order to get to her boss and Karl in case they were in danger. As soon as they had the address and post-code, Cara had rushed down to the carpark to get the car whilst Gill went to inform Chief Superintendent Pau.

It was the first time she'd ever had to knock on Pau's office door. She even paused before doing so because she was so nervous. When she heard Pau call for her to enter, she went into a sweat. Standing before the Chief super was like being a naughty schoolgirl summoned to the headteacher. She explained the situation and told Pau that she and DS Matthews were going to drive out there. Pau's face expressed deep concern. She insisted they shouldn't go on their own, so picked up the phone and ordered back up. The result was the three squad cars in pursuit with lights flashing and sirens blaring that were struggling to keep up with Cara's high-speed skills. She didn't slow until the sat nav directed them to take a sharp left turn. Luckily, the gate was open, and it was only after driving some way along the loose gravel track when Cara slowed down.

The fields to the left of the track looked overgrown. She could see an outbuilding of some sort in the distance. Neither Gill nor Cara spoke as the car made its way towards it, which grew bigger and more defined as they got closer. The rain was still pelting down at a considerable rate, so they could only get a snapshot of the building with each stroke of the windscreen wipers. Gill thought the bottom of the large stutter door looked odd, twisted almost. And then she saw the car wedged under it. The car screeched to a halt. Gill recognised the figure sitting against the wall.

'There's Deacon.' She quickly left the car and ran to him. 'Are you Ok?'

Deacon gave a short laugh and coughed. 'I've been better,' he whispered. He pointed to his throat.

Gill turned to Cara, who was standing next to their car, talking on her mobile phone. 'Have we got any water?'

Cara gave a thumbs up, reached into the car and came over with a bottle of sparkling water, handing it to Deacon. He gave a smile and took gulps. After a few more coughs, Deacon cleared his throat.

'Have you got any paracetamol's, by any chance? My head's killing me.'

'The medics are on their way, sir,' said Cara.

Two of the uniformed officers from the accompanying squad cars went into the outbuilding on Cara's request to ensure there was nobody inside and to check around the place for anything untoward. The other two officers called for the detective's attention. Cara went over to see what they wanted. Gill turned to Deacon.

'You look like shit.'

Deacon gave a smile. 'And you don't look too bad yourself, Gill.'

She put her hand on his shoulder. Cara called Gill's name. As Gill approached the body, she recognised the suit, even from the back. The blood matted into the hair surprised her. She'd have thought the rain would have washed it away.

'He's alive, said the officer. It looks like he's taken a big blow to the bottom of the head and neck. I don't want to risk moving him in case it causes more serious injury. We've called for another ambulance.'

'I appreciate that, thank you.' Gill knelt down beside Karl and put a hand on his still body. 'Hang in there, Karl.' She felt a wave of guilt, realising she hadn't really spoken to him outside of the team briefings since he joined. In fact, she knew nothing about him other than him being very organised. Was he married? Did he have a girlfriend? What were his hobbies? She made a conscious decision to correct that if he pulls through. God willing, he will. She walked back to Deacon, who was gazing at her.

'Karl?' he asked.

Gill nodded. 'He's alive, but he doesn't look good. He's still unconscious.'

They could hear the faint sound of a siren in the distance.

'Hopefully that's our call and they can sort him out. Did you see who did it?'

'No. But I know who it was.' He gathered his thoughts.

'Do me a favour. Put out a warrant for James Hawthorne's arrest for the murders of Terry, John and Danny McGregor.'

'James Hawthorne? Are you sure?'

'Very.'

Gill put the call through to the station. Meanwhile, Deacon sat quietly for a while before escaping from his thoughts.

'Gill. Margaret Wilson. He's going to go to her house.'

'But she isn't in there. Remember? We have her in the nick.'

Deacon massaged his temples with his fingers before rubbing his eyes. They seemed clearer, although still tainted by the pounding of his head, blurring slightly with every beat.

'We know that, but he doesn't. We need to get over there quick. I think he'll go there to finish the job now he knows we're onto him.'

'We can't. The paramedics need to check you over. You probably have concussion, so you need to be assessed, sir, you know, to ensure that you're...'

'Being rational?' said Deacon sharply.

He needed Gill onside; she normally was. She was right. After all, he'd received a blow to the head and been half poisoned by exhaust fumes, but now wasn't the time to be righteous as far as he was concerned. And it didn't go unnoticed that Gill had acknowledged him as "sir", something she normally avoided. Was that through genuine concern on her part or just being patronising? In his current state of mind, he neither knew nor cared.

'Just help me get up, Gill. We need to get in the car. He might be at Hawthorne farm, but I doubt it. I would imagine he's already there.'

Deacon could feel his head and his thoughts getting clearer, although his head was still painfully pulsing to where he felt sick.

Deacon called Cara over.

'Check at Hawthorne's farm to see if James is there. If he is, arrest him for the murders of the McGregors. But be careful, we know what he can do.'

Cara looked behind at the squad cars and returned her gaze. 'I'll take a few of the uniforms with me, and we'll find out if he's there. If not, I'll let you know.'

Deacon was wondering if he was getting paranoid in his current state. Cara seemed less enthusiastic than her normal self—reluctant, almost. Maybe she was worried about his health. Most likely concerned by what Pau would say when she found out that she and Gill let him continue without having a medical assessment.

'Cara. Whatever happens later, just say I ordered you to take the actions that you did. Do I make myself clear?'

'Yes, sir.' She threw her car keys to Gill. 'You take the Skoda, I'll go in the squad car.'

Cara and Gill grabbed an arm each and dragged Deacon to his feet. He felt a little unsteady at first, walking gingerly, more like Frankenstein carefully placing one step in front of the other towards the car. There seemed to be some sensation in his legs again. Because of his walking, he hoped the blood circulation would improve. By the time they reach Margaret Wilson's home in Oakham, they would be a bit more back to normal.

'You walk like you've got piles,' quipped Cara.

Deacon laughed, 'Thank you,' he said, 'but don't make me laugh. My head is killing me as it is.'

After getting into the passenger seat of the car, he let out a long sigh. Why? He didn't know. Gill started up the Skoda and made a sharp U-turn, following Cara, who was in the police car in front. At the road, Cara's car turned right towards Hawthorne Farm, and Gill went left towards Oakham.

'So, where does Margaret live?' asked Gill.

'I can't remember off of the top of my head, but I'm sure it'll come to me once we get into the town.'

'Brilliant,' came the flat reply.

Gill drove at speed. The rain had eased somewhat from earlier but was still hitting the car in sufficient volumes for the sensors to keep the wipers working at high speed. Deacon stared out of the side window at the hedgerow racing by. How green everything had become. The leaves, the fields, the grass verges and the trees. Different shades of green yet strong. He'd often noticed that. When it rains, it seems to give even more depth of colour to the landscape. Was it because it washes the leaves or feeds them or simply that the wet surfaces give the effect from a glistening surface? The contrast against the swirling grey clouds emphasised the phenomenon further.

The buzz from his jacket took Deacon by surprise. He scrambled, putting his hands in all of his pockets to find the source, finally pulling his mobile phone from his inside pocket. By the time he'd retrieved it, the buzzing had stopped. He looked at the screen and, not for the first time, let out a long sigh.

'Let me guess,' said Gill. 'The Chief Super?'

Deacon smirked and rested his head against the headrest.

'Just give it a second.'

The ringtone of the hands-free burst into life. She glanced at Deacon.

'I'm going to have to answer it.'

Meanwhile, Cara arrived at the Hawthorne farm and rushed up to the front door with the two police officers by her side. She banged on the door with her palm. The door remained closed. She banged on the door again and called Rosemary's name. Nothing. Cara was worrying something was wrong and was looking around for a boulder of some sort to break the window of the door to enable her to open the latch from the inside. Finally, there was a click of the latch, and the door slowly opened. Rosemary stood with her head and shoulder resting on the wall. She let the door creak open. She looked a mess. Her hair was all over the place, partially pulled out from the ponytail. She wore no makeup. Her eyes were red, and cheeks wet from tears. It looked like someone had pulled off the top two buttons from her top. There was a slight cut just above her breasts. Cara got the impression the lost buttons and cut resulted from Rosemary being grabbed by the shirt, hence the creasing around the lost buttons, and guessed that the slight cut resulted from a fingernail.

'Is James here?' asked Cara. Rosemary shook her head. 'Where is he?'

'He's gone,' replied Rosemary in a whisper.

'Where?' Cara found herself shouted now.

'I don't know,' came the whispered reply.

'Oh, come on, Rosemary. You must have some idea?'

'I-DON'T-KNOW,' shouted Rosemary into Cara's face, which took her aback.

Cara pointed at the shirt and the cut. 'Did James do this to you?'

Rosemary stood silently for a few seconds, glaring through tear-filled eyes, before nodding.

'Can we come inside?'

Rosemary opened her arm and gestured for them to enter. The two officers quickly rushed in to ensure that James was not still in the place.

'Shall we go in?' asked Cara.

Rosemary stayed where she was. 'I need the fresh air.'

Cara touched Rosemary's arm in comfort. 'What happened?'

'He came rushing into the house and grabbed his weekend bag from the bedroom and began throwing any of his clothes into it that were lying around or in the wardrobe.'

'When was this?'

'I don't know. Earlier.'

'I know that, Rosemary. How much earlier?'

'Who knows? Two hours maybe.'

That certainly fitted the timeline Cara had created in her head from when Deacon and Karl left the station to when she and Gill arrived at the so-called disused barn. 'Then what?'

'I asked him what was wrong. What had happened? But he just ignored me and kept rushing about the house collecting his stuff. I was pleading with him to tell me what was wrong. In desperation, I grabbed his arm with both hands to get him to stop for a minute and tell me what was happening.' Rosemary stared at the floor. Small drops of tears dropped from her cheeks and onto her foot.

'Did he hit you?'

Rosemary shook her head. 'He just went into a rage and pulled me up towards his face by my top. His eyes. I've never seen him like that before. The hatred in his eyes and the anger. He was shouting at me through gritted teeth to leave him alone. He told me I was a slut, and I should be lucky that he didn't rip my head from my neck.' She was shaking now. Staring blankly in front of her. Reliving the moment, Cara guessed.

'Then what?'

'He left. Never looked back like he always does, never gave me a wink as he usually did. He just walked out with his bag and left me.'

'Have you any idea where he went?'

Rosemary shook her head.

'I'm sorry for the questions. I take it he was in his Range Rover.'

Rosemary nodded at first but frowned. 'No. The whole thing was upsetting, unsettling, scary, but when I watched him go, I felt there was something that wasn't right. He never had his Range Rover with him.'

'What was he driving?'

'A black Mercedes.'

The sheer venom in Chief Superintendent Pau's voice was unnerving, even for Deacon who had known her for many years and engaged in many a good argument over a host of things. Both working together as police officers on undercover operations and, to differing degrees, climbing the slippery tree of the police ranks. But this time Pau was vicious. He can't recall ever hearing her like that. The sheer anger. And yes, she was right; he had broken protocol by clearing off from the scene without being medically assessed, and she had every right to remove him from the force, and he was in no doubt she probably would. Maybe she was right. He hadn't been ready to return to full duties and was making irrational decisions and, endangering his colleagues, making her look stupid. But what really hurt and made him feel like complete shit was the fact that she accused Gill and Cara of professional incompetence and acting obsequiously towards him, and that she would decide whether to discipline them or transfer them out of her sight.

Part way through the rant, Gill had pulled over into a layby. Deacon could tell the comments and threats hurt Gill and quietly took it on the chin, so to speak. He thought he could see tears in her eyes. DI Gill Foster, one of the toughest and best police officers he'd ever worked with, male or female, brought close to tears, and all because of him and his stupid insistence on following things up rather than seeking medical help. And worse still, forcing Gill and Cara to go along with it. His head was no longer thumping against his skull, or if it was, he didn't notice it, because the guilt he felt was eating away at him.

Gill's mobile rang again. This time, she disconnected it from the car and took the call outside. Deacon loved his job. He didn't want to lose it. What else could he do? He would face the music. With his years of service, the pension would be good, and the mortgage was now paid since the passing of his wife. He tried to imagine what she would say if she were still alive. It would certainly be something like, "You've got nothing to lose, just fight it. If they throw you out of the force, you'll be able to live comfortably on the pension. And if you remain in the force, you'll be equally happy". The car door clicked open, and Gill sat down in the passenger seat.

'That was Cara. I told her what Chief Superintendent Pau said.'

'Gill, I'm sorry. I promise you I'll take full responsibility for my actions and fall on my sword. It was nothing to do with you or Cara. I made the calls as your superior officer. So, please. Let's get back to base and I'll sort this mess out, I promise.'

Gill stared out of the window as he spoke. She started up the car and screeched out of the layby onto the road at high speed.

'The station's the other way, Gill.'

'But we're going to Oakham, to Margaret Wilson's house. If the Chief Super is going to discipline us or even transfer us, we'll make it worth her while. Cara agrees. You've never hung us out to dry, never missed the opportunity to promote or highlight anything we've ever done to enhance our profile. And more to the point, you've never suggested we are not good enough because we're female. So, we're on your side. Cara and the boys are on their way now. By the way, Hawthorne's driving a Mercedes. So, let's catch this bastard, shall we?'

―――――

The car came to an abrupt standstill outside the neat, detached house behind a black badly parked Mercedes, with its front wheel up on the pavement.

'It looks like he's here,' said Deacon.

'He certainly parked in a rush. Cara's about fifteen minutes away. I'll call for extra back-up.'

Deacon got out of the car as Gill made the call. He felt considerably better after the drive and noticed his legs were functioning relatively normally again. Approaching the front door, he tried to turn the handle, but it didn't move. He could hear crashing and banging inside, so looked through the windows, but the curtains were closed. Under the windowsill were a number of cigarette-ends, spent matches covered with a sprinkling of silver ash, like someone had emptied an ashtray out from the window. Supporting himself by grabbing the windowsill, he picked up two of the used matchsticks, walked to the driver's side of the black Mercedes and removed the dust caps from the two wheels, folded the matchsticks into three and wedged them in the tyres' valves. He could hear the gentle hiss of air escaping as he carefully stood and steadied himself.

Gill stared at him, slowly shaking her head. 'You never cease to surprise me.'

Deacon shrugged his shoulders. 'If he gets away from us, he won't get far. Shall we wait for the cavalry or try the back door?'

'Whatever decision we make will be wrong in our glorious leader's eyes. So, in for a penny, eh?'

Deacon smiled and led the way around to the back of the house, by the empty driveway and through a black iron gate. The smashing and crashing noise was much louder as they neared the open back door. Someone had smashed the glass of the door's window to gain access to the key in the lock on the inside. Deacon still couldn't believe the amount of people who leave their door keys in the door. A burglar's dream. What struck him was the sticky tape used on the glass. An old trick. By applying a few layers of tape on the glass, it produces little or no noise when broken. That suggested an element of planning. An intention. Deacon's impression was that James Hawthorne was in a panic to get away, yet in his enraged state to close the loop and kill Margaret Wilson, he still used the tape? Was it always his intention to complete the job and take out the fourth monkey?

'Shall we go in?' asked Gill. Deacon nodded.

They walked into the kitchen, which was large, spacious and modern, with white granite worktops stretching around the room like arms from a large stainless steel multi-oven and a white ceramic hob. Neatly placed pan sets were on two of the walls and low hanging stainless steel pendant lights hung at different heights. The white-tiled floor was spotless except for the odd piece of glass now lying upon it. As they moved into the living room, the damage and devastation was overwhelming. The room he remembered when he visited with Karl to question Margaret Wilson was now a space that was smashed, broken, torn, and bent. A sudden bang on the ceiling let them know that the room above was undergoing the same makeover. Deacon pointed to the stairs.

As they reached the landing at the top of the stairs, an almighty crash happened which slammed the door of a bedroom shut. It literally made Deacon jump, much to Gill's amusement, as he saw her laughing, as quietly as she could, with tears in her eyes. He gave her the middle finger in response. Gill's mobile buzzed. She looked at the screen.

'Cara and the boys in blue are here,' she whispered in Deacon's ear.

'Send her up. Have the uniforms guarding the front and back,' he whispered back

Once Cara joined them on the landing, Deacon made his move.

'James!' he shouted. The room went silent. 'I'm Detective Chief Inspector Deacon. I don't believe we've met, but you've met my colleagues who are here with me now, DI Foster and DS Matthews.' Silence. Deacon pressed more. 'We know what happened, James. We know what Dudbridge Holdings did, taking away your family's land, the hurt it caused your father, the beating you took when you confronted them.'

'You know nothing!' came an angry sounding reply. 'Nothing! John McGregor, Terry McGregor, Danny McGregor and their fucking stabbing piece, Margaret fucking Wilson, are four of the most vindictive, egotistical, self-centred and greedy pieces of scum I have ever met.'

'But you can't take it on yourself to deal out justice. It needs to go through the proper channels. People like that always get caught, eventually.'

'Bollocks! And if you believe that, you're a fucking idiot. The McGregors stitched up my brother and my dad and effectively stole two thirds of our land. They conned it from them and left them with nothing in return. And when I tried to unpick the fraudulent, criminal elements to return it to my family, that bitch, Margaret Wilson, and the McGregors made my family's lives a misery. Margaret threatened my dad with potential consequences while I was in another room with those three arrogant scumbags. I don't know everything that she said to dad because I wasn't there, but he was trembling all the way home. I kept asking him what she said but he wouldn't tell me, but it terrified him. Two days later, he died. Now she was the only person who was with my dad when he wasn't with me. As I've said, the others are scum, and I gave them what they deserved. But Margaret Wilson needed her to suffer longer. To be looking over her shoulder, to be shitting herself. I don't know if she did. She seemed to tick along nicely on her own, keeping the business running, and that has really grated on me. So, I needed to seal her fate. But she's not here. But I'm happy to say that I've broken up everything here that she owns. Even her fucking dildo.'

'I'm genuinely sorry for losing your dad, James.'

'So am I.'

'And your brother.' There was a long silence. 'Are you there, James?'

'Y-yes, I'm here.'

'Did you hear what I said?'

There was a pause before James Hawthorne answered. 'About Steven, yes.'

'What's bothering you about Steven?'

Long pause. 'I don't know what you mean?'

'You knew about Steven and Alison McGregor, didn't you?'

Long pause. 'Yeah.'

'Did you approve?'

'I didn't care what he did, to be honest.'

Deacon decided to take a risk. 'And it gave you the opportunity to sleep with Rosemary, while he was away.'

He thought he heard James laugh. 'Needs must, I suppose. Rosemary wanted love and attention, and I could oblige. She was happy. I was happy, and Steven was happy. A win, win, win.'

'So, why did you kill Alison McGregor?' Gill and Cara turned to each other.

There was no response.

'James. Are you still there?' asked Deacon.

'Yeah.'

'I'll repeat the question. Why did....'

'Because I had to. I'd already decided what I was going to do. How I was going to pay those bastards back. But I needed help. And Steven, as soft as a bloke he can seem, was as strong as an ox. He knew what the McGregors had done to dad, but that wasn't enough to get him on side. But for him to think that they killed Alison - that would tip him over the edge and get him on side. As it happens, it worked out even better, because as I drove towards her, I saw him out of the corner of my eye. It was perfect. I had a scarf around my face and wore a baseball cap so no one would recognise me. And the car is one I normally have locked away, so he would never have seen it.'

'Are you saying that Steven was your partner in crime, so to speak?'

Again, there was a long pause. 'Why do you think he killed himself? I needed revenge, I needed retribution, and so did he. But I'd fought in Iraq. I've seen things done to people that no-one should see. Men, women, children. It didn't matter who they were, how old, if they were pregnant. If they needed to be dead, they would be. I was hardened by it. Steven wasn't. That final evening with him when he was up the tree with the wire around his neck will live with me for the rest of my life. Unlike the McGregors.'

'It's over now, James. You've achieved all you wanted to do. Settled the scores and suffered the loss of your brother. Enough is enough. Why don't you come out of the room?'

'When Margaret Wilson's dead, I'm done.'

'We've got her locked up at the nick.'

'You're lying. You're talking shit.'

'Why would I lie, she's not here is she? Have a think.'

Once again, there was a long pause before they could hear furniture being moved. The door opened. A tired and beaten looking James Hawthorne stood upright, covered in sweat and with some minor cuts to his face and arms. He clasped his hands and reached out towards DS Cara Matthews, who dutifully applied the handcuffs and read him his rights.

CHAPTER TWELVE

THE TEAM WAS SITTING around Deacon's office, enjoying their slices of pizza. The mouthwatering aroma wafting around the room from the four steaming, partially eaten bases, enticing them to eat more. Sitting at the table, Karl, complete with neck brace, was carefully chewing away. The blow he received by James Hawthorne to the back of his head resulted in a fractured neck. However, the results from the CT scan were positive and the doctors and medics who gave him the initial care and attention when he arrived at the hospital were confident he should regain all neurological functions. And all the signs were that he would make a full recovery from his injuries, as there was no sign of damage to Karl's spinal cord, which was a relief to the team. And he'd already expressed his desire to return to duties as soon as possible.

Considering what he had been through, Deacon thought Karl seemed in good spirits. His hair had grown since he last saw him, and Karl was now supporting a beard which wasn't overly long but would benefit from a trim. Then again,

Deacon would guess that shaving wouldn't be high on Karl's list of priorities and difficult or comfortable to do with a neck support. What was noticeable was how much Karl seemed to gel with the other members of the team. Initially, he could be aloof and prickly and difficult to engage with. But now he seemed more embracing and relaxed around his colleagues. Everyone had commented over the past hour how immense his role was in solving the McGregors' case. And as the investigation progressed, Deacon warmed to him more and trusting his ideas and opinions.

The mood in the room was fun and light-hearted. Over the past four weeks, Deacon, along with the rest of the team, he would guess, had reflected on the case. Deacon, Gill and Cara had gone through the process of being reprimanded by Chief Superintendent Pau. She certainly made sure they all got a piece of her mind. However, from what the rumour mill led them to believe, Pau couldn't take the disciplinary action she clearly wanted, because of Area Commander Taylor. He'd made a personal visit to Pau to congratulate her 'super' team and great leadership in solving the murders. There had been some loose ends that needed tying up since James Hawthorne's arrest. But effectively the case was shut for now until it made its way to court, anyway. But James wouldn't contest it. As far as he's concerned, he did what he needed to do and takes full ownership.

'So, how did it all finish up, guv?'

'I'm sorry, Karl. Of course, you wouldn't have been in the loop. So, I'll try explaining the cause of events.'

'When James returned to the family business following his stint in the military and his time studying for his business diploma, he was to learn that two-thirds of his family's land had gone. The land you discovered, Karl, and earned us an almighty headache!'

Karl managed to laugh along with Gill and Cara.

'Dudbridge Holdings, effectively stole the land from the Hawthorne family, taking advantage of Steven and his father's lack of business knowledge. James was more clued up business-wise and took issue. He began to pressurise the company into returning what they'd dishonestly taken, threatening legal action. It appears that the McGregors called his bluff. They probably guessed that the Hawthornes were in no position to hire a lawyer and risk losing.'

'So, James arranged a meeting with The McGregors and Margaret Wilson at their offices to try to sort it out. He planned to reason with them that his dad was an old man and didn't really understand what he was doing. He took his dad along hoping they'd feel the injustice and have sympathy for him. After all, the land was of little use to them if they couldn't sell it on. But they never budged. Eventually, John and his boys got up and left the room and asked Margaret to show James and his dad out. James said he followed the men and tried to plead with them to change their minds. They ignored him and kept walking, but eventually Terry turned and threw him to the floor. When he went back to the office, he could here Margaret speaking in a raised voice but couldn't hear what was being said. When he entered the room, Margaret clammed up. He said his dad looked petrified. She wouldn't tell James what she had said, telling him it was none of his business and led them out of the building.'

'The next day, James went back to Dudbridge to try again. As he arrived, he bumped into Terry McGregor in the carpark and asked him to reconsider. He said Terry laughed at him and said that if his dad and brother were so thick, they deserved to be turned over. That was when James saw red and made a bit of a mess of Terry McGregor's face. Later that day, while at his office in Beeby, where he ran his property business, Terry turned up. He saw him park and wondered if he'd reconsidered their position. Clearly not, because no sooner had he stepped outside, the McGregors beat him to within an inch of his life. The next thing he remembered was being pulled from a ditch and put in an ambulance. And as you discovered Karl, he ended up in the hospital.'

Deacon grabbed a couple of pizza slices from the table. He sat back down.

'And it was at that point where he made his mind up that he'd do something about it.'

'By killing them,' said Karl.

'But with a lot of thought and preparation and several years to fester.'

'To send a message to Margaret Wilson,' said Gill.

'The three monkeys thing. It just seems too Hollywood. And excuse my language, guv, but it takes some sadistic sick bastard to do what he did.'

'I agree, Karl, but there's something we didn't know at the time but came to light after we arrested him. Cara, tell Karl what you found out.'

Deacon leaned back in his chair and bit into his pepperoni pizza slice.

'Ok. We knew he was in the army and was part of the ground force in Iraq at the start of the gulf war. And the MOD told us he ended up in a military hospital when an IED exploded during a house-to-house search. They also told us at the time on medical grounds he was retired. So, we assumed because they offered nothing else, it was because of his injuries.'

'I'm getting the feeling it wasn't,' said Karl.

'Correct,' said Cara. 'Following the release of James' name in the press after his arrest, the fellow at the MOD contacted me again. He read the full report and basically, it wasn't as straightforward as he thought. Yes, an IED seriously injured

James, but he recovered. In fact, he went back to his unit and full duties, and wanted to go back. Apparently, following such traumas, the army closely monitors soldiers to ensure there are no underlying problems - you know, mental scars and suchlike. And it was during this period where they started noticing a difference in his behaviour. PTSD can affect people in different ways. And James became more violent towards prisoners in particular. People he considered the enemy. The final straw came when they sent him out to collect a war prisoner. He later arrived back at the camp on his own, claiming the prisoner had escaped. Now, this happens occasionally. However, a few days later, they found the body of the prisoner with his head virtually cut off. Apparently, it was only the spinal cord that kept it attached. And there was a knife plunged into the victim's right eye. James Hawthorne's knife.'

'Jesus Christ,' said Karl.

'Now, what my contact at the MOD couldn't tell me was how he escaped a military court and a court Marshall. He can only assume they didn't follow procedure, or for political reasons. It was best to keep it quiet. So the army retired him on medical grounds with full pension and benefits.'

'Thank you, Cara,' said Deacon, 'and that goes some way to explain how he could commit such terrible murders.'

'I still don't get how he could take three men and kill them on his own—especially the way he did it,' said Karl.

'He didn't,' said Deacon. 'His brother helped. And I mentioned earlier that he spent several years planning for his revenge. Part of that process was getting the relevant chess pieces into place. And I guess it was a stroke of fortune in some ways because Steven was having a secret relationship with Alison McGregor. James knew about it because his brother had told him at some point. He knew Steven loved her to bits, so he killed her and blamed the McGregors for being vindictive and wanting to teach her a lesson. Purely by chance, when James drives into her in York, who witnesses it, but Steven—but he doesn't see the driver. So, he assumes it's the McGregors and James stokes that thought. From that point, Steven wanted revenge, too.'

'I'd like to pick up on that,' said Gill. 'When did you know it was James that killed Alison, because it wasn't until we were at Margaret Wilson's house you said that?'

'A good question. Weirdly, in my strange fuzzy state of mind, some things became clearer. If the McGregors wanted Alison dead, they wouldn't do it themselves. And in truth, they wouldn't be stupid enough to hire someone to do it, because all the lines of enquiry would go back to them. In truth, she was out of the equation anyway, as her daughter, Libby, had said. So why take the risk? But I would guess the fact it happened, and they don't know who's responsible, must have unsettled them. I'm pretty certain Steven would never have even dreamt of doing such a thing to Alison. Certainly, after talking to Libby, who was the go-between for her mother and Steven. And even from what James said. Margaret Wilson? No, she's brave when with her masters, but I don't believe she had the guts to do it. And again, she had a very close association with the family. So, unless there was a player we knew nothing about, that left James.'

'And that's why you're a DCI. Ooh, pizza. I'll have a nibble if you don't mind.'

The team turned to see Chief Superintendent Pau pulling a slice of pizza from the box.

'Please, don't mind me,' and she bit into her slice as she grabbed a seat and sat next to the food.

'James and Steven went to Three Gables armed with a handgun each, and were prepared to smash the door down, but they rang the bell and Danny opened the door and they rushed in, had them face the wall and threatened to blow their heads off. James said there was no bravado. The McGregors did as they were told. They tied their wrists behind their backs, gagged them and marched them into the back of their livestock trailer and took them to the building that you discovered, Karl.'

'And where we received the whack on our heads?' Karl said with a smile.

'Indeed. Gill, I'm talking too much. Do you want to tell him about the building?'

'Ok. Pretty much everything happened in there. And again, they prepared everything like a military operation. From what we understand, they laid out the polythene sheet on the floor. James had acquired disposable suits, shoe covers and gloves years ago in preparation, which is why we never came across any evidence of purchase. They also had a box full of masks from Covid. They killed Terry in front of the others. Steven held him down as James hammered the hook through his eyes.'

'Jesus wept,' said Karl. 'And Steven was actively involved?'

'Yes, but he had his eyes closed, apparently,' said Cara.

'They placed him in the livestock trailer, wrapped in polythene again. They made John sit in the Mercedes, which they were using to tow it. Apparently, Danny was shaking with fear and left tied up in a chair at the outbuilding, while James, Steven and John drove over to the Timmins' farm to latch the body to the tractor.'

'Why there?' Karl asked.

Deacon answered. 'Purely because James had noticed the open field whilst driving in the area. It just so happened that it led to the Timmins farm. It was bad luck on their part.'

'And following placing Terry's body, they drove out Tilton way to sort John out. They forced an old rag into his mouth that was soaked in petrol. James said that once the petrol was in his mouth, he was quiet.' Gill sighs. 'We understand Steven helped his brother carry John's unconscious body into the little building and lay him in position on the floor, and waited in the car for a few hours as James lit the material and kept the fire going.'

'I have to say,' said Pau, picking out another slice of pizza, 'the man is absolutely insane. How he could carry out such barbaric actions on another human being is beyond comprehension.'

'I agree. It's frightening, who can lurk within society,' answered Deacon, 'But he did. And he was sociable, kind and generous, but there have been plenty of examples in history where people like that hide a dark side.'

'And after tormenting Danny by witnessing the death of his brother and certain death of his father, it was his turn,' said Gill. 'Apparently, Steven wanted out of this whole situation, but James made him hold Danny's head as he drilled through it, again with polythene on the floor, and disposable suits. According to James, Danny screamed far longer than he expected. The idea was to drill from ear to ear, but it was more difficult than he expected to keep the drill straight. Anyway, as soon as the deed was done, they put him in the jet washed trailer on top of a polythene sheet and drove to Dudbridge. Steven was in the back of the trailer holding him to ensure there was little sign they'd moved him to the location.'

'Wow. And what was Margaret Wilson's role in all of this?' asked Karl.

Deacon held up his hands. 'Only she knows. I certainly don't think she's innocent in any of the dealings that went on in Dudbridge, but we can't find enough evidence to stick. But look, the McGregors are out of the equation, as is James Hawthorne. We should be happy with that result.'

'My God. When I joined the force, I never in my wildest

dreams would have thought there were such people in society. This is the stuff of horror films.'

'But it's not, DC Goodman. This really happened. And you, along with everyone else in this room have stopped James ever doing this again,' said Pau. 'When everyone's shouting about how useless the police are, they don't follow up on burglaries, petty crime and public disorder, you know what a difference you've made.'

Deacon smiled. He couldn't have said it better himself.

―――

It was a hot and muggy evening, and having the window open didn't really make a great deal of difference to the temperature. But it at least allowed the smoke to escape. The stars glistened in the sky, with not a cloud in sight. She took a sip of her wine and placed the glass down with a clink on her new glass table. Staring out at the street, she could see the 'For sale' sign fixed to the fence near the front door. This chapter of her life was over. It had high points, it had lows. She considered herself lucky to have met John, Terry, and Danny McGregor. They'd been good to her. They were protective, yet gave her the opportunity to progress in the business. And her intimate relationships with all three of them had been consensual. She was heartbroken at their deaths.

But it was time to move on. Libby had scuppered her dream to run the company. The bitch was still a partner in the business without her knowledge. Why Libby had to come out from the shadows to tell every news agency prepared to listen, that Dudbridge holdings were a poisoned brand, she couldn't understand. And the comment she made, 'a fish rots from the head down' made the headline in three of the nationals. And had the reporters at her door, making it impossible to continue in her role.

Margaret lit another cigarette and took a long draw on it. Her eyes closed, enjoying how the toxins within the smoke relaxed her. Against her wishes, Libby's suggestion to sell the business and give all employees an equal cut of the profits forced her hand. She knew Libby didn't like her and was probably doing this to hurt her. But Margaret also knew things she would tell no one. Accepting she would have to go with the flow, her plan was to sell up and move to Spain. She couldn't stay here. Not after the break in, and her private space being violated. It made her feel vulnerable. And now her name had appeared in newspapers and bulletins in relation to the arrest of James Hawthorne and her role at Dudbridge Holdings Ltd. The vitriol emails and posts had begun.

Libby McGregor sipped her coffee, trying to think of what message she could put on the card. It was a lovely picture on the front of the beautiful gardens of Down House, the former home of the naturalist, Charles Darwin. She felt happy but was unsure why, because lots of people dear to her had lost their lives. But there were mysteries solved, and a murderer caught, and long-lasting gripes put to bed. Detective Chief Inspector Deacon had come good. She never really trusted anyone after the McGregors invaded her life. They took away every decent strand of fairness and dignity that her father possessed. But Deacon did. Her heart felt heavy as she thought about her mother and what she had been through. Losing her father. The relationship and marriage to John McGregor, who betrayed all the trust she gave him. And the happiness that Steven Hawthorne injected into her spirit before being killed. But now she felt in a position to let go of the past and live a life without such a weight around her neck.

Libby simply wrote 'Thank you' on the card. Should she write more? No. It says it all. She could now move on with her life. She put the card into the envelope and wrote the address on the front. After pressing the stamp into the top right-hand corner, she wondered if Detective Chief Inspector Deacon would know it was from her. She smiled. Having solved this case, it would be funny if he didn't.

Deacon found it enjoyable in some respects. He doesn't normally. In his mind, going to 'visit' someone at a cemetery was tokenistic. They're not there. Long gone. You were just staring at a headstone and a small plot of land and pretending that your loved ones were there, watching and listening. But tonight, he suggested to Susan that they go and 'say hello'. He didn't know why, but he knew it would make his daughter happy and he wanted to pay his respects. The pair of them sat at the bench that faced Claire's burial space. The evening was warm and clammy, and the stars covered the sky like tiny diamonds. He and Susan held hands as, once again, they shared stories of a fantastic wife and mother. His eyes welled up when Susan told her mum that her hero dad had caught a very dangerous criminal and was all over the news. But what broke his defences was when Susan told her mum that she was right. Dad is a very special man.

When they returned to the house, Deacon made them a spaghetti Bolognese. While Susan was tucking into her food, he slide over an envelope sized box. She stopped eating.

'What's this?'

'Look.'

Susan opened the box and held up the gold chain. 'This is what mum bought for you on your fortieth birthday,'

'It was.'

'So why are you showing me?'

'I'm not showing it. I'm giving it to you. I can never wear it at my job. God knows how many times I'm grabbed during arrests. It deserves to be worn. To be seen. Your mum didn't buy it to be kept in a box. You wear it for me. For her.'

Susan's eyes teared up as he clipped it around her neck.

'Our princess,' he said with a smile.

ENJOYED WAGES OF SIN?

Please take a few minutes to leave a rating and review on Amazon.

There's good news. DCI Deacon and his team will be back in 2025 with another case in 'Dance With The Devil.'

ACKNOWLEDGMENTS

I would first like to thank you for choosing the novel and reading it. I hope you enjoyed the story and warmed to the characters as much as I did while writing it. Interestingly, I mapped out the story many years ago, but only committed to writing it last year. Nonetheless, I can assure you the follow-up will be available next year!

Many thanks to Wendy Griffiths, who meticulously read through the manuscript and pointed out subtly (and not so subtly) that it wasn't as clean a draft as I claimed it to be. I appreciate the time you dedicated to the endeavour.

A big thank you to W.A. Kelly, writer, podcast host, producer... the list goes on, for the book design and formatting. It was at that point that my labour of love turned into reality. Also, I really appreciate your advice and guidance.

It's fair to say, I would probably never have considered writing a novel had my dear friend, Simon Catchpole, not suggested it. He has always encouraged and championed my work and felt a novel would be the natural progression from my short story writing. So, here it is in print as a thank you, Simon!

Lastly, but by no means least, my heartfelt love, thanks and gratitude goes to my wife, Karin, who allowed me the space to fulfil this dream. Finding the time to write around a demanding job and life in general has been challenging. I started writing at the weekends, but additional evenings throughout the weeks soon crept into the routine. So, for ten months, Karin saw very little of me as I was at my computer, typing away - although in truth, I get the impression she enjoyed the peace!

ABOUT THE AUTHOR

Shane Payne was born in Leicester and has lived and worked in and around the area for most of his life. He currently lives in a village in rural Leicestershire with his wife and dogs. Upon leaving school, he trained as an engineer before moving into teaching and academia and achieved the award of Doctor of Education. Along with his writing, his lifelong passion has been music. From a very young age, he has played drums with various bands and musicians.

Printed in Great Britain
by Amazon